The Two Worlds
of Isabel

Giulia Martinez-Brenner

Dedicated to my family. However cliché it sounds, they never stopped believing in me, and never let me give up.

CHAPTER 1

WHEN YOU READ this, you'll probably think what happened to me is cool. Think again.

My name is Isabel Maria Yates, I'm thirteen years old, and believe me, I was exactly like you—wishing for an adventure more than anything. I not only admired my storybook heroes, I also envied them. I convinced myself that it wasn't fair they got to have their own stories and I didn't.

But be careful what you wish for, because adventure, even though it offers plenty of thrill and excitement, can also bring sadness.

So the next time your birthday comes around, and you plan on wishing for an adventure when you blow out your candles, don't. Don't waste that wish. Hope for world peace or the end of climate change instead.

I learned this the hard way.

It started out like any regular school morning: woke up a bit late, splashed cold water on my face instead of waiting for it to warm up, and had some toast for breakfast. At eight o'clock, I slung my backpack over my shoulder and started the walk to school.

During first period, we got our grammar tests back. I got a B+, which I was pretty proud of considering I am quite a failure in English; math and science are more my subjects. Everybody was whispering, asking each other their scores. Obviously Elena got an A, and everyone else got Bs or Cs.

Next period was Art, which I hate. I mean, I like drawing and stuff, but the teacher is so narrow-minded. Whenever I draw something original and cool, she throws it back in my face like the day she insisted the sky could only be colored in using horizontal strokes. It wasn't the first time she'd told me stuff like that, but since I hate it when people tell me what to do, I usually break the rules just to get on her nerves. So, yes, Art can be stressful.

At snack time, a big drama raged about some guy and his girlfriend and everyone crowded around the people involved, whispering and demanding details. And even though I usually like drama, this time I just ignored the spectacle. I needed to put my concentration into reviewing my physics assignment I would have to orally present to the class later that day. As I said before, I am quite good at science, especially in physics, but those little butterflies of anticipation fluttered nervously in my stomach all the same.

Finally, when the bell rang for third period, I rushed back to the classroom, thankful for the hour of math before science. In the middle of class, though, the school secretary walked in and glanced at me with an expression on her face I couldn't understand. My best friend, Josie, punched my arm lightly to get my attention and whispered, "Ooh, what did you do this time?"

I have never really gotten in trouble before, and if I have, it was never something big enough to call in the secretary. I guess there was that one time, not so long ago, when I got sent to the principal's office, but that was my moron teacher's fault, so I didn't include it. (Seriously, it was not my fault. My teacher was being a big, fat, unfair jerk, and I told him so, in not so many words. As you can imagine: big mistake. I spent the rest of the month in detention.)

Ms. Florence had just whispered something to Mr. Tuckers, and now he looked at me and motioned for me to come to his desk. With the rest of the students' eyes burning into my back, I slowly walked to the front of the class.

"You should pack your bag and go with Ms. Florence," Mr. Tuckers said quietly.

Still clueless, I did what I was told.

I walked out into the corridor and the first thing that came to my mind was the hope that I wouldn't be gone for so long that I'd miss science. Even though I was a bit nervous for my oral presentation, I still loved talking in front of an audience and being the center of attention. It's a weakness of mine. And a weakness of many others, in my opinion. But not one a lot of people like to own up to.

I had just passed the computer lab when I noticed that Ms. Florence's steps were much longer than usual, forcing me into a jog to keep up with her pace. Then I realized the color in her cheeks had drained away, leaving her face pale. I wondered what had happened to leave her so unsettled.

"Um, Ms. Florence, is something the matter? Are you sick? Did I do something wrong?"

"You have done nothing bad, but . . . but . . ." She took a deep breath to steady her shaky voice. "Best your mother tells you."

Now I was getting kind of freaked out, but I kept my mouth shut (which, for me, is quite an accomplishment).

We had almost arrived at the door of the office when it burst open and my mother, with puffy eyes and wet cheeks, rushed out and whispered in a hoarse voice, "It's Tom, sweetie. He's at the hospital. Your brother, he . . . he . . ." Her voice cracked and she dissolved into tears again.

My older brother was in the hospital? How? Why? When would he get out?

"Mom! Mom, what happened?" I grabbed her arm and asked forcefully, even though my voice trembled.

Seeing that my mother couldn't answer, Ms. Florence said, "Your brother's in a coma."

My brother? Coma? I could hardly get this information registered into my brain. My knees buckled, and I fell to the floor, but I was too stunned to bother getting up.

*

That night at dinner, there was no talk, no laughter like there usually was.

Well, you wanted excitement, didn't you? I thought later in bed. Yes, I did, but not this kind. While falling asleep, I found myself taking back the wish that I had wanted for so long. I wanted nothing to do with books or adventures ever again.

The next day I woke up hating the world for being so cruel. I lay in bed with the pillow over my face and cried silent tears.

When I finally got up, it was already lunch time, but I had no desire to eat. Instead I took a hot shower and stood there under the steaming water, feeling it soak my hair and wash away most of my sadness. Then I got dressed and looked around. My house felt so empty. No parents (they had gone to the hospital), no brother. Stop. Don't think about Tom. I had cried enough already.

I didn't want to stay in my room, and for some reason I found myself wandering into Tom's bedroom and wishing with all my heart that I could be with him.

Protagonists in stories are always a little bit afraid, but I still always imagined that if I had an adventure, I wouldn't get scared. And yet the feeling I got when I stepped into Tom's room couldn't be described as fear.

What I felt was pure terror.

I had expected to find his room in its usual mess, but what I did was step into a brilliant, bright light. "What the . . ."

5

The world began to spin. My eyes watered.

The floor of my brother's room had become a swirling vortex.

I began to scream, but my heart was pounding too fast. . The floor sucked at my feet, trying to pull me down. I felt myself sinking and thinking that nobody would know what had happened to me.

I was on my own.

I blacked out.

CHAPTER 2

WHEN I WOKE up, all I saw were . . . these weird creatures, if you could even call them that. About eight of them stood over me. They had the form of people, but their features were hazy, and black. Their outlines blended into their surroundings so you couldn't really see where their bodies ended. When I looked at them, the only thing that came to mind were people made of smudged charcoal like we used in Art class.

I quickly scrambled to my feet and instantly the color of my surroundings struck me head-on. It almost blinded me! The sun in the sky shone brighter, the grass that I had been lying on was a shade of emerald green that I had never even seen before, and the sky gleamed such an intense turquoise that I gasped.

Once I had gotten over all the different shades and hues that surrounded me, I realized that there was something else—something new and unfamiliar but I couldn't put my finger on it. Then it hit me. It felt like the density of the air had decreased so that when I moved my arms, they cut through the air with amazing ease. For a second I felt like laughing at my new agility, but then my situation came rushing back to my mind and whatever hint of amusement I had quickly faded.

My head and my heart pounded, but I ignored them both. "Where am I?" I demanded, loud and clear. "And who are you?"

The black smudges had begun to shift slightly and they looked at each other. "Another one?"

"What should we do?" another asked.

"I don't know!" a trio of them responded in unison.

There was a small pause before one of the smudges started yelling, "We should take her to the Fading Castle!"

Confused and scared, I started screaming, "Take me home! Don't you dare touch me! Take me home!"

They slowly advanced. I backed away.

When they understood they wouldn't get anywhere this way, the smudges swarmed and started pushing me along.

In my panic, my breathing came to me in short gasps and all of my thoughts whirled around in my mind, making it impossible for me to think clearly.

They dragged me to an enormous castle made of giant slabs of black rock. There were some places where the wall of the building changed from stone to glass, but I couldn't see through them as the sun was reflecting straight into my eyes.

When we arrived at the base of the castle, instead of finding a big oak door, like I had expected, only a small set of sliding doors stood in a wooden frame that lead us inside.

The smudges pulled me toward the entrance but that was when I put my foot down. No way would I be dragged like a rag doll by these strange creatures, forced to go somewhere I didn't want to. Already I felt sick just being in this weird new land, and this wasn't making it any better. Where was I? How had I gotten here anyway? What had happened in Tom's room?

But first, concentrate on the matter at hand, I told myself.

I turned to the smudge nearest to me and hissed in the most menacing tone possible, "Let go of me. Now."

It took a step back, surprised, and in that moment, I wrenched my hands from its grip and lashed out at the other creatures surrounding me.

"Leave me alone!" I shouted. I was hopelessly outnumbered, but they were obviously startled at my little explosion.

"We don't want to hurt you. Really." one of them said in a masculine voice.

I glared at him. "Do you really think I'd fall for that crap?"

"Just come with us," another one piped in. "We want to help you!"

I just scoffed and said, "You guys must think I'm really stupid to actually believe you."

The smudge that had spoken first made a move to

9

grab my arm. Just as I felt him touch me, I jumped back and tried to slug him in the stomach. My hand passed right through his body. His insides were warm.

I instantly pulled my arm back and doubled over, feeling like I was about to puke.

"Leave her alone, Rick," said another smudge to the one who had tried to take hold of me. Then he turned to me and continued, "We have one of you! The sick one!"

"What?"

"Just come with us, and we'll show you what we mean."

I had to admit I was curious, but I also knew that they could be lying and leading me to some sort of trap. But what did I have to lose? I had no idea where I was or how to get back home, which was the one thing I really wanted to do.

Before, I hadn't really been thinking about it, but now I understood the full gravity of my situation. I was stuck in this strange, unknown land. By myself. Far away from home and from everything else familiar to me.

Alarm rose in my throat, and I managed to choke out "fine" before silent tears flowed in little rivulets down my cheeks.

"Oh, don't cry," a smudge said, trying to be comforting.

I remembered that they were staring at me, and I angrily brushed the back of my hand across my face. I couldn't let them see me as weak. I had to be strong and tough. With confidence in my steps, I marched up to the sliding doors and, with all the smudges following me, walked in.

Once we had entered, the smudges arranged themselves in a circle around me and led me down the corridor. The interior of the castle looked like one of those really expensive hotels with smooth marble floors, air-conditioning in every room, and chandeliers of twinkling crystal lighting up your every move.

We stopped in front of an elevator door, and they nudged me to step inside. The doors closed behind us with a ding, and the elevator shot up so quickly that my stomach dropped into my feet. I had to hold onto the sides so I wouldn't fall.

When we stopped moving and got out, I saw a long staircase winding up in front of us. The smudges started to climb without hesitation. Seriously? How far up did we have to go?

It didn't take long for me to get out of breath. My leg muscles burned, and I would have asked for a break if I had a smaller ego. The stairs rose higher and higher. Other staircases broke off and headed in different directions, but whenever I tried to glance at where they led, I was bustled along further before I could get a good look.

The smudges finally stopped on a landing, filed into a room, and started chattering excitedly. I looked up and realized I stood in front of a long white bed surrounded by a shimmering silk cloth.

The smudges' chattering stopped and a sad silence

spread over them as I moved the cloth aside to see who (or what) was on the bed.

There, pale and weak, lay Tom.

"Tom!" I yelled and threw my arms around his frail body. After a second I pulled away because the smudges were staring and Tom was finding it hard to breathe. I gaped at him. "What are you doing here? I'm dreaming. This can't be real! But you're supposed to be in the hospital! You're supposed to be in a coma!"

"Wait. What are you doing here?" he demanded.

"I don't know. I just walked into your room and suddenly I was here! Are you alright? Where in heck are we?"

"Calm down," he rasped. "I have a lot to explain, and it will take me a while in this condition, so you'd better sit down."

Only that short sentence had made him wheeze. Hundreds of questions bubbled up inside me, but I managed to push them all down because Tom had already started talking again.

"I'm dying."

Not a good start.

"I'm going to try to make this as simple as possible and go right to the point. There are two worlds. I mean, there's an alternate reality of Earth."

"Whoa. What world?"

"This alternate reality, we are in it at this very moment. This other world is right next to our world, but hardly anyone can see it. Well, I'm one of the very few who can. I didn't even realize it until not so long ago.

But I've been seeing this alternate reality for as long as I can remember: in my dreams and in visions that I have. Then one day, this vortex thing came into my room and I got transported here. The smudges explained to me where I was and now they're taking care of me."

"But why? Are you sick?" I asked.

"Well," he said and took a deep breath, "it's complicated. You see, before any of us were alive, at the beginning of time, the Earth wasn't like it is today. It was full of magic. But then there was an all-powerful, very evil person who decided he didn't like the world that way. So using some kind of complicated black magic, he Divided the planet into two different worlds, Earth and Eeba, and made it so they were invisible to each other. And it's still like that today. But . . ." He stopped speaking and started coughing. Before he could say more, a smudge left and a moment later returned with a glass of bubbly, dark purple liquid. Tom took a long sip, then continued, "But he made a mistake when he cast the spell, so once in awhile, a person from Earth can see Eeba, and somebody from Eeba can open the portal from one to the other."

All this was so much to take in. I felt dizzy and just plain confused.. I had so many questions and I wanted so many answers. Knowing this, Tom nodded, so I knew I could start talking.

Trying not to let all the questions rush out of my mouth at once, I said, "How do you know all this?"

"The smudges told me," he responded.

"What are the smudges, exactly?"

His face darkened. "Well, the person who Divided the Earth doesn't want anybody to know that these two worlds exist, so when someone finds out about the alternate reality that he created, he . . . sucks their soul. That's what's happening to me, and that's what happened to the smudges."

I gasped. "So all of those smudges were once people from Earth?"

"Yes."

"Will you become a smudge?" I whispered, afraid of my own words and the answer I would get.

"If the Soul Sucker succeeds, then yes," he said with an amazingly calm tone, almost without emotion. But I knew he couldn't be . . . pleased with his fate. How could he be talking about this horrible future with such tranquility? Just hearing it made rage rise inside of me. You see, I'm not one to get sad. I get mad.

"Does it hurt?" I asked.

"No, it just feels . . . empty. Like you aren't you anymore. And you feel weak, very weak," Tom said, misery seeping into his voice.

"Oh, I'm so sorry," I said, my voice drifting off. I felt a lump growing in my throat. I took my brother's hand and said, "It's going to be okay. I won't let this happen to you."

A weak smile played across his lips. Squeezing his hand even tighter, I asked, "Is there any way to stop the person doing this?"

"I don't know, but I don't want you trying to do anything, do you understand me? This is a dangerous person we're messing with, and I won't have you taking any risks for me!"

"You aren't the boss!" I protested stubbornly, but Tom had used so much energy talking that he had fallen asleep.

I needed some air. I looked around and realized there weren't any windows. All of the light in the room was coming from a glowing sphere that hovered right above the bed. I made for the door and, surprisingly, the smudges didn't try to stop me.

One of them even said, "Go. We will call you when he wakes up." Another opened the door for me.

In the corridor I turned left, then right, then went down a small flight of stairs. I had no idea where I was going. I just knew I had to get some air before I threw up all over my favorite sweater.

Trying to calm down but still a wreck, I almost missed it, but at the last moment I turned and saw a door. What looked like daylight shone from underneath, so I pushed it open. It led out to a huge terrace. I stepped out and a cool breeze met my skin. As I looked around, letting the wind whip my hair out behind me, I noticed smoke. Just a small dot on the horizon to my right, but it was definitely smoke. I didn't like it. It made the back of my neck tingle.

On the same side as the smoke, a giant blue lake glittered, miles of trees and grass surrounding it. On the left, a vast city thriving with noise and life.

Suddenly something cold and velvety passed over my shoulder. I jerked my head around and saw it was only one of the smaller smudges. "That's Malsama," it told me.

"What?"

It pointed at the city. "That's Malsama."

"But I thought it was Eeba."

"No," it chuckled. "Eeba is the planet. Malsama is the city."

"Oh," I said, feeling like an idiot.

"But enough chitchat. You have to come," it said, more urgently. Then it motioned for me to follow.

I stopped in front of the familiar door that led to Tom's chamber. As I entered, I braced myself. All the smudges had gathered around my brother's bed. Tom's breathing was shallow and his hair, soaked with sweat, was plastered to the sides of his face.

No. This couldn't be the end. I had to do something, now!

I sat down on the floor and buried my face in my hands.

But what could I do? Nothing. No, don't think like that. I told myself to be positive. As long as Tom was still breathing I had a chance!

"Isabel," Tom rasped. I slowly uncovered my eyes. "Go with Ian. He'll take you to Grandma Martha, and you can trust her. Go."

"Wait! Who's Ian?"

"I am," came a voice from behind me.

I whirled around and saw an adult-sized smudge.

"I'm Ian," he said. "Your brother gave me strict orders to take you to Grandma Martha, so that's what I'll do. Come with me, and be quick about it." And he started walking briskly down the hall.

I gave one last look at my brother and kissed him on the cheek. Then I took off after Ian. After walking for a few minutes, he stopped in front of what looked like a closet door. "After you," he said.

"Excuse me? I thought you were going to take me to this Grandma Martha lady, and unless she lives in the broom closet, I think you've made a mistake."

"Just go in!" he said impatiently.

"Fine!" I opened the door, rolling my eyes, and then . . . whooooooooooooosh!

The floor dropped from under me and I found myself falling down a giant slide, in the dark, at what felt like a hundred miles per hour!

I screamed for what seemed to be years and all the time I was sliding, I couldn't see anything. After I got over my shock, I started to enjoy it. This was the coolest ride ever! I realized that instead of taking the stairs, they had a slide to get to the bottom of the castle. Sweet!

But then I thought, What will happen when it ends? Will I slam into something and die? That got me screaming all over again!

At one point, I felt the slide straightening out beneath me and I realized I was getting to the end. I braced myself. The slide curled up and I was launched into the air, carried forward by all the momentum that had built up from the enormous fall.

"AHHHHHHH!" I shrieked, my voice hoarse from all the yelling. Was I going to die like this? Was I going to bang into the floor and smash my skull into a million pieces?

Gravity took its hold on me, I was going down, and . . .

I landed on something soft and bouncy. I was okay! But I still couldn't see anything. Wasn't there a light in here or something?

Oh. My eyes were closed. Oops.

I opened them and found myself in an enormous room. At the very end, there was a tiny little door that looked like it led to a little cupboard. But I knew better. I will never underestimate closet doors again!

I looked down and realized I was sitting on a huge, orange beanbag! And there were lots of different colored ones covering the ground of the room. I was still gazing at all the colors, when I heard a shout, "Look out below!"

Ian. I had to move out of the way unless I wanted to be squished by a smudge!

I glanced behind me, where there was a giant hole in the wall. Before I knew it, Ian was sailing out of that hole and shooting up to the ceiling. My eyes followed him up into the air, and I calculated that he wouldn't land anywhere near me but rather on a pink beanbag on my left.

I was right.

He landed and then stood up as if nothing had happened.

"What was that?" I demanded. "You couldn't have warned me about the small, unimportant fact that I was about to fall down a massive slide?"

"Sorry, it's so much quicker to use the slide instead of the stairs, but I thought you would be scared if you knew and wouldn't want to go."

"I guess I would have been, but next time tell me."

"Okay, Isabel."

Ian led me to the other side of the room and he opened the tiny door. It led straight outside. It felt so good to feel the wind and sun on my skin.

As we stepped out into the open, I heard Ian mutter, "Pink. Why do I always get the pink beanbag?" I guessed even smudges had annoyances.

Eeba was amazingly beautiful, even if I could only see the plain of grass and a small part of the lake on the horizon. I just couldn't get over the vibrancy of it. Everything was brighter and more cheerful.

"Come on," said Ian.

I turned to him and gasped. At his side was a roofless mini-hovercraft. My jaw dropped. "No way! Can we ride in it?"

"Yep." Ian smiled. "Hop in."

"Do you also have, like, jetpacks and stuff?" I asked as I buckled myself in.

"Yes, we do. We have hovercrafts, jetpacks, wings . . . "

"Wings?"

"Of course! This is Eeba! You'll be blown away when we reach the city! I still remember my first day on Eeba. It was fantastic, and it still is!"

"Your what?" I asked, confused, then I remembered that as a smudge, he had also come from Earth but had had his soul literally sucked out of his body when he found out about Eeba. "Oh. I'm so sorry Ian, I . . . I forgot."

He scowled, but I knew it was just his way of covering up his sadness. "I still think about my family, but I will never be able to see them again. Once your soul is gone, you can't go back to Earth. It doesn't matter anyway. My family is dead by now."

"Why would they be dead?"

"I discovered Eeba a long time ago and now that my soul is sucked, I will have to stay here forever and never be able to die. But meanwhile, time on Earth will still go on. It's been so long that it isn't possible that anyone I knew is still alive."

"Oh," I said quietly. I racked my brain for something comforting to say, but it remained blank. I felt so sorry for Ian, and to think, the same thing would happen to Tom! I tried to persuade myself that I hadn't just seen my brother for the last time. We would both make it through this and live long, happy lives but doubt still prowled around my heart.

Only then did I realize that I hadn't even said goodbye (nor did I realize that it could happen to me too).

"Don't you want to know what Earth is like now?" I asked Ian, trying to take my mind off of Tom. "I'll describe it to you if you want. We have so much new technology, nothing like hovercrafts but—"

Ian cut me off. "Isabel, don't," he said, with pain overflowing in every word.

"Why?" I whispered. I cursed myself as soon as that one word flew out of my mouth. Why couldn't I have just kept my mouth shut? Why did I have to take it that one step further?

I didn't expect Ian to answer me, but he did after a minute of tense silence. "I'm not going back to Earth, and I have to accept that. Please don't make it any harder by talking to me about it."

I didn't respond, and he knew I understood. For the rest of the journey we whizzed along, just a few feet above the grass, hardly speaking.

We passed the lake but at a great distance, so I couldn't make it out. We drove in the direction of the city, and after about an hour we reached Malsama.

Looking out the window, I asked Ian to slow down.

Instantly the hovercraft steadied to a slower pace and lowered closer to the ground.

I gazed around, at a loss for words.

Malsama is probably the hardest thing I've ever had to describe, but I'll do my best: The cobblestone streets weren't just pieces of rock; roses and daffodils sprouted from the gaps between the stones and nuggets of gold and diamonds were wedged inside the road. I gaped, but nobody seemed to notice the precious jewels being trampled under their feet.

As casually as I could, I bent over the side of the hovercraft and brushed my palm over a diamond. I curled my fingers around it and tugged as hard as possible, but it was stuck fast. I tightened my grip and prepared myself to try again, but Ian drove a little farther, forcing me to let go of the glistening rock.

The buildings were astounding. Some were modern,

sleek and classy with glass walls and geometrical roofs. Others were old-fashioned with small windows and red wooden doors. Still others were made of fire and water and a few even looked like they were sculpted from pearl and fur. There was one that looked like a stand-still tornado! Everywhere there were people—walking, riding in hovercrafts, flying in the air. Men in tuxedos and men in suits of armor. People wearing cowboy costumes. Several dressed as ladybugs. Women in puffed dresses and glass slippers, some in ninja gear, and others in motorcycle jackets. Many men had twirly mustaches or big bushy beards, though, of course, there were also some with no hair at all. And there were also some that just looked normal, meaning the kind of people you would see every day on Earth.

Children, both girls and boys, had elaborate hairdos, green beehives, and pink mohawks, but otherwise looked like miniature versions of the adults, playing with . . . were those elves?

Oh. My. God.

As I looked closer, I could see little elves babysitting children and fairies with flowing golden locks and dragonfly wings. Dwarves and gnomes, mini dragons and manticores, unicorns and baby mammoths, purple frogs riding donkeys. It was insane.

Ian chuckled as I stared in amazement. We turned a corner that led into another street, a bit less crowded than the first. I glanced up and saw a little sign that read "Plausible Quarter." I wondered what that meant but as I looked around, I understood. Compared to the rest of the city, this street seemed entirely ordinary with small suburban houses and little gardens in front of every home.

A group of little kids sat in one of the yards making mud pies. "Hi!" I called out to them. One of them turned to me, picked up a lump of mud, and hurled it at my head. Thankfully it missed my face, but it hit my shoulder full on.

"Hey! What the hell was that for?" I shouted at them, but the little boy who had thrown it just laughed at me. As he snickered, I noticed his mouth was full of little pointy teeth. As I looked at him more closely, I wasn't so sure if he was actually a little boy. Or that anything could be ordinary in this place.

Ian looked at me. "I'm sorry. Imps can be pests."

"Humph," I grunted as I tried my best to peel off the quickly drying mud. It was useless. My sweater was in dire need of a wash.

Finally we parked in front of a small house and got out of the hovercraft. Ian knocked on the door and a small old lady with frizzy grey hair stepped out. She gave us one look and quickly beckoned for us to come in.

The one huge room, which was just inside the front door, was filled with furniture that told me it was the living/dining room. Every shelf and every table had at least ten things on it. Piles and piles and piles of stuff everywhere. I could describe it as a cluttered granny house, but it felt just like a house that was . . . lived in.

"Hello, Grandma Martha! How are you?" asked Ian, clasping his hands together in front of him.

"I've been better, but considering, I'm just fine," she replied. Her voice was warm and smooth, reminding me of hot chocolate on a cold snowy day. "This is the girl, Isabel, I suppose?" she said, turning to me.

"Yes, I am," I said before Ian could answer for me. "But, excuse me, why exactly am I here? And how do you know my name?"

"Ian told me Tom had ordered him to bring you here once he knew you were in Eeba."

When could he have told her that? Tom hadn't known I was here for very long. Oh well. I had more important things to think about.

"And as for the other questions," Grandma Martha continued but quickly glanced behind her at the sofa and back at me. "Well, why don't you sit down before I start blabbing on? I'll get you some tea?" she offered with a smile. She led me to the part of the room that had a few armchairs, a couch, and a coffee table. I sank down into the couch as Grandma Martha yelled, "Zach! Get the tea for our guests! And hurry up!" behind her shoulder.

"All right! All right!" a young male voice shouted back. A minute later a boy about my age walked into the room, balancing a tray on one hand and holding a pot of tea in the other.

He had scruffy, blond hair and warm brown eyes. I grinned. I could tell when a guy was cute or not, and he was definitely the former. He placed the tray, filled with cakes, cookies, and teacups and saucers, on the small coffee table.

"Well? Say hello to our guests!" scolded Grandma Martha.

"Hi, Ian. Hi . . . ?"

"Isabel," I told him.

"Oh, you're Tom's sister. Granny said you would be coming." He smiled and I noticed his eyes traveled to the space on the couch next to me.

Smiling inwardly, I nodded and gracefully moved aside to allow him to sit next to me. As he took the space I had just freed I quickly adjusted my hair, and when I turned back to him he grinned. Grandma Martha handed me some tea and a cookie and I thanked her.

As she gave Ian and Zach their tea and treats, I thought a bit more about this boy next to me. He wasn't like the other "cool boys" at school, most of whom were just arrogant jerks. Zach was hot, and he probably knew that my heart melted a tiny bit when he smiled, but it didn't seem to make him conceited in any way.

At that moment I became very aware of just how dirty I was, and I silently cursed that little creature that had thrown the mud. And then I remembered why I was there. Focus, Isabel!

"Yeah, so, about Tom," I said, bringing the conversation back around to what was important while trying to keep my voice level. "His soul—"

"He's Fading," finished Grandma Martha, shaking her head. "Yes, we know." Her voice was deeply saddened. "I am sorry, Isabel, but there is nothing you can do to help your brother. Once the Soul Sucker has his hold on him, that's it." She looked down into her teacup. "Isabel, I have seen many good, innocent people Fade, only because they have seen something they shouldn't have."

There was silence for a moment as tears welled up in my eyes, then, "Oh Zach, be a good boy and get the almond cookies from the pantry," Grandma Martha said, trying desperately to lighten the mood, even though we all knew it impossible.

"Right." He jumped up.

"I'll come with you." I said, following him out of the room, roughly wiping my eyes with the back of my hand.

As he opened a cupboard and took out a cookie tin, I studied him. I had hardly known him for more than two seconds, but despite his mischievous, boyish grin, he had kind, confident eyes and an honest expression on his face. I decided to have faith in him.

"Look, Zach, I hardly know you, but I think I can trust you. I don't care what your grandmother says. I mean, I'm sure she means well, but I'm going to go and try to save Tom despite what she says. Will you help me?" I whispered so Ian or Grandma Martha couldn't hear.

We made eye contact. "Please? All you need to do is keep quiet and give me information, anything you know could be useful . . ."

Zach held my gaze. "I'll do everything I can," he said and held out a hand to shake.

"Thank you," I said, my voice full of appreciation as I took his hand as requested. .

By that time, he had filled a plate with almond cookies, so we made our way back to the living room, where Ian and Grandma Martha were deep in conversation. When they saw us they instantly stopped talking to each other.

Zach put the plate on the table, and we sat down on the couch again.

"I don't mean to be rude," I said, "but why am I here instead of with my brother?"

"Well, first of all, we thought it would be too hard for you to be with Tom in this difficult time. We didn't want to make it any more difficult for you than it already was. Secondly, we have to find a way to send you back to Earth before the Soul Sucker finds out you're here," replied Grandma Martha and then bit into a cookie.

I swallowed hard. "What happens if he finds out I'm here?" I whispered, my eyes wide with fear.

Nobody said anything.

"Tell me!" I demanded, pounding my fist on my leg.

"He would have your soul sucked too," Zach murmured.

"Zach!" exclaimed Grandma Martha.

"She wanted to know!" he protested. "She has a right to know," he said under his breath.

They kept talking, but I was no longer listening. I would turn into a smudge. I would never be able to go back home. I would never see my parents again. I would never see Josie again. I would only be a husk of what I once was.

No way was I going to let that happen to me or my brother. And there was no time to be scared or discouraged. I had to make a plan (preferably one that would work) and execute it. Now.

I stuck my chin out and said, with more courage than I knew I had, "Well then, I guess we'll just have to make sure he doesn't find me, won't we?"

They all looked up, eyes wide. Grandma Martha said, "Isabel, you are strong. This world needs more confident females like you. I have a feeling you will do great things."

I felt my face heating up and when Grandma Martha saw my discomfort she quickly changed the subject. "It's getting late. I'll go make dinner. Zach, you show Isabel the guest room. Ian, why don't you help me in the kitchen?"

With that, she and Ian went into the kitchen while I followed Zach to the other side of the room and up a small flight of stairs. He led me down a hallway, pointing out the different rooms of the house.

Finally, at the end of the hall, he opened a door to a cozy little room. Against the wall opposite the door was a bed with a fluffy, orange duvet and pillows. A tiny window adorned in matching curtains sat high on the left wall, and underneath it was a small wooden desk and chair. Beside the door there was a small mirror and a shelf with a few books. It wasn't much, but I thought it was adorable.

I sat down on the bed and Zach took a seat next to me. "Zach?" I looked into his eyes. "How did I get here?"

He looked away. At first he didn't respond, and I was about to ask him again when he turned back to me said, "Since you've trusted me, I'll trust you. I—I can do something. I don't know how, it's just . . . I mean . . . "

Seeing he was having trouble saying whatever it was, I urged him on. "Yes?"

"Well, I have this thing that I can do. I just wish for it, and then it happens."

"Well, what is it?" I said, a bit impatiently.

"I can open a kind of door to Earth. The first time I did it, your brother came through it. I've been wanting to open another portal just for fun, but Grandma won't let me."

"Why not?"

"Dunno. It's dangerous. Maybe if I didn't open it, he wouldn't be in danger now."

"But that doesn't make sense! If you didn't open it again, how did I get here then?" I pondered it for a second, then I added, "Zach, could you please open the portal again? Just so I can see?"

"Um, I guess. I just hope Grandma doesn't find out." He knitted his eyebrows in concentration. Suddenly the floor started spinning. It was exactly like what had happened when I was brought to Eeba.

"Stop!" I yelled, panic rising in my stomach as the sight brought back the memory of falling from Earth to Eeba.

He closed the portal straightaway. "That was it," I

said. "You must have opened the portal that brought me here. There's no other explanation."

Zach shook his head. "But that can't be! I only opened it once!"

"I wish I could open the portal. That would be awesome."

No sooner had I spoken those words than the floor liquefied and started to spin. "Oh my God!" I yelled. "Zach, close it!"

"It's not me! It's you!"

Before I could question his theory, I said, "Close." And remarkably, it did.

We stood there, looking at each other, amazed. Zach was the first to speak. "You can open the portal too! This is fantastic! I'm not alone!"

"So I brought myself here? You didn't do it! This is so cool!"

It took me a second to realize that we were holding hands. I instantly tore mine out of his, and we turned away from each other, both of us equally embarrassed.

After a moment of awkward quiet, we heard Grandma Martha yelling from downstairs. "Zach! I'm sure Isabel would like to get clean for dinner. Why don't you let her take a shower? Get her some of Sage's clothes!"

"Okay!" Zach shouted back.

"Who's Sage?" I asked him on the way to the bathroom.

He handed me a clean towel. "Just my stupid older sister," he scowled.

I didn't think it appropriate to ask why. He showed

me into Sage's room and opened her wardrobe. Inside, skimpy dresses hung from a bar and low-cut tank tops were stacked in neat piles.

Now let's get something straight: I'm not unfashionable. I like dressing up and feeling pretty but this was just a bit . . . too much.

I pulled a dress off a hanger and held it out before me: short and sleeveless with a black and grey aztec print across the top part. I must admit, it was pretty. But then I held it against my body and my self-esteem dropped to the floor. There was no way I could fit into it. Sage may have been older than me but her body type was one I could only have dreamed of having. Eyes stinging, I jerked the dress back onto its hanger and shoved it into the closet.

That wasn't the first time, and definitely wouldn't be the last either, that I felt like trash because of the way I look. I always think I'm over it, but some days it bothers me more than others. And that dress was just another reminder that beauty seems to come in only one size. Contempt for myself boiled up inside me. I'm supposed to be a strong feminist! Who cares about society and its beauty ideals?

But I couldn't help myself, and I angrily shut the wardrobe door.

"Isabel?" asked Zach. "Is everything all ri—"

"I'm fine." I said, being as convincing as possible. I've had a lot of practice in this department. I covered my face with my hair as I wiped my eyes in a desperate attempt to save my eyeliner.

Zach raised his eyebrows. "Are you sure you're okay?"

Did it look like I was okay? Are boys so dumb as not to even understand when someone is upset when they so obviously are?

"Of course I'm okay," I said.

Hearing footsteps behind me, I turned around to see Grandma Martha coming into Sage's room. "Come on, Isabel," she said. "Go take a shower and give me your clothes so that I can wash them and have them ready for tomorrow."

I looked at her outstretched hands and then down at my muddy shirt. I couldn't say no. "Fine."

"Good." And she walked out of the bedroom.

I turned back to the wardrobe, opened the door, and began the hard task of finding something decent to wear.

When I finally walked down the steps to the dining room after a long, hot shower, I realized with embarrassment that they had all been waiting for me to eat.

I quickly walked over to the table and said, "Oh God, you guys shouldn't have waited for me!" I took a seat next to Zach on the couch.

Mistake.

I heard a little girl's voice say in a sing-songy tone, "Ooh! Zach's got a girlfriend!"

I whirled around to see a short, ten or eleven-year-old girl with straight brown hair and cheeky brown eyes. She was wearing overalls over a simple striped shirt. I secretly wished Sage had taken more after this little girl's style.

"No!" Zach and I said at the same time, but she just giggled.

"Who is she?" I whispered to Zach.

"Just my little cousin, Maya. Ignore her."

Ian called us to the table and he motioned for me to sit opposite Zach; Maya was on my right. The food was delicious, but I hardly got to eat it because Maya was a nonstop talker. Whenever I'd bring a bite to my mouth, she would ask me another question.

We were right in the middle of the meal when there was a knock on the front door. Grandma Martha let in a tall, skinny girl with the same blond hair as Zach. Make-up covered her face but—even though it was a little too much—you could tell it had been put on by a pro. She sauntered in wearing a red top that showed off her belly button, a matching skirt, and black heels.

The first thing she said was, "Who is this girl wearing my clothes?"

"This is Isabel, Tom's sister," said Grandma Martha.

"Oh, Tom." For a moment her girly, sarcastic expression was replaced with a dreamy smile. But then she snapped out of it, dumped her purse on the floor, and plopped down on the free chair next to me. "Sorry, forgot my keys but... oh my God! You actually look quite adorable in my clothes! I'm sure even Zach thinks you're cute!"

Zach rolled his eyes, and I turned redder than her shirt.

I became even more embarrassed when Maya added, "Oh, he already does!"

"Well! Does he now?" Sage exclaimed, winking at me.

"That's enough teasing your brother!" scolded Grandma Martha, but I could see a hint of amusement in her eye.

Once we had all finished eating, I took Zach aside. "Look, I really think we should tell them about my power. They might be able to tell us more about it."

When he only raised his eyebrow, seemingly unconvinced, I insisted. "Come on, let's do it!"

He hesitated a moment, then said, "Fine, but you do the talking."

We sat down again at the dinner table as everyone was stacking their dirty plates. I nervously cleared my throat. Once they were all looking at me, I said, "Zach and I have something to tell you."

"Engaged already?" mumbled Maya into her glass, stifling a giggle. Grandma Martha shot her a "cut it out" look, and the little girl stopped snickering.

"As I was saying," I continued, "you already know about Zach's power that brought my brother here to Eeba, but the way I got here was still uncertain. Well, we found out that I have Zach's same power! We can both open the portal to and from the worlds!"

Grandma Martha gasped and put a hand to her heart. "That's not possible! That has never happened before! Not in the whole history after the Great Division! Two of them at the same time . . ."

"What?" Zach and I cried in unison.

Ian was the one who responded. "Children, we have some things to explain to you."

Everyone stayed quiet and waited for him to speak. For some reason, at that moment my physics assignment popped into my head. I realized that at the beginning of this whole thing, I was supposed to be doing the talking. But then throughout the whole day, I was the one listening as everyone else told me new things. I noticed that I much preferred being the one who talked as opposed to being the one who listened. I know it's a rather selfish thought, but I also know it's the truth, and I have no problem admitting that.

"As you all know," Ian began, "Tom isn't the first person from Earth to see Eeba. I, myself, was one of the people who saw it in their dreams. Well, since Eebians are like the people of Earth, neither knowing about the other, we smudges have noticed a pattern in history: whenever there is a person from Earth that glimpses Eeba, there is always a person in Eeba that has the special ability to open the portal between the two alternate realities. But throughout all history there has only been one person at a time, and that person has always been from this world. We already knew that you, Zach, were that person, but now Isabel has that power too! And she's from Earth! Something very strange indeed is happening. I think it's a sign."

Grandma Martha sighed and smiled. "I have a feeling you two will bring hope to Eeba and Earth."

There was a moment of silence while we all let that news sink in. Hope? Why would Earth and Eeba need hope? I could understand why Tom would need it, and maybe also the other smudges, but what was wrong with the world the way it was now? They said that the Soul Sucker had Divided the world. Why? And they had called him evil. Taking souls out of people's bodies was wicked for sure, but was Dividing our planet also bad? Then I reminded myself that this person was literally taking away Tom's life, his very essence. Anyone who did that was evil at the core. Hatred boiled inside me.

Finally the silence was broken by Sage. "That's not fair!" she said.

Then Maya huffed and piled on, "No, it's not! They get to be all amazing while I sit at home being a no-body!"

"Girls!" scolded Grandma Martha. "It's not like now that they have this ability I'm going to let them go off to save Tom! Absolutely not! They are going to stay safe under this roof until we send her back to Earth!" She glared at me, though the look felt more protective than menacing.

Zach and I glanced at each other, and we both knew what that glance meant. There was no way I would stay here, waiting for my brother to lose his soul. As soon as I could, I was out of there, and if Zach wanted to tag along . . . well, I wasn't one to object at having to share a journey with a cute guy.

"Now children, off to bed. Except for you, Sage. You can help me with the dishes," said Grandma Martha as she rose from the table. Sage responded with a loud groan.

The rest of us dashed upstairs before Grandma Martha decided that she needed our help, too.

CHAPTER 3

I WOKE UP to a knocking on my door and the sweet smell of maple syrup in my nostrils. I jumped out of bed, then jumped right back in again with a yelp when I realized I was wearing only a t-shirt and my underwear, and Zach stood right outside the room.

"Don't come in yet! Just hold on!" I yelled and frantically looked around for my jeans. On the chair next to the desk I found my jeans, shirt, and sweater washed, ironed, and folded. It felt great to be wearing my clothes and not Sage's.

I met Zach outside in the hallway, and we walked to the kitchen together. "We have to find a way to get out of the house." I stopped myself. I hadn't even noticed I had said "we" instead of "I." I glanced at Zach to see if he had noticed the slip up. He just nodded.

What did that mean? I didn't really expect him to actually come with me to try and save Tom. I mean, I was fine if he did, don't get me wrong, but he barely knew me or my brother, and this could get quite dangerous.

Dangerous.

When had I ever done anything dangerous in my life? Wait, let me count the times. NEVER. I had done stupid things that could have turned into dangerous, but not anything as big as this. Going to save my brother from the grasp of an evil sorcerer? Yes, that was definitely as dangerous as it got for me.

I almost laughed from the ridiculousness of it all. Here I was, using the word "sorcerer" when not talking about some fantasy story. This was real life. Looking back, I realized I had simply accepted all of it. Never objected to all the crazy ideas of there being two worlds that had come from one. Or the imps and the hover-crafts or any of it. Ever since I could read I had imagined myself being part of an adventure full of magic, wonder, and surprises. And now I found myself right in the middle of one! So why did I feel so . . . sad?

I jerked myself back to the present by looking at Zach again.

"So . . . ," I said, waiting for him to finish the thought.

He obliged. "So we have to find a way to get out of here without Grandma thinking it suspicious."

I knew I must have looked like a fool, but even so, I couldn't stop the enormous smile lighting up my face as I realized I wasn't alone on this.

Zach responded to my smile with his own wide, mischievous grin.

God, he really was hot.

"But what are we going to do once we're out?" Zach asked.

I had already thought of it last night. "I say we go out and get some supplies, and then go to Earth and make a plan there. It seems that the Soul Sucker would be stronger here, otherwise why would he stay on Eeba? This way we'll be safer, and he might not be able to . . . you know . . ."

Zach nodded. He understood what I meant. I wouldn't be able to help Tom at all if I were in the same condition as him.

He thought about it for about ten long seconds. "Okay," he said, finally. "Just leave this to me."

After our delicious breakfast of waffles and maple syrup, Zach turned to Grandma Martha and asked, "Granny, could I give Isabel a tour of Malsama? And maybe we could even get the groceries for you while we're out?"

Grandma Martha jerked her head up from her coffee to look at us. "I don't know, Zach. We have no idea what the Soul Sucker knows. He could be completely oblivious to Isabel's being here, or he could be waiting outside."

"Please?" I begged. "It's so amazing here in . . ."

"Malsama," prompted Zach.

"In Malsama. Right," I said. "Pretty please? I promise we'll be extra careful."

"Remember, Granny, yesterday she just drove right up here and nothing happened," Zach added.

Grandma Martha gave in. "Fine. I'll give you the grocery list. But then come straight back. No dawdling! Then we'll send you off back to Earth. Alright, Isabel?"

"Perfect," I said with finality and we both turned to go.

We only got to the front door before Grandma Martha warned us one more time not to draw too much attention to ourselves. As I was closing the door behind me, I noticed Ian staring at us with one raised eyebrow. He hadn't said a word throughout the whole morning, and he remained silent even now.

We had just closed the front door behind us when it opened again and out came Sage in black skinny jeans, stiletto boots, and an open back shirt that was actually quite cute..

Zach opened his mouth to say something, but Sage silenced him with one look. "Wait," she mouthed.

We walked in silence down the street, but as soon as we were out of view of the house, Zach started protesting, "Why are you here? I don't recall asking for your incredibly agreeable company."

"Listen, I'm not a moron, even though you may think I am. I know that something's up when my brother offers to get groceries. If you're planning to go save Tom, which I have a feeling that's what this is all about, then count me in." Sage flashed a lipstick-covered grin and sashayed down the road.

Zach stared after her, his jaw hanging down. "What? But . . . she can't!" he spluttered.

I just shrugged and followed her. "She might as well

come along. If she doesn't, she'll just tattle on us, and besides, the more the merrier, right?"

"Not if my sister is one of those 'more,'" he muttered but followed me anyway.

Once we both caught up with Sage, Zach said, "Wait! If you insist on coming along, at least listen to us!"

His older sister stopped and spun around on her heel to face him. "Fine, Mr. Know-It-All. Tell me your plan."

Plan. The problem was that we didn't have one.

"Well, the thing is, we don't really . . ." I trailed off, embarrassed. "We have a step one, but that's about it."

Sage rolled her eyes. "Great. Tell me the first step then."

"Only somewhere private, where we won't be heard," Zach said looking around him. "Remember what Grandma said."

"Follow me," Sage said, grabbed his arm, and started plodding forward.

Zach groaned and glanced at me over his shoulder. "So now she's in charge?"

"Are you saying I can't be a leader?" Sage snapped.

"Guys!" I yelled as I caught up to them. "Nobody's in charge, we are doing this all together!"

Zach and Sage stopped and turned their backs to each other and crossed their arms, each clearly annoyed with the other. Now it was my turn to roll my eyes. "So where is this private place?"

Zach and I followed Sage down the street and into a narrow alley that ended at the door of a tent. Sage gestured to the tent, and Zach and I walked in, looking all around us. "What is this place?" he asked.

"A bar, kind of low-key. Everyone here has something to hide, so everybody minds their own business. This is the perfect place," replied Sage.

The tent was filled with a noxious, suffocating smoke, mixed with the scent of beer, meat, and sweat.

"Um, I don't really think this is a safe place. It looks like a bar for criminals or something," I said, my eyes shifting from one scary-looking bar patron to another.

"Just relax, and don't make eye contact," advised Sage.

The whole time Zach had remained silent, and now that I looked at him, he seemed a bit pale. "You okay?" I asked him.

"All this smoke. I feel like I'm going to barf."

"Well, just don't do it on me," I said, taking a step away.

"You're sympathetic," he mumbled, the sarcasm clear in his tone.

Once we sat down at one of the tables, I said, "Zach and I are going to save Tom."

"I thought so," Sage said, like it wasn't a big deal.

"Don't go tell Grandma Martha or Ian, otherwise we'll never be able to save my brother. They would never allow us to do anything like this," I pleaded.

"Oh, I won't. As long as I can come with you," she said.

"We already discussed this. You can come, but it's not going to be safe," I warned.

"Yeah, there's going to be all kinds of dangers, black magic, monsters, and death!" said Zach, trying desperately to scare his sister into not coming.

"I'm no chicken," she replied with a straight face, not the slightest bit fazed by what the boy had said.

I looked at her more closely. Was she really that fearless? Or was she just acting brave? There was fear in her eyes, mixed with a stubborn determination, which told me she hated that Zach thought she was a stupid girly girl. I mean, she was definitely a girly girl, just maybe not a stupid one.

I told her about my idea to go to Earth, and why.

"But if he was the one who Divided the world in the first place, wouldn't he also be able to travel from Eeba to Earth?" Sage objected.

"He's obviously stronger here than there. Why else would he stay here on Eeba? So it's better for us to be on Earth," snapped Zach.

"Shut. Up," said Sage as she squinted her eyes at her brother. Zach rolled his eyes in return.

"Um, one quick question," I said before they could get into an argument. "People on Earth don't know about the two worlds, and Grandma Martha said neither did Eebians. Then how come you guys know?"

Zach shrugged. "Grandma has always talked about it. I don't know how she knows though."

Sage nodded her agreement. She had taken out some mint gum from her pocket and popped it in her mouth and was now absentmindedly chewing with loud, obnoxious noises.

Zach glared at her. "Will you cut that out? You sound like a cow!"

"No." She opened her mouth even wider with each chew.

He threw up his hands. "I can't stand her!"

Christ. This was going to be harder than I thought.

"Enough talking," I said. "Let's just leave. We can't open the portal here in the middle of a bar or we'd have a whole bunch of Eebians to explain back on my home planet."

We stood up and started walking out. We had almost arrived at the door of the tent when a man stepped in front of the opening, blocking our way out.

My heart jumped into my throat and began beating ten times the normal speed. Who was this person? Was it the Soul Sucker? Had he come to take us away?

Zach tried to edge around the bulky person that was preventing us from leaving.

"Not so fast," he grumbled in a low, gravelly voice.

I gulped. We were doomed.

"I haven't seen you 'round here before. What's your business?" the man demanded.

When nobody answered, I realized he had directed the question to me. "I'm, I'm new in town," I stammered.

"What's your business?" the man repeated.

"I, I don't understand—"

He took a menacing step towards me and looked straight in my eyes. He didn't move for a while, and all I could do was stare back at his stormy, grey irises and hope he wouldn't kill me. After a torturous minute had passed, he looked up, satisfied, and announced, "I'm pretty sure this is the one. Oh boy, will the boss be happy with us."

Some instinct gave me the feeling that "the boss" had very much to do with the Soul Sucker.

"I really don't think this is necessary, sir," said Sage as she stepped forward. "She is—"

"Did somebody ask you?" the man raged.

Sage squealed and scurried back.

Zach yelled, "Don't talk to my sister that way!" with a bit of a tremble at the end that showed he immediately regretted ever opening his mouth.

"I think these two have to learn a lesson, 'cause nobody talks to me like that," said the man in an ominous whisper.

"Please don't. We don't want any trouble," I begged.

But the man ignored me. "Get 'em. All three of 'em!"

Four other men, twice the size of the man in front of us, made their way towards us from various places in the tent. They were all massive mountains of muscle wearing tuxedos and black shades over their scarred faces. I caught a glimpse of gun holsters attached to each of their legs. And they were not empty.

"Run!" yelled Zach.

Sage and I needed no more encouragement. We ducked under the first man's arm and raced out into the street.

"This way! Follow me!" shouted Zach.

We all sprinted away from the bar and onto a busy

road with the men right behind us. People crowded in front of us but, being smaller, we easily ducked around them. Luckily for us, the bulky men chasing us had a much harder time dodging the throngs of people. But even if we had this small advantage, we could never outrun them.

Ahead of me, Zach turned down into a narrow street covered in graffiti. I followed him, but when I glanced behind me to see if Sage was keeping up, she wasn't there. A bit further down the road, I saw her struggling with her high-heeled boots. I groaned. We were running for our lives, and she was worried about her shoes?

"Ditch them for God's sake!" I shrieked at her.

She mumbled something under her breath but took them off and clutched them in her hands.

We were all in the alley. "Quick! The portal!" screeched Sage.

I willed myself to be back home and for the portal to open. Before I knew it, the ground ahead of us had begun to spin. "Let's go!"

Sage and Zach jumped into the vortex without delay. I hesitated for just a moment. Long enough to see the five men rounding the corner and their flabbergasted faces.

Then I leapt through the portal as well and was whisked back to my reality.

CHAPTER 4

WHEN I OPENED my eyes, I found myself sprawled across the sidewalk of Oak Street next to the door of a coffee shop. I glanced around and saw Sage and Zach already standing there. I abruptly picked myself up and hoped that nobody had seen us magically appear.

"Well," I said to the two of them, "this is Earth." Two frowning, disappointed faces stared back at me.

"This is it?" asked Zach. "It's so . . . plain."

"No it's not!" I said, defensively. But then I observed my surroundings more closely. He was right. In comparison with Eeba, Earth looked so grey and boring. But Eeba wasn't a whole lot better. It was too overwhelming and intense in a forceful sort of way.

And that was when it struck me.

On their own, the two worlds were on opposite sides of the scale, and what we needed was just one world that was right in the middle.

We had to bring the two worlds together.

It was the very opposite thing that the Soul Sucker was doing.

I was about to tell Zach and Sage my idea when my eyes fell on my watch. Oh my God. I had completely forgotten about my parents! They were probably freaking out. I had been gone for over a day without telling them anything!

"Look, guys," I said, anxiously, "I really have to go. My parents—"

"I understand," Zach said, cutting me off. "Go. We can take care of ourselves, and we'll make sure to be discreet."

"But—"

"Go! We'll be on this street when you need us."

I gave him a gracious smile, and dashed home.

*

I wanted to bang open the door screaming, "I'm back! I'm okay!" but of course I didn't. Instead I walked in calmly and called out, "Mom? Dad? Anybody home?"

Instantly, a ruckus broke out. I hardly had time to see what was going on when my mom and dad enveloped (and almost suffocated) me in a huge bear hug. Looking up, I saw that they were both crying freely in front of the police officer that stood behind them.

"Don't, don't you ever do that again, do you hear me? You had us worried s-sick! Isabel Maria Yates, where on Earth were you?" sobbed my mother.

Oops. I hadn't thought about that. What should I tell them?

"I was, er, out, um, with some friends. I thought I had told you."

"Out?" yelled my dad. "Do you realize what your mother and I are going through right now? Your brother is in a coma, and then you disappear! You don't respond to our phone calls or messages, not even Josie knew where you were, and then you come back and all you have to say is you were out? You are grounded for . . ." he paused as he struggled to think of a time limit. "For infinity! Now go to your room, now!"

With my head hanging, I trudged up the stairs, barely believing that I was grounded forever. If they forced me to stay home, how was I supposed to see Zach or Sage again? How was I supposed to save Tom in time?

I threw myself on the bed and fell into a half sleep. Falling through a vortex was exhausting. I was awoken by the sound of my bedroom door opening. Mom came in and whispered, "Isabel, I'm sorry we were so mad, but it was just because we were worried about you. You understand?"

I nodded and hugged her again. "I love you, Mom."

"I love you, too."

When we finally broke away she said, "Your father and I are going to the hospital to see how Tom is doing. Do you want to come?"

I didn't even try to understand how he could be in two worlds at once, and to tell the truth, I didn't even care that it was scientifically impossible. All I knew was that I had to save him, not sit there watching him Fade away!

But on the other hand, I didn't want to tell my parents the real reason behind Tom's coma. They would probably think I was crazy and take me to get some mental health care. I mean, I hardly believed it myself!

So for the time being I had to act normal, and that meant having to go to the hospital.

*

When I saw his face my eyes filled with bitter tears.

It just wasn't fair!

My amazing brother, once so full of happy energy, was now in a deep, evil sleep, and I didn't know if he'd ever wake up.

I was drowning in waves of sadness as I remembered all those happy times with my dear brother. Like when we went to the lake for my birthday and we spent so many amazing hours, splashing and playing in the water. Or at night, when I was little, and I would sneak into his bed, and he would whisper to me so many stories full of magic and hope that would gently put me sleep. And even the times when I was lonely, walking to school by myself because Josie was sick. He would excuse himself from his friends and come to walk with me instead.

"Has there been any improvement?" I asked, even though I already knew the answer. When my mother didn't reply, I looked into her face with more attention. All her usual cheerfulness had vanished from her eyes, replaced by a heavy, tired sadness. Only then did I realize just how much this hurt her. At least I knew the real cause of Tom's coma, and I could try to do something about it. But my parents? They didn't know anything.

I realized that I had to succeed, not only for my brother's life, but also for my parents' and mine.

Tears were now rolling freely down my cheeks, and I whispered to myself again and again, "I'll save you, I'm not going to let you die. I'll save you."

*

A day had passed since I had returned from the other world. I was still officially grounded but that wouldn't stop me. I was planning on sneaking out to get Zach and Sage, but my parents had other ideas. No matter how much I protested, or how much I begged, they were intent on my going to school.

I tried as best as I could, but eventually they won the argument.

So the next day I was walking to school when I bumped into Josie.

"Hey stranger," she called. "I tried to call but you never answered. Then Mrs. Nickle had a talk with the whole school about your brother. Izzy, I'm so sorry!" She gave me hug.

I hugged her back but I didn't say anything. I was trying to decide whether I should tell her about Eeba or not. I had just made up my mind to not confide in her when she said, "Hey, if you have something to tell me, go ahead. I have a feeling you're hiding something from me." She gave me her suspicious look, with the one eyebrow raised. My mind flashed to Ian's raised eyebrow, and before I knew it, I was pouring out my whole story to her. She listened in silence, breaking it only to gasp or mutter little noises of amazement.

When I finally finished she didn't say anything. I was beginning to regret ever opening my mouth when she said, "Wow."

"You believe me?" I asked anxiously, hoping against hope that she did. I couldn't bear having my best friend thinking I was insane. But she nodded and stammered, "Yes . . . yes, I believe you."

There was a long awkward pause, then Josie glanced at her watch and cried, "Oh my God, we are so late!" We tore down the street toward school.

We barged into the classroom out of breath, and it was already second period. Math with Mr. Tuckers.

"Sorry we're late, Mr. Tuckers," we chorused.

"Late? I think it's a bit more than late! I will have to call your parents about this, young ladies!"

Josie and I put on our best we-are-very-ashamed-and-we-won't-do-it-again looks, and he shooed us into our seats. We knew his calling our parents was a bluff. Or at least we hoped it was.

*

It felt like years had passed until the lunch bell finally rang. I could tell Josie was just as eager as I was to talk about what I had been through. After I had politely re-fused to sit at the boys' table (Aaron and Sammy especially wanted me to sit with them. We had been friends since kindergarten, and they felt like cousins to me), Josie and I picked out a separate table. We had just sat down when Ashley, followed by her little gang, came to our table.

"Oh, hi, Isabel! I hardly noticed you were here. I've gotten so used to not seeing you!" Her gang sniggered.

"Missed me?" I asked, not even looking up.

"Oh please, don't think so highly of yourself!"

I snapped back, "Ashley, why don't you go pick on something with a brain the same size as your own? For example, the toilet seat."

For a moment she remained flustered, searching for something to say until finally she retorted, "But I thought I already was talking to the toilet seat."

"That just proves how incredibly stupid you are," I replied while calmly unwrapping my sandwich.

"Look who's talking!" Ashley snapped back. Obvi-ously annoyed at my seeming indifference to her comebacks, so she decided to take it a step further. "You know, school has been so much nicer without you . . . or your brother."

Now her group remained silent. We all knew she had gone too far.

I was aware of my fist rising, about to fly into her face, when Josie came to my rescue.

She yanked my hand down and pulled me back into my seat. Then she turned back to the mean girl and started cursing her in ways that would have made the rudest sailor proud. Which is just the sort of thing to capture the attention of the teacher.

"Girls, what's going on?" asked Mrs. Erickson.

"Nothing," said Ashley, as innocently as possible.

"Then why don't you go sit back down at your table?"

They stalked off and Josie turned to me. "That could have gotten a lot uglier than it already was."

"You are very right," I said as I bit into my sandwich.

We ate in silence for a bit and then she said, "So when are we going?"

I looked up, confused. "What do you mean?"

"When are we going to go get Zach and Sage? To talk about a plan?"

"We?" I said. "Josie, listen to me. I would love for you to come, but I can't have you taking that risk!"

Josie snorted. "Oh please. Stop sounding like my mom!"

"But there's magic involved! Dark magic!" I protested, a little too loudly. The other kids at the tables next to ours peered over at us.

"Er, just talking about a book I read," I explained to them. I turned back to my friend. "Look, I've known you since I was, like, two years old, and I wouldn't be able to live with myself if something were to happen to you."

"I guess we'll have to make sure that nothing happens, then, because I'm coming," she said. "Seriously, you didn't actually think that I would let you do this alone, did you?"

"I'm not alone," I pointed out. "I have Zach and Sage."

"And you prefer them over me?" Josie cried out, pretending she was offended.

"You know that's not what I meant!"

"I'm coming," Josie said as she wiped her mouth with a napkin. "And that's that."

I didn't know whether to keep arguing or leave it at that. I loved her, but if she got hurt—or worse—I would never forgive myself. Still, I knew I could use her help and support and that I could never do anything as big as this without her.

I gave in. "You are so annoying," I said with a grin.

She took another bite of her sandwich. "I know."

"Idiot," I responded, still smiling.

Josie cleared her throat, pointed her index finger in the air, and said, "And I quote: 'Never argue with an idiot. They will only drag you down to their level and beat you with experience.' And I sure did beat you."

I laughed. "Who said that? Mark Twain?"

She shook her head. "Guess again."

"Uh, George Carlin?" I said, choosing a comedian that Josie and I loved to watch on YouTube.

"Yup." She continued eating her lunch.

I must admit I was grateful for how stubborn she was. I felt like a bit of the burden had been taken off my shoulders now that I was sharing it with my best friend.

All of a sudden I felt something cold and wet sliding down my back. I whipped my head around and saw Ashley standing behind me with her now-empty milk carton clutched in her hand.

"Oops! I am soooo clumsy! I'm sorry, Isabel." The way she said "I'm sorry" sounded more like, "I wish you were a cockroach I could step on and then flush down the drain."

She tossed the carton onto my table and went off to flirt with Colin, her gang trailing behind her. That group reminded me of the smudges, just hollow shells with nothing inside. Actually, the smudges probably had more personality than these morons.

Then I felt the slimy milk soaking into my shirt and dripping into my underwear.

I saw red.

I vaguely remembered Josie's hand clamp down on my wrist as she dragged me to the bathroom.

"Isabel, just take a deep breath. Isabel, listen to me. Try and calm down so we can sort this out. You can't get into trouble now with Tom's life hanging in the balance and Zach and Sage wandering around on Oak Street."

I sighed. She was right, and I had to focus. As I peeled of my wet shirt, I called Ashley all the bad words I could think of. Some of them I even invented on the spot.

Josie continued to be practical, saying in a soothing voice, "Okay, here's what we're going to do. I'll give you my shirt, and I'll put my sweater on, then you put yours in your bag to dry out at home."

"Thanks a million, Jo."

I felt so tired. After all I had been through: Tom, a magical world, and school bullies. I just wanted to crawl into a ball and dream it all away.

The rest of the school day was long and uneventful. Josie and I just waited until the final bell so we could proceed with our plan, and Ashley made herself scarce, which was probably the smartest thing she's ever done, considering I was just longing to give her a nice kick in the pants.

*

Back at home, I crumpled down on my bed and lay there for a second as I calculated how much time it would take to sneak out to Oak Street, passing by Josie's house, and meet up with Zach and Sage. I would have gone to get them straight after school if my mom hadn't decided to come pick me up. I guess Mr. Tuckers hadn't been bluffing when he said he'd call my parents. Then I looked around my room to see what things would be useful to bring to Eeba. I began to get restless. I wanted to get out of here! I crept out of my room and tiptoed down the staircase to my parents' room. I peeked in to see if they were busy and maybe wouldn't notice I was gone, but unfortunately at that very moment my mom turned around and saw me looking in.

"Oh, Isabel, I was just about to call you! You and I are going out to dinner," she said.

"Crap," I muttered under my breath. Then I noticed that my dad wasn't in the room. "Where's Dad?" I asked.

"He's at the hospital, and I don't feel like cooking so we're going to go to Charlie's. Buffet night, okay?" said my mom.

"Yeah, sure," I grumbled.

Once we were in the car and on our way to Charlie's, I thought more about how I was going to save Tom, and how I was going to bring the two worlds together. And something occurred to me.

A crazy, amazing idea popped into my head, and I knew why the Soul Sucker did what he did.

I was so wrapped up in my own thoughts that at first I didn't notice we had arrived.

Or who was standing at the end of the buffet table.

Ashley, in designer skinny jeans and ballerina flats, with her straight blonde hair hanging in front of her eyes, was leaning on Colin's shoulder.

Luckily, they had their backs to me, so I easily slipped into a chair at the table where my mom was already sitting.

Mom turned to me and said, "You go on and fill your plate. I'll be right after you."

I shuffled to the buffet table and started putting food on my plate. As I got closer to where Ashley and Colin stood, I only had one thought: payback time.

I faked a stumble and sent my plastic plate, contents and all, flying towards Ashley's shirt.

Bull's eye.

Pasta, salad, and mashed potatoes smeared all over the back of Ashley's Abercrombie & Fitch top.

She slowly turned around to face me.

"Oops. It slipped," I said, batting my eyelashes and using every ounce of my self-control to not burst out laughing.

Ashley's cool went out the window.

Her face went as red as her lipstick. She blindly grabbed at the table for something to throw back at me but only succeeded in knocking over a cup with her elbow.

The contents of the cup spilled all over Colin—and in an area that made it look like he had wet himself. He stared down at his wet spot, then at Ashley, completely mortified. "This isn't . . . I mean, I didn't . . . ." He turned and sprinted to the men's room.

There were a few moments of silence. Servers and other restaurant personnel started shouting at once. Some tried to clean up the messes, both the one on the floor and the one on Ashley. Others just yelled for no particular reason.

In the midst of the confusion, I grabbed another plate, scooped up whatever I could onto it and raced back to my table.

"Isabel, what took you so long? And what's happening over there?" asked Mom, craning her neck in the direction of the buffet.

I realized that she hadn't seen anything, so I mumbled, "Um, I don't know. I think someone might have spilled something. No big deal."

I stayed close to her for the rest of the night since Ashley wouldn't try to kill me with my mom around.

I hoped.

As we were driving to the hospital to pick up Dad, I was relieved to remember that the next day was Saturday. I had a whole weekend before school started again, and by then, hopefully I would be on Eeba, saving Tom. And if I wasn't, maybe in that time Ashley and Colin would forget about the incident at Charlie's.

But somehow I doubted that.

CHAPTER 5

AS SOON AS I woke up on Saturday morning, I called Josie. We had planned to meet at the park, and since it was right next to Oak Street, we would try and find Zach and Sage. Still in my pajamas, I went downstairs, where my mom was sitting by herself at the kitchen table, staring into her empty coffee cup.

"Uh, mom?" I whispered, not wanting to disturb her thoughts. "It's okay if I go to the park with Josie today, right?"

Lifting her sad eyes to meet mine, she replied, "Isabel, don't think I've forgotten that you're grounded."

"But Mom! I'm just meeting up with her at the park, and then we're going to the library to do some research for a homework assignment." I lied.

"Uh huh, Isabel. You really think I'm stupid, don't you? To believe an excuse like that?"

I groaned silently. This was going to be harder than I thought. "Come on!" I said. "My time period for being grounded is almost done anyway!"

"Oh, so infinity has already passed?" asked Mom, slightly amused.

I was getting nowhere. I had to come at this differently. I sat down at the table next to her.. "Mom, Josie's my best friend. Please let me go see her so I can talk to her about . . . all this." I said, quietly, clearly meaning Tom's coma. "I need to talk to someone. And right now, I want to talk to Josie."

I felt a little guilty, lying like this to my own mom about something so important, but I had to do it if I wanted a chance to save my brother. And, technically, we certainly would be talking about Tom.

My mom took a deep breath, and for a moment, just stared ahead of her. The despair was heavy in the room. Then she whispered, "All right."

"Thanks." I said, giving her a hug.

As I turned to go, Mom spoke up. "Why don't you get some money from my wallet so you can have lunch, too. I'm leaving in a little bit to meet up with your father."

After I had gotten the money and brushed my teeth, I slid on high-waisted jeans and a loose grey tank top. I bent down to put on some socks, and as I did, I caught my reflection in the mirror. I stared at the girl that looked back at me: I was a bit short and had olive skin, full lips, and thick brown hair that fell in wavy locks a little bit past my shoulders. My mom calls me "curvy," but I see myself more round. Definitely more thick around the chest and thighs than I would have liked at thirteen. Stepping closer to the mirror, I drew a thick line of black over each eye and added some mascara. Once satisfied with my makeup, I adjusted my hair and smiled at my reflection.

I looked good.

Remembering my little, um, "self-esteem crisis" just a few days ago, I looked down at my hands in shame. The one thing I didn't want to be was one of those girls who thought that being gorgeous and skinny is the most important thing to be. I always get so depressed when girls call themselves fat and ugly—even when they aren't—and act like their value in life as a person is directly proportionate to their appearance.

I need to be the person who helps those girls—not be one of them!

Well, I still have a long way to go.

That said, I should probably tell you a bit about Josie.

Josie was absolutely stunning. Tall and slender with glossy black hair that contrasted beautifully with her sky blue eyes and a smile that drove the boys at school crazy. If you judged her by her looks, you would have imagined her to be in Ashley's group, but her attitude was the complete opposite of theirs: polite, smart, sure of herself, and as cool as a cucumber. The big difference between our personalities was her prudence and thoughtfulness, contrary to my impulsiveness.

I glanced at my watch and realized I should get going. I threw on a cute, cream-colored sweater to protect me from the chilly outside air and was on my way. I cruised down the smooth streets on my skateboard towards the park.

When I arrived, Josie was already there waiting for me.

"Jesus, what took you so long? I've been dying to talk to you! I've—" I heard a buzzing sound and her hand flew to her pocket. A scowl crossed Josie's face as she pulled her phone out to answer the call. "He has been busting my butt all morning," Josie muttered as she put the phone to her ear. She doesn't swear often, so I understood that she must be pretty pissed off.

"I told you not to call me again!" she hissed. I couldn't hear who was on the other end, but Josie was obviously at her limit. "I don't care! You know what? Just . . . good-bye!" And she hung up. Then she turned to me, took a breath, and said, as if nothing had happened, "I've been thinking about Eeba all night!"

I raised an eyebrow. "Josie? Um, who was that?"

"Just Andrew." She said, rolling her eyes.

"Excuse me?"

"Andrew," she repeated. When she saw my confused face, she said, "Andrew, as in the guy who took me out to the movies? Ring any bells?"

"Oh, right!" Finally I remembered. "Well, what happened with him?"

"Long story. Let's just say I'm done with him."

I smirked. I was so glad I didn't have to deal with stuff like that.

"Anyway," I said, "first we have to find Zach and

Sage. They said they would be somewhere on Oak Street, but it's been quite a while since I last saw them. I hope they're okay."

We hurried up and down the street, peering into alleyways and places they could be hiding, but they were nowhere to be seen.

Time ticked by, and we started to get hungry, so we decided to have lunch and then continue our search.

At the café, we sat down at a table for two and were about to order when I heard a familiar voice yelling, "Isabel!" I spun around and saw Zach and Sage sitting at one of the tables.

"What the heck are you doing here?" I hissed.

"Hey, chill out. We have to eat something!" said Zach, picking up a menu.

I felt a bit guilty since I had practically abandoned them to fend for themselves. But instead of saying anything, I just slapped my forehead. "How will you pay for it?"

Zach grinned, mischievously.

I rolled my eyes as I got up to go their table, which had two empty chairs. "Well, this is my friend Josie," I said, motioning toward her as she got up from our table. "Josie, this is Zach, and she's Sage."

They all greeted each other and we sat down.

Sage whispered to me, "Does she know? About . . ."

"Yep. Josie's going to help us."

We all ordered and waited for our food in an awkward silence. Sage shifted uncomfortably in her seat. "So, do you have any other ideas? Zach and I have been thinking. Well, actually you need a brain to do that, so let's just say I have been thinking."

Josie snorted into her glass and even I had to keep back a giggle.

Zach only sighed, as if he knew there was no point in arguing. "Whatever."

I leaned forward into the table and said, "I actually do have something, but I think it would be better if we talked about this at my house. My parents aren't there so it would be fine. If anyone heard us talking about Eeba in here, they would probably think we're all crazy."

The others nodded their approval.

*

After wolfing down our food, we rushed back to my place. When Zach saw my skateboard he cried out, much to my embarrassment, "A hover-board!" And I had to quickly explain to him that it was a hover board that didn't hover, which made him even more confused.

The whole way to my house, in fact, Zach and Sage gaped at the normality of Earth. Even though they had already been there for a while, they kept looking up at the sky, half-expecting to see people flying around with jetpacks or something. I also noticed they were both having a hard time moving around. I remembered that the air particles had been a lot less dense on Eeba, so it was only natural that walking around Earth would feel a little strange.

We entered my house and everyone got themselves comfortable in my bedroom. Then they all looked at me. I realized they were all counting on me to lead them in this adventure.

I gulped. This wasn't a responsibility I wanted, or one that I thought I was ready for.

"Well, er . . . ," I started, "We're going to save, er, Tom, um, and—"

"Yes, but how?" interrupted Sage.

"That's, um, a very good question, er . . . ," I scanned their faces, unsure of what to say. But then I saw Josie's encouraging gaze, and I began again with renewed self-esteem.

"Well, last night I was thinking, and I may have a theory." I looked at them to make sure they were all paying maximum attention before continuing. "I asked myself why the Soul Sucker takes away your soul instead of just simply killing the person? What I think is that he uses the souls' power for something."

Everyone sat alone with their thoughts for a moment before Josie asked, "But what?"

"That's the problem. I don't know. " I didn't say anything for a second, and then another thought came to my mind. "I also had this feeling, a few days ago, when I had just arrived back here, that Earth and Eeba were too different on their own, and that they should be joined again."

"You mean undo what the Soul Sucker did all those years ago?" asked Zach.

"Remember when Grandma Martha said that we

would bring hope to Earth and Eeba?" I asked. "That must be what she meant."

"Supposing what you say is true," Sage said, "what does that have to do with Tom? Or the souls?"

We all pondered this for a minute or two, but nobody could think of anything. "Well, whatever we do, we have to go back to Eeba," Sage said. "And somehow we have to get to the Soul Sucker."

We all nodded with understanding, and then Zach said, "I have an idea." A huge grin of triumph spread across his face, signaling his belief that he'd thought of something that could be important.

We all gathered in close with excitement to hear the boy's proposition.

"Remember that bar we went to? And those men who tried to catch us? I have a feeling they are the Soul Sucker's helpers, or henchmen or something. Who else would be looking for Isabel? Well, what if we go back there? Hopefully they'll still be there . . . and we get caught on purpose!"

"You're crazy," I said almost before he finished speaking.

"No, seriously. They wouldn't kill us; they would take us to the Soul Sucker! You said so yourself that he uses the souls. Why would he waste ours?"

"But I don't know for sure! It was just an idea!" I protested.

"You know Isabel, it may not sound like a solid theory to you. And it isn't really, but you do have a point." Josie said, turning to me.

"Alright. For argument's sake, let's say my hunch is right. Is turning into a smudge that much better?" I said.

"Whoa, who says we'll be turned into smudges?" Sage interrupted. "If we start thinking we'll fail, then we will. We have to be optimistic."

"I guess . . . we could . . . try it," I said, then looked at the clock on my bedside table. "But you guys have to get going. My parents could be here any minute."

"Okay," said Sage, "but where are we going to sleep? I'm sick of spending the night on a cardboard box in an alley."

"Oh, sorry about that. I couldn't come and get you any sooner," I said with a shrug.

"You can stay ay my place," offered Josie. "My parents are away for the weekend, and I'll just tell Lisa, my older sister, that you're friends of mine coming for a sleepover."

"That's a great idea," said Zach.

I looked away so that Josie wouldn't see my annoyance at Zach's staying at her house. When they turned to go, Zach smiled and said, "See you tomorrow!" So that made me feel better at least.

CHAPTER 6

I HAD SET the alarm for five in the morning, so I could wake up early and get out of the house while my parents were still asleep.

Dringgg went the clock, the noise slightly muffled since I had placed it under my pillow so no one else could hear it. I tore myself up from bed and away from my nightmares.

I brushed my teeth, got dressed, and grabbed the backpack that I had prepared the night before. It was filled with water bottles, snacks, money, blankets, a mirror, and flashlights. Then I slid my handy Swiss Army knife into my pocket. Hopefully that would be enough stuff, plus, Josie had said that she would also bring some supplies.

I sneaked down the hall and peered into my parents' room. They were sound asleep. I felt horrible about leaving without telling them anything. The thought of how worried they would be when they woke up and found me gone was almost too much to bear.

After a lot of consideration, I made up my mind to write them a note, just telling them that I was fine and that I would come back as soon as possible. As I fixed the piece of paper onto the fridge, I wondered what would happen if I didn't succeed—if I never did come back. My parents would be crushed.

Only then did I realize just how much my friends were sacrificing for me. They, too, were risking not ever going back to their family and friends, only for some silly idea of mine.

But it was too late to turn back now.

I pushed the bolt to the front door back as silently as I could and slipped out into the sunrise.

I was the first one to arrive at our meeting point behind the elementary school. I sat there in the first rays of sun, waiting for the others.

Josie showed up next with a humongous bag weighing her shoulders down. As soon as she saw me, she gave a sigh of relief and dumped her bag on the pavement. "Just ... a few ... things," she explained between pants as she caught her breath.

Tilting my head to the side, I looked at the backpack. "A few?"

"Oh, stop giving me grief! Somebody on this mission needs to be prepared and responsible!"

I looked over her shoulder. "Where are Zach and Sage? I thought they were with you."

Josie nodded, "Oh yeah, they're right behind me, but

they started arguing about something or other. Whatever. They'll be here in a sec," she assured me.

She then plopped herself down next to me. "You okay?" she asked.

"Sure," I lied. Seeing her, I was reminded that if anything were to happen to her or Zach or Sage, I would never forgive myself.

As if reading my mind, Josie said, "Isabel, remember, I'm coming with you on my own accord. You didn't force me. Actually, I kind of forced you. This was my decision so I will live with the consequences. Whatever happens, don't blame yourself."

I got so choked up that I couldn't speak. I turned to her, my eyes shining with tears, and hugged her. "Thank you," I whispered.

"I hope the same thing goes for Zach and Sage," I said, once I got over my emotional moment.

Josie grinned.

"Oh! Zaaaaach!," she said. "I know what's going on!"

"What are you talking about?" I cried out.

"I see the way he looks at you! Isabel, you can't hide anything from me!"

"You're insane," I muttered, but secretly, I was pleased.

No sooner had I said this than I heard a whoooo. It sounded like a really bad impersonation of a bird.

"What the . . . ?" said Josie. We stood up and saw Zach, half-hidden by the shadows, with his hands cupped around his mouth.

Whoo whooo.

I rolled my eyes and went over to where he was.

"Nice," I said, sarcastically but with a smile.

"Weirdo," I heard Sage mumble, and I had to stifle a giggle.

Josie stopped any further argument between the two siblings by saying, "Which one of you will open the portal?"

I went forward, but Zach said, "Step aside. Better let the pro handle this."

"Yeah right," I responded, teasingly, but Zach had already closed his eyes to focus.

While he was summoning the portal, I felt a pinching on my arm. I turned to see Josie clinging to me. I reminded myself that she had never seen the portal before and had no idea what to expect. But before I could whisper any words of comfort to my best friend, the ground before our feet began to swirl. Josie let out a little yelp and jumped back.

"Well," I said, "after you," and gestured to Zach.

He jumped through and the rest of us followed suit.

*

"Oh damnit!," cursed Zach. "I totally messed up."

"What did you do?" groaned Sage.

He looked at us sheepishly. "I forgot to specify that we wanted to land in the Plausible Quarter, so now we've landed in the Pixie District."

Sage groaned again, but I didn't understand what on earth they were talking about. "What does that mean?" I asked them.

"There are different districts in Malsama," explained Sage. "We live in the Plausible Quarter; that's where the more Earth-like people are. That's why Zach and I look pretty much like you, and we aren't too different from your people. But the other districts have all the other kinds of inhabitants of Eeba. And we are in the Pixie District." She rolled her eyes.

"That's so cool!" cried out Josie.

Zach and Sage looked at her, wide-eyed. "You don't know pixies," Sage said.

"No, I guess I don't," said Josie, looking to me. I shrugged in response.

"Here, 'pixie' means trouble," warned Sage.

"Oh." Josie sighed.

"We'd better get out of here as quickly as possible," said Zach. We all nodded and began to walk towards the end the street.

"Where are you guys going?" said a shrill female voice from behind.

We all stopped in our tracks and slowly turned around to face who had spoken.

A pixie, her flaming red hair in perfect spikes, hovered a foot above the ground right behind us. The wings that kept her aloft were as pointy as her hair. She reached the height of a small child, but her features were those of a teenager. She was pretty, in an angular sort of way, and her pointy purple nails tapped on her side, showing she was an impatient creature and that she didn't like not getting her way.

"Um, we were just leaving," I stammered.

THE TWO WORLDS OF ISABEL

"But why? I couldn't let you go out all by yourselves," she continued in her high voice.

From what Zach and Sage had said, this pixie shouldn't be trusted. I didn't know exactly what she would do, but I knew we should get away from her as soon as possible. I could see Sage and Josie were thinking the same thing because they were both slowly backing away. Zach, however, hesitated.

The pixie glided over to Zach and slowly ran her sharp nails through his hair. "I insist you come with me. My friends would love to meet you! We don't get many visitors these days, especially ones as handsome as this young man."

"Oh, I like her," said Zach, a stupid grin plastered on his face. I would have rolled my eyes, but I was more concerned than disgusted by Zach's behavior. He, himself, had said pixies were dangerous creatures, so this one must have put some sort of spell on him.

The pixie had started to drift down the opposite end of the street that we wanted to go down, and Zach followed her like a puppy.

Sage, Josie, and I exchanged worried looks and went after them. I had my pocketknife ready, and Sage offered to take Josie's bag for a bit since Josie's karate skills would be of more use if she could actually move. I smiled at Sage's suggestion. She was changing; I doubted she would have made the offer to carry a big backpack a few days ago.

Luckily, my bag didn't weigh so much, so I could carry it and still take action. Once we caught up with them, I saw Josie nudge Zach discreetly on the shoulder. "What are you doing?" she hissed. But he didn't respond. He just continued to gaze happily and obliviously at the redhead.

The pixie had been flying ahead of us, but now she stopped in front of an open double door. Dance music blared from inside. It was so loud that I could feel it thumping in my chest. My head started bopping automatically, but I instantly stopped when Josie roughly tugged at my arm.

The spiky-haired creature ducked into the place and Zach obediently followed.

I saw him disappear after the pixie, and I knew that if we entered that place, we would have a hard time getting out again with Zach all in one piece by our side.

"Come on," I said, determined.

Beams of different colored light cut through the air in every direction. Tons of other pixies were rocking out on the dance floor and drinking who knows what. I instantly got more nervous. Not because party animals make me anxious, but because who drinks four shots in a row at seven in the morning?

"Roxie!" I heard a voice yelling. I turned and saw a blue-haired pixie making her way to where we stood. The first pixie that we had seen (Roxie, apparently) yelled out to her friend. "Hey, Skylar! Look who I found!"

Only then did Skylar notice us. "Well, well, well. Cute." She stepped closer to Zach, who could only stare helplessly into her eyes, clueless grin still on his face.

Sage and I took defensive steps towards him. "Don't touch my brother," threatened Sage.

"Yeah," joined in Josie, "or you'll have to deal with us."

Skylar and Roxie turned to face us, momentarily forgetting about Zach. "Oh we're so scared," mocked Roxie.

Skylar giggled. "Dealing with you would be so easy, it's not even funny."

"Try us," I said, hopefully sounding braver than I actually felt. I glanced at Sage and watched her subtly edging around the two pixies and finally making it to the enchanted Zach.

Josie's scream got me back into focus.

Roxie and Skylar were morphing into grotesque monsters. Their teeth sharpened and elongated so that they protruded out of their mouths. Their eyes popped out of their sockets and their hair started to flame.

My breath caught in my throat. I was paralyzed.

I snapped out of it when they started breathing fire. Keeping my hand behind my back, I flicked open my pocketknife. My plan (if you could even call it that) consisted in not provoking the pixies—not starting a fight that we could never win. Instead, I decided to hold them off as long as I could just by backing away slowly.

I wish I could say this strategy worked, but it didn't.

Roxie and Skylar lashed out with their sharp nails, and Josie and I had no other choice but to defend ourselves and try to fight back. I brought my knife up from behind my back and struck out at Roxie. Josie looked around desperately for something she could use as a weapon, but, coming up empty-handed, she began just throwing random kicks and punches.

Out of the corner of my eye I saw Sage trying desperately to wake Zach up from his trance. She looked up for a second and we made eye contact, and her feelings were clear to me: however annoying Zach was to her, he was always her younger brother, and she felt responsible for him.

I glanced at Josie. She was doing pretty well, considering she had only her fists as defense. Thank God the pixies didn't have weapons other than the fire and their teeth, otherwise we would really be goners.

Josie's face scrunched up with pain as her knuckles got badly burnt. Without thinking, I stepped in front of her and began kicking and waving the knife with renewed vigor, trying to fight off both of the pixies at once.

Sage saw my difficulty, but she was torn as to what she should do. Try to break the spell on her brother? Or help me so I wouldn't die a painful death?

I'm glad she chose the latter.

Rushing to my side, Sage crouched down and in one swift motion, took off her boot and flung the sharp heel towards Roxie's face.

The boot met its mark.

With Roxie out cold and Skylar so shocked that she had momentarily forgotten about us, I knew it was time to make our exit.

I grabbed Josie's wrist and hastened out of the disco.

I turned around to see Sage struggling with her reluctant brother and trying to put her shoe back on. Behind me, I heard Zach protesting, "Leave me alone! I think they're nice. What do you mean monsters? I think you're overreacting a bit!"

After encouraging Josie to get out of there, I went over to Zach and said, "Sorry about this, but—" and I delivered a big slap across his cheek. He blinked and looked around, confused. "What the . . . ? What are we standing here for? There's a monster over there!"

Skylar's shock was quickly changing to a boiling fury, and we all bolted down the street to catch up with Josie.

The furious buzzing of Skylar's wings was getting louder and louder, making us run faster and faster. "How dare you hurt my friend? You will pay for this!" she screamed at us, in a surprisingly powerful voice.

We were all panting, trying to catch our breath. Just as I started to lose hope, I saw a familiar figure in the distance—a figure that looked like smudged charcoal. "Help!" I yelled, waving my arms frantically so it would notice us.

"Isabel? Is that you?"

"Ian!" I shouted. "Help! That pixie wants to kill us!"

Once we neared him, he yelled, "Hurry up! Jump into the hovercraft!"

We all launched ourselves into his vehicle, and the moment we touched the interior cushioning, Ian cranked the gas. We zoomed off leaving Skylar behind.

As soon as Skylar saw us cruising off in a hovercraft she gave up. I looked over my shoulder to see her changing back into the blue-haired pixie she was before. She waved her fist, shrieking something incomprehensible, then zipped away, presumably to the disco to help Roxie.

I breathed a loud sigh of relief. "Ian, thank God we saw you!"

"I'm glad, too! But that doesn't excuse you from running away!" He looked down at us, and Zach, Sage, and I hung our heads.

"Sorry," we mumbled.

Ian waved our apology away. "Don't apologize to me! Apologize to Grandma Martha when we see her! She's been worried sick!" Then, keeping his eyes on the road, he leaned towards the backseat where we were all crammed next to each other and said in a quieter voice, "Don't tell Grandma Martha, but I agree with you." He leaned back even further so we could hear him better and added, "I suspected you were off to save Tom, and I think you should! In my opinion, you all have a good chance on defeating the Soul Sucker."

"You do?" asked Sage, surprised.

"Yes, yes I do," he replied. To me he sounded like he was telling the truth, but he said it like it pained him. I wondered what was the matter?

"So you won't take us to Grandma Martha?" I asked.

"No."

We all thanked him. Then he said, "Now who's this little lady?"

"This is Josie," I explained. "She's my best friend, and she's going to help as well."

Josie smiled, timidly. "Nice to meet you, Ian."

He nodded then continued driving in silence.

In that moment of quiet I moved my gaze to the street where I saw huge piles of leaves lining the road. There weren't many other drivers out, but I could hear faraway buzzing in the air behind me, and I imagined all the creatures flying through the clouds.

Zach whispered to me, "I'm sorry. I feel so stupid that I was enchanted so easily, and that I messed up bringing us here in the first place." He looked down, ashamed.

I felt bad for him. "It wasn't your fault that you got caught up in Roxie's pixie magic. It could have happened to anybody," I reassured him. "And besides, it's hard to open the portal. I probably would have messed up, too!"

He shrugged. "What exactly happened when I was under her spell? All I remember is just a blur . . . Until you slapped me. And although I can't say it was enjoyable, thanks anyway."

I laughed and gave him a brief recount of what had happened, exaggerating a bit on the horrible monsters the pixies had become. But he wasn't so shocked about that part. What really had an effect on him was what his sister had done. "She really did that?" he asked. "Wow." When he saw me grinning, he abruptly stopped praising her, and said, "Whatever. Anybody could have done that." He tried his best to look unimpressed, but it wasn't working.

I looked past him at Sage. She had heard what he

had said, and she tried really hard not to seem too proud of herself. But she wasn't doing a good job; I'd never seen her more happy.

"So, what's your big plan to rescue Tom?" inquired Ian, glancing back at us.

Everyone looked at me to explain. "Well," I began, "what we're going to do is get caught on purpose by the Soul Sucker's secret police guys so we can get to the Soul Sucker's lair without him suspecting that we're going to save Tom."

Ian nodded. "Hmm, very clever. And what exactly are you going to do once you get there?"

I was about to say, "That's as far as we've got," but Josie's loud scream interrupted me. "Watch out!" she cried.

Ian's attention was pulled back to the road where an enormous parrot, almost fifteen-feet tall, careened towards us. It tried to slow itself down, but it couldn't and ended up banging into our vehicle. The parrot went hurtling to the side and the hovercraft tipped upside down. Somehow Sage, Josie, and Ian stayed inside, but Zach and I were tossed into the air and landed on the ground in a heap of crunchy leaves. Thankfully, we weren't gravely hurt.

As I sat up slowly, I watched the hovercraft with my friends in it, sail up into the air, then I saw it start to come down again. I held my breath.

I was just waiting for it to smash down, but it didn't. Instead, it floated down in a composed glide. I peered inside to see that Ian had managed to gain command over the controls and that everyone was safe.

"Watch where you're going, you morons!" squawked a rude male voice. We all turned to see the giant parrot in a lump next to the empty road.

"Sir, are you all right?" asked Josie.

"I guess I'll live. But next time, try looking at the road!" he retorted.

"We're very sorry," apologized Josie, "Mr . . . ?"

"I'm Eket," said the parrot. "And you are?"

Once we had all introduced ourselves, he softened. "Is everyone all right?"

"Oh we're all fine, thank God," Ian assured him.

"Sorry I was so rude to you," he said. "I guess it was partly my fault. I think I may have had too many baked beans at breakfast."

"A bird? Eating baked beans?" I asked.

"Why of course!" Eket exclaimed. "But they make me awfully gassy, and then I get cranky, and then—"

"Whoa!" interrupted Zach. "Way too much information!"

Eket laughed. "Well, I'd better get going," he said. "I'm on my way to a concert. I guess you can come if you want . . ."

"Oh, no thank you." I said, quickly. "We're kind of in a rush."

"Okay, suit yourself. Bye then!" With a wave of his colorful feathers, Eket flew off into the sky.

Once Eket left, we all climbed back into the slightly beaten up hovercraft. Luckily it still worked okay. We arrived in the Plausible Quarter, where Zach and Sage lived, not too long after that.

"You can drop us off here," Zach told Ian. He obediently slowed to a stop, and we all hopped off.

"Thank you so much, Ian!" I called out to him. "You're the best. We know we can count on you!"

He just nodded and said, "Yes, yes, just hurry up and go save Tom." And then he zoomed off.

As I watched him go, something nagged at my brain, something that made me uneasy, but I couldn't pinpoint what it was. I asked myself why I felt like that, but nothing was coming to mind. Maybe it had to do with the way Ian had behaved. I mean, it's nice that he believed we could save Tom, but would a responsible adult really act like that? Well, I was just glad someone had confidence in us!

As we walked down the street of the Plausible Quarter, I couldn't help feeling very, very nervous. Most of our plan had been built on mere feelings and hunches, not really any concrete facts. What if those men weren't the Soul Sucker's henchmen? What if the Soul Sucker didn't even care about the souls' power? What if . . . ? Thankfully Zach interrupted my negative thoughts before they could go any further.

"Our best shot is to go back to that bar where we first saw the Soul Sucker's goons," said Zach.

And if they weren't there? Or if they weren't connected to the Soul Sucker at all? I kept my doubts to myself.

As quickly as we could, we made our way back to the smoke-filled bar, hoping those macho men would be there.

Once the tent came into view, Josie whispered, "If

they're there, and they catch us, we have to act surprised and struggle a bit, got it?"

"Yeah," said Sage. "Okay, let's go."

We strolled up to the tent, trying to act as natural and casual as possible. We hadn't even sat down yet when I felt a pair of strong, meaty hands on my shoulders. I jerked my head around and saw the four men from our previous visit.

Even though this was part of the plan, I felt a scream simmer inside me. The others were pretending to struggle and fight against the men, yelling, "Let me go!" I joined in. But even if we hadn't been faking it, we could have never have fought and won against these guys.

One man bent my arms behind my back, making my eyes water and preventing me from moving. I felt my backpack sliding down to my wrists. I tried to shift my arms to get my bag back up to my shoulders, but it was impossible. Then the man laughed cruelly, grabbed the knapsack, and tossed it on the ground.

I looked briefly over at the others to see if Josie's bag had been taken away, too. It hadn't.

They dragged us out of the bar and into a long black limo with ease. Despite myself, I gasped at the interior of the car, and I could see everyone else doing the same.

"Buckle up," said one of the men in his gravelly voice. "This limo's fast."

"Just how fast—?" Josie tried to ask, but the man at the wheel revved the engine. Two rockets darted out of the back of the car and we shot forward. Faster than anything I had ever ridden, including amusement park rides.

I clung to the sides of the car and concentrated on not throwing up. The only thing Josie could utter was a small, "Oh."

After a while, I got over my nausea and managed to take a peek out the window to see where we were going. Unfortunately the windows were tinted, and we were going so fast I couldn't make anything out very clearly. However, I could see that we had left the streets of Malsama a while back, and now we were just driving over flat plains of grass.

I had just gotten the courage to ask the driver if he could slow down, when there was a deafening THUMP.

The limo stopped so abruptly we all jerked forward, hard, against our seat belts. We definitely would have flown through the front window if we hadn't had them on.

The men filled the air with loud curses. One of them opened the door, climbed out, and was instantly snatched up by a giant claw.

The other men jumped out to see where their cohorts had gone, but the huge claw snatched them up as well!

"P-please don't hurt us!" I screamed at the claw. "We haven't done anything!"

"Now why would I do that?"

"Eket?" I asked, trying to see beyond the claw to the body it belonged to.

"The one and only," the giant parrot said proudly.

"But what are you doing here? Where are those men?" said Zach.

"Well, I was on my way to the concert, when I saw

those men putting you in the car, and I'm a loyal friend, so I decided to save you! Jeez that car went fast, but not fast enough! Ha! I threw those men somewhere over there." He jerked his massive beak towards the way we had come.

I tried to understand where we were, but we stood in the middle of nowhere. Malsama was obviously behind us, but I couldn't see it at all, and I knew there was a lake somewhere near here, but I couldn't see even a glimpse of it on the horizon. The only thing to be seen were little rolling hills covered in carpets of grass. It was beautiful, in an empty peaceful sort of way. Even though we hadn't driven for very long, we had obviously gone a long way. Probably had something to do with the rockets.

"Well? Aren't you going to thank me?" Eket asked, a twinge of disappointment in his voice.

"Oh yes, thank you!" said Josie. "But . . ." she looked at me, "should we tell him?"

"Eket? Can you keep a secret?" I asked him.

"Of course I can!" he said, looking offended. I thought about it for a second. We couldn't go around telling everyone we met about Earth and Eeba, but then again, Eket looked so innocent and childish even if he was fifteen feet tall. And plus, if he decided to help us, he could be really useful for fighting off other bad guys. So I gave him a quick summary of everything about Tom, the two worlds, and how we were actually just pretending that we had gotten captured by those men.

When Eket heard that he had just ruined our plan, he looked crestfallen. "I-I'm sorry," he said with a sniffle. "I thought I was rescuing you. If there's something I can do to help you, I'll do it."

"Hold on, Eket. Let me talk to my team," I told him.

Zach, Sage, Josie, and I had a group huddle. I made the proposal: "Why don't we make Eket part of the team? An awesome bird by our side could come in quite handy, don't you think?"

"Yeah," Sage agreed. "With his claws and wings we would be practically impossible to defeat!"

"Okay, so that's settled." Then turning back to the parrot, I said, "Eket? How would you like to help us?"

"Well, I guess it's the least I could do since I ruined your plan."

"So now you're part of the team. Great!"

"I'm part of the team? Cool! And could we have a secret handshake and code names? I could be Mr. Cotton Candy."

I looked around to everyone else, who had equally puzzled looks on their faces. Then I turned back to Eket. "Umm . . . okaaaay," I said. "But first can you do me a favor?"

Eket nodded vigorously.

"Could you fly me up? I have to see where we are, and where we should go."

Eket crouched down, and Josie helped me onto his back. "Does anyone else want to come? I think I have enough strength to hold one other person," he said.

I expected them all to start fighting about who would come with me and get to ride on the giant parrot's back, but instead they all quickly refused.

When Eket just stood normally, I was already pretty high up on his back. Then he started flying, and I freaked out—in a good way.

"Woooohoooooo!" I yelled. I was having the time of my life!

The wind slashed and stabbed at my face, making it almost impossible for me to open my eyes. I looked briefly over my shoulder. My friends already looked like tiny dots on the ground. The higher Eket went, the colder it got, so that little bits of frost formed on my eyelashes, and I could see my own misty breath in front of me.

"You can stop now," I told the parrot in a small gasp.

I looked around. The castle where Tom rested stood a great distance away but a part of it was still visible. Behind us, a long way off, the city of Malsama spread in different directions. The lake wasn't very far off. Then my eye caught on something else: that speck of smoke that I had seen from the balcony of the castle. It seemed so out of place—the colorful world with a smear of grey. As I looked at it, my skin tingled as it had done at the castle, and I had a hunch that the smoke had to do with the Soul Sucker.

"You can fly me down now," I told Eket.

He obediently did as I said. The return flight was a lot more scary than the ascent, and I clung to his red back feathers with all the strength I had.

When Eket finally touched down, I slid off his back and jumped to the ground. I wobbled for a second and then collapsed in a heap at my friends' feet. My legs had become shaky from the flight, and they had given way from under me. The sound of giggling got me to stand up fairly quickly.

"Right," I said, dusting myself off and ignoring the chuckling from the others. "From what I saw, Malsama is behind us, and there's a big lake right ahead."

"That would be Korral Lake," said Sage.

Zach looked at her in surprise.

"What?" she said, crossing her arms. "I, unlike somebody I know, studied geography."

"Anyway," I continued, "on the horizon there's what looks like smoke. I have a feeling that the smoke is where the Soul Sucker is."

"Another feeling?" Zach asked with a smirk.

I liked Zach, but even when a cute guy makes fun of me, I give him a piece of my mind. I shot him a dark look. "I would shut up if I were you, Mr. I'm-too-scared-to-fly-on-Eket's-back."

Zach responded by rolling his grey eyes. But in the end, I saw another small grin spark across his lips.

"As I was saying," I continued, "I think we should start towards this smoke, passing by Korral Lake."

"It would be a shame to leave the limo behind though," said Zach.

"Eket, can you hold all of us on your back?" asked Josie. "Eket?"

"Did someone say my name?" Eket wanted to know. While we had been talking, he had been absentminded-ly picking his beak.

Josie sighed in disgust and repeated her question.

Eket looked at her wide-eyed. "Are you crazy? I mean, I'm strong but not that strong!"

"Well, what if Eket flew ahead but not too fast? And we followed him in the limo?" Josie suggested. "That way Eket doesn't have to carry all of us, and Zach doesn't have to leave his beloved limo behind." She laughed and gave Zach a light punch on his arm. Then she quickly pulled her arm back when she realized she had just made a very boyish move. She turned around and hurried into the limo.

Zach and I exchanged a shocked expression, then we, too, made for the car. Zach picked up Josie's bag and reached for the door to the driver's seat—at the same time I did.

"Sorry, I'm driving," he said.

"I don't think so, buster. Step aside," I told him, teasingly.

"No way! I got here first."

"Whatever, dude. I'm driving, and that's final."

"No. I should drive—I'm the man here."

"And, why does that matter?"

"Guys!" yelled Josie. "Cut it out! Sage should drive. She's the oldest."

At the sound of her name, Sage looked up. "I don't care. Do whatever you want." That got us arguing all over again. We finally stopped when Eket boomed, "Isabel drives until the lake, then Zach drives, and that's final!"

Zach sulked while climbing into the back as I slid into the driver's seat. "I've always wanted to do this," I muttered to myself.

"Isabel, just be careful," warned Josie.

"It's okay," I said. "We're surrounded by grass with nothing to run into!" With that, I turned the keys in the ignition, put the car into gear, and hit the gas. I had watched my parents, and Tom himself, drive enough times to know the routine by heart. The car jolted forward. I didn't put on the rockets, because I didn't know how but also because I was actually a bit afraid. I mean, I was only thirteen. I wasn't technically ready to drive an actual car, let alone drive it with rockets!

Eket was already in the air and soaring towards Korral Lake while I followed him in the limo. At first the ride was jerky, but when I finally got the feel of it, the trip smoothed out.

"Oh yeah!" I shouted with glee. "Check it out, I'm thirteen and driving! Now that's what I'm talking about." I tapped my fingers on the steering wheel in a little rhythm.

After a few hours, though, I was getting really bored. It had been a while since I had even turned! And without having anything to steer around, I was practically just sitting there with my foot on the pedal. Then Eket's voice called down to us, "We're almost at Korral Lake!"

I stuck my head out the window and saw a thick line of blue coming up ahead. As we neared the lake, the sun's rays reflected off the water and into my eyes, making it hard for me to see where we were going Finally, I felt the wheels of the limo having to work harder to spin, and I realized we were driving on sand. I pushed down on the brake. "Here we are!"

I scrambled out of the limo and stretched my cramped body. Ahead of me Eket was curled up, his head under his giant wing.

"Come on guys!" I yelled, banging on the window. "We're here!"

The three others, who had fallen asleep during the long car ride, dragged themselves out of the car, groggily extending their stiff limbs and rubbing the sleep out of their eyes.

As soon as Josie saw the great expanse of clear blue water, she sprinted towards it, screaming, "Oh my God! Look how clean it is! It's beautiful!"

She kicked off her shoes, took off her sweater so she was in just jeans and shirt, rolled up her pants to her knees, and waded into the water. Zach joined her without a second thought, but I held back.

"We don't have time to play! We have to go!" I shouted.

Zach turned to face me, "Come on, Isabel. Just a tiny break. We have to eat lunch anyway, so why don't we have a picnic and have a little bit of fun for once?"

"I guess," I said but wondered what this delay could mean for Tom.

He laughed. "Then come on!" he grabbed my hand and pulled me to the lakeshore. I glanced back at Sage, who had her arms folded across her chest and her eyes downcast.

"Do you want to . . . ," I began to ask.

"No. You go ahead." With that, she trudged off and sat down in the shade of a tree.

Before I could ask what was the matter with her, Zach gave my arm another tug, and I forgot about Sage as I splashed into the cool water.

After a bit, Josie got out of the water and announced, "Time to eat! I'm starving. I'll go prepare some food."

"I'll help you," offered Zach, walking out of the lake as well. The two opened up the trunk of the car to get Josie's supply bag.

I frowned, but on the whole, I tried to ignore how much it bothered me that Josie and Zach were alone together.

Worried about Sage and without anything better to do, I walked over to the tree she was sitting under. As soon as I plopped myself down next to her, she looked up, and I was surprised to see tears in her eyes.

"Sage! Are you sick? What's wrong?" I asked while putting my hand on her arm.

"Isabel, I have to get something off my chest. But promise you won't tell Zach or Josie or anybody else."

"I promise," I said without hesitation. It struck me as strange how she had all of sudden blurted out that there was something on her mind, and why would she tell me? We hardly knew each other!

"You see, about Tom. I've seen him many times," Sage said softly.

"How?" I asked, turning to look her straight in the face.

"Do you know how he saw Eeba? He saw it through his dreams. And I saw him through my dreams."

"What?"

"I know, I hardly understand it myself, but somehow, through our dreams, we met and got to know one another. After a long time of seeing each other, well, I don't know . . . we fell—"

"You fell in love," I finished in a whisper of amazement.

She smiled. "Yes. I know sixteen may be a bit young, but it feels so real."

I sighed. "How romantic! Falling in love in a dream!"

She giggled. "I know." Then her expression became depressed again. "But now that might all end." Another tear trickled down her cheek.

"No, it won't," I said, hoping I sounded a lot more confident than I actually was. "We will save him."

"I needed to hear that," was all Sage said but she also squeezed my hand while saying it. Were we actually becoming friends?

Wanting to change the subject, I said, "I think Josie and Zach have just about finished getting lunch ready. Come on, I'm starving, and you must be, too."

CHAPTER 7

"WOW!" I EXCLAIMED. Josie and Zach had organized a fantastic picnic with little sandwiches, slices of melon, and chocolate muffins.

"How did you . . . ?" I asked in disbelief.

Zach grinned. "What did you think that giant bag was filled with?"

We all laughed.

"Hey!" squawked Eket. "I'm going to go find something more appetizing for myself. Will you guys be all right?"

"Of course!" said Josie. Eket spread his wings and with one mighty flap he became airborne.

After we had all devoured the picnic, Sage got up. "I think I might have a quick dip before Eket comes back."

She tugged off her boots and dove into the rippling

waters, clothes and all. Just as I reached for the last muffin, I heard a shriek coming from the spot where she had just jumped.

In a second we were all on our feet, running towards the shore of Korral Lake. "Sage!" we called out. When there was no response, Zach walked deeper into the lake, swirling the water between his fingers and shouting out to his sister.

Suddenly Zach, too, vanished!

Josie and I searched desperately, screaming their names. Then, unexpectedly, something covered up the sun, putting us in the shade. I looked up, expecting to see a cloud.

Oh boy, was I wrong.

Emerging from the water was a colossal jellyfish-like monster. It blocked out the sun's rays with the pinky-purple hat thing at the top of its body.

I barely had time for this fact to sink in, when a sharp, blinding pain shot up my leg, and I was dragged underwater. For several seconds, panic fogged up my brain, and I could only think of the throbbing in my leg and that I couldn't breathe.

I looked down and saw that the jellyfish had wrapped one of its tentacles tightly around my ankle. Still underwater, my lungs burned for air. Abruptly, I was pulled out of the water and realized the giant jellyfish had one of its tentacles curled around every one of my friends. They, too, were held out of the water, about ten feet above ground.

I heard everyone else screaming, but I didn't have the

strength. I used all of mine just to keep myself conscious. The pain in my leg kept getting stronger and stronger. I didn't know how we were going to get out of this one.

Zach yelled over and over, "Keep fighting it! Keep fighting it!"

I kicked and struggled more ferociously, and I saw the others doing the same.

Suddenly the jellyfish monster began moving the tentacle that held Josie, bringing her closer to him.

"He's going to eat her!" I shrieked, overcome by dread. "Oh my God. Oh my God!" I knew I was getting hysterical, but I couldn't help myself. This was way too much for me to take in. I fought even more, but the monster was too strong, and its sting had made me weak and tired. The others were losing energy as well.

"No! Leave Josie alone!" I tried to yell again, but it came out as a whisper.

I felt my consciousness slipping away from me. I was about to pass out when I felt a big gust of air. I looked up. "Eket?"

The giant bird didn't respond. Instead, he swiped his talons at the jellyfish, trying to make it lose its hold on us. But the jellyfish was too big, and he had the advantage of his many tentacles.

Eket realized he would never be able to take down the monster like this. As he looked around, his eyes rested on the limo. He flapped towards the car, lashed out, and grabbed it with both claws. The limo clutched in his talons, he flew back over to the jellyfish.

The parrot took a deep breath and flung the limo at the bell on top of the monster's body. The car slammed into it with a big squeeeelch noise, and the jellyfish sank down again into the water.

Its hold on my ankle loosened, and I felt myself falling down back into the water. I remember seeing Eket's beak in my face as he picked me up as delicately as he could and carried me safely to shore. Then black closed in around my eyes, and I passed out.

CHAPTER 8

"SHE'S ALIVE!"

I sat up shakily. "Of course I'm alive, Eket," I groaned. I looked over to see Zach and Sage already sitting up on the sand beside me.

"What about Josie?" I asked, looking around frantically for my best friend.

Eket replied, "She still hasn't woken up." I quickly scrambled to my feet, disregarding the aching in my leg. "How is that possible?" I demanded. "She was one of the last people to get caught by the monster. She should have been the first to wake up!"

I spotted Josie, motionless on the sand, and ran over to her. I looked closer to make sure she was breathing.

Thank God she was.

I stared at Josie's leg where I could see that all the skin around her ankle had gone a blue-black color. I presumed this was where the beast had gotten its hold on her.

I checked my own leg to see if I had the same thing, but I found only a small ring of bruises and a bit of swelling.

"I don't know," said Zach, shaking his head. "It looks like he may have stung her more than he did the rest of us."

"Josie!" I yelled. "Josie, wake up!" I turned to the others. "What should we do?" They shrugged.

I grabbed her shoulders and gave her a good shake. A gasp escaped her mouth, and she coughed up lake water.

"Oh, thank God!" I exclaimed, hugging her savagely. She whimpered as I embraced her. "Oh, sorry," I said, letting her go.

"W-water," she murmured.

Sage seized a water canteen and held it gently to Josie's lips.

After she had drunk, she managed to sit up and talk more clearly. "What happened?"

I responded, "Eket came and crushed the monster with the limo."

The giant parrot puffed out his chest proudly. "That's what I did."

"The limo?" Zach exclaimed. "I loved that car, and now I won't even be able to drive it!"

Sage rolled her eyes. "No, but you're alive. And at least all the supplies weren't inside when Eket threw it!"

"I remember being stung by a monster. It was horrible!" Josie sniveled. Then she glanced at her leg and winced. It seemed like she was about to start crying but instead she just poured some water from the canteen over the discolored skin.

"It's all my fault," said Sage, hanging her head. "I studied Korral Lake in geography last year. I should have warned you about the Galdur."

"The what?" I asked.

"The Galdur is that jellyfish monster. It lives right in the center of the lake, and when it senses that another creature is in the water with it, the Galdur goes and attacks it for food."

In my head I thought that yes, that was probably information we would have found useful, but I didn't want to make Sage feel any worse than she did. "Well," I said, "I'm just glad Eket came in time."

"Mr. Cotton Candy," Eket corrected.

"Of course," I said with a quick smile.

"But how are we going to get to the Soul Sucker now that the limo's gone?" asked Zach.

Sage answered, "If I remember correctly, Korral is surrounded by lake tribes. There should be one not too far off. We should try to find them and see if they will help us."

"Great!" I said. "Will we be able to walk there?"

"I guess so," she replied. She checked the time on her watch and then looked up and studied where the sun sat in the sky. "We have to go east, which is that way," she finished, pointing in the direction we had to go in.

"Perfect. Now, Eket, why don't you carry Josie since I

don't think she's strong enough to walk just yet, and Zach, since you're the man you should carry the big backpack."

"What?" he spluttered. "I'm not—"

I grinned. "Good grief, just do it!"

Once we got ourselves organized, Eket hovered up in the air with Josie resting gently in his claws. Sage and I followed closely behind him on the ground, and Zach trailed after us, grumbling about destroyed limos and annoying girls making him carry heavy bags.

After a while, I whispered to Sage, "I don't know what we would have done without you. I'm so glad you came with us."

She grinned and said, almost embarrassed, "You probably won't believe me, but I'm not all about fashion and makeup. I mean, I do like those things, but I also like learning and knowing stuff and being outside. Some people just take one look at me and instantly put me in the 'stupid pretty girl' group. I hate when people judge me."

I nodded sympathetically. It felt kind of weird to be making an older girl feel better, but I understood what she meant. "You mean like Zach judges you?" I asked.

"Yeah." She paused and took a quick glance behind her. "And by the why, he likes you."

"What? That's crazy," I protested, attempting to sound annoyed, which was difficult with that ridiculous fluttering in my heart.

"Maybe, but it's true."

I was about to tell her she was crazy when Eket called

down, "Hey! I think I see a village or something in the distance!"

"That must be the lake tribe!" I shouted back. "Leave Josie with us and fly on ahead! Ask them if they can help us!"

"Got it, Agent Banana Split!" he squawked back.

"What did you just call me?"

"Agent Banana Split. That's what I decided your code name should be! Don't you like it?"

"We don't need . . . ," I began to object but then decided to just let it be. "Yeah whatever. Just go!"

He flew down to the ground and placed Josie delicately in front of us. Then with a great flap of his colorful wings, he took off in the direction of the little lake village.

"So we'll just wait here until he comes back?" Zach asked, doubt in his voice.

"I guess," I replied. But as soon as I had said that I was doubtful, too. Maybe it wasn't such a good idea sending Eket over there by himself.

"But what if he doesn't come back?" insisted Zach.

Josie's eyes fluttered and she said weakly, "Yeah. What if they're evil and kill him before he even gets to open his beak?"

"Now guys, let's be optimistic," I said.

"But what if that happens?" said Josie.

"Well . . . " I looked to Sage. "Don't you know what this tribe is like?"

She raised her hands defensively. "My textbook just

THE TWO WORLDS OF ISABEL

said there were tribes around Korral Lake. It didn't go into details."

"Well, I still think we should just wait. There is a possibility that the tribe is a nice one, and if it isn't, I doubt we would have a chance if Eket didn't . . ." I trailed off, hoping with all my heart that Josie was wrong.

After about fifteen minutes of anxious waiting, we heard a familiar sound of beating wings. "Eket!" we cried. "You're alive!"

He landed next to us.

"What are you wearing?" Zach asked.

"Oh, this," Eket said, waving at the flower necklace that was now hanging around his neck. "Things were really weird. It seems this tribe, the Erinav tribe, worships birds. So they see me as some kind of . . . divine being." His cheeks reddened. "It's rather embarrassing, really."

"But at least they didn't kill you on sight!" I said.

"Well? What are you waiting for?" Sage demanded. "Take us to this Erinav tribe!"

"Oh, right! Come on, then!"

He reached to pick up Josie but she said, "No thanks, Eket. I feel strong enough to walk."

So Eket walked ahead in front of us, and we followed behind.

I glanced behind me to see Zach struggling with the bag. I felt kind of bad about dumping it on him so I walked up to him and offered, "You want me to take that for a while?"

"No, it's all right," he replied, to my surprise. I expected him to park it on me in a second, but he didn't.

"Um, okay," I said awkwardly, not knowing what else to say.

I then marched up to Josie. "Are you sure you're okay?"

She grinned. "Who do you think I am? Colin?" We chuckled. It felt so good to laugh, to get some of the heaviness out of the situation in that simple action.

As soon as I saw a small group of houses up ahead, there was a loud trumpet noise and then came an amplified voice. "Oh, Great Eket return with friends!" it blared.

I turned to see Eket blushing and fidgeting in his flowery necklace.

"Erinav tribe welcomes friends of Eket!" came the voice again.

We were about twenty feet from the nearest hut when all of a sudden, a throng of people came rushing out of the houses, all of them carrying flowers, or food, or different kinds of shells.

They swarmed around Eket, giving him their offerings, saying things like, "Take flower, make I happy."

As the giant parrot tried desperately to move through the crowd without hurting anyone, the mob of people suddenly parted to make a large space in the center. Then someone of obvious importance started walking down a kind of catwalk. He wore necklaces of shell and coral and a small crown of feathers.

He came to a stop in front of Eket, knelt, and declared, "Great Eket dine with I! And friends of Eket, come!"

He made his way back down the walkway, with us

following him. The other people on the sides of the pathway bowed their heads as we passed.

We made our way through the village until we came to a small cluster of bigger huts. There were three. We entered the middle one.

"Who lives in those houses?" I asked, pointing at the other two buildings.

"Me explain inside." The man took a step towards the door then said sadly, "Sorry, but Eket not fit!"

"Oh, that's okay," said Eket. "I'll just sit outside and stick my head through the window."

"Eket very wise," the man praised.

"Oh, it was nothing," Eket said, again blushing.

We entered the house. The air had an exotic smell of cinnamon, sandalwood, and incense. There was a low table of dark wood in the center of the main room, surrounded by tasseled cushions of all different colors.

"Please, sit," the man said, gesturing to the pillows. Then: "My name Taiko. Me King of village."

"Oh, Your Highness!" exclaimed Josie.

Taiko smiled. "Yes. In other huts live Queen and Shaman."

Zach looked confused. "But wouldn't the Queen be your wife and live in the same house as you?"

Now it was Taiko's turn to look confused. "No, no," he said shaking his head. "In Erinav tribe, Queen and King no husband and wife." Then he continued, "After eat, we go see Queen Prizma and Shaman Oring."

We all nodded and looked at each other without saying anything for a few seconds.

"So," said Zach, breaking the silence, "what's for dinner?" He was answered with a sharp poke between the ribs from Sage. "What? I'm starving!" he said in his defense.

King Taiko just chuckled. "Yes! Me get dinner right away!" He clapped his hands and a plump woman rushed in with a tray full of steaming food. As soon as she had laid it on the table, a young man came out of the back with another tray balancing in the palm of his hand, this one holding different beverages. Then a third person went outside with a gleaming silver platter to serve Eket.

The man and woman served us and then bustled back to what must have been the kitchen.

Zach instantly dug into his meal and the rest of us quickly followed. The food was rich and spicy, unlike anything I had ever tasted. At one point, Taiko tried to explain what it was, but all the names of the vegetables and spices meant nothing to Josie or me. Zach and Sage knew some but most were unfamiliar to them, too.

As I was taking a pause from huge bites and sipping some sort of sweet, creamy drink, I heard a loud snapping noise, over and over. It took me a moment to figure out it was Eket, opening and closing his beak, rapidly, as he, too, gobbled up his dinner.

Finally, when we had all eaten our fill and were watching the flames in the fireplace crackle and spark, King Taiko abruptly jumped up. "Now you see Queen and Shaman and explain what you do here." I was relieved since we really had no idea what was happening with Tom and I wanted to get to him as quickly as possible—but I also didn't want to be rude and push the King to get moving.

He took my hand and led us out the door into the twilight. He promptly knocked on the second hut's door. It creaked open and a round, but beautiful face stuck out of it.

"Queen Prizma! Is King Taiko!" announced the King.

"Oh!" said the woman who had opened the door. "Enter! Enter!"

We did as we were told, and Eket copied the arrangement that he had in King Taiko's home.

As soon as Eket's head peeked in from the window, Queen Prizma practically threw herself at him. "Please, Great Eket, must take mine best perfume!"

"Um, actually I don't really use perfume," objected Eket.

"Please! Make I happy!" persisted the Queen.

"Argh, fine!" huffed Eket, clearly not pleased with what he had just said. Queen Prizma ceremoniously took out a small glass bottle from the inside of her blue robes and sprinkled a bit of the mixture onto Eket's feathers. A strong fragrance of pineapple, passion fruit, and a starry night sky enveloped all of us. (How you get the smell of the night in a bottle, I have no idea, but that's what it smelled like).

After she had done this, Queen Prizma said, "I go call Shaman Oring, he also want hear what you say."

She stood up, elegantly rustled her peacock blue garment, and walked out of the house.

I turned back to King Taiko to see him scowling. "What's the matter?" I asked.

"Oh, just that Queen Prizma so fancy, and me no. No proper for King wear pretty thing, but girls yes."

While Queen Prizma wore regal colors and long, flowing dresses, King Taiko only had stiff brown robes tied at the waist with a bright blue cord.

"Aw, it's okay," I said and patted his back. "I think you should wear whatever you want. Who cares what people think! You should dress to make yourself happy, shouldn't you?"

Taiko's eyes widened as if that thought had never occurred to him. "You is right Isabel! Me is King and do what me want!"

I smiled, "Exactly. You have the power to remake the rules, so do it!"

Just then, Queen Prizma entered, accompanied by another man. He was younger than King Taiko, but his skin was darker and more weathered-looking. He wore the same brown robes as the King, but he also had a large blue turban that kept on sliding off his head.

"Greetings to Mighty Eket and friends!" he said, shifting the turban back in place. "Us very honored!"

"Yeah, we've noticed," mumbled Zach, causing Sage to elbow him in the stomach again.

"What did you want to ask us?" I said quickly before Zach and Sage started arguing.

"What you do here?" Shaman Oring asked. "No one come in many time."

"Why not?" Josie asked. "I would think lots of people would visit around here. It's so beautiful."

King Taiko shook his head. "No much people leave Malsama."

"Yes," Queen Prizma agreed. "This part of Eeba very flat—not much mountains, only few hills. People want make Malsama everywhere. Already we fight them to leave our land alone."

"Oh, I understand," I said. "They wanted to destroy the territory by expanding Malsama."

"Yes," King Taiko confirmed.

I tilted my head so I could whisper into Josie's ear, "Sounds a lot like Earth, doesn't it? Urbanizing everywhere?"

"Uh huh," she agreed. "How come the two worlds have to be similar in bad things?"

I clicked my tongue with displeasure.

"But why does that make you surprised we're here?" Zach asked.

Queen Prizma shrugged. "Don't know. Just few person visit."

"That's a shame," Josie sympathized, but broke off when a big yawn erupted from her mouth. She tried her best to stifle it, but she didn't do a very good job. "Oh my goodness, excuse me," she said.

But the yawn was contagious, and soon everybody's mouth was open wide with weariness.

"I'm pretty tired," murmured Sage, announcing what we all felt.

"Where is mine manners!" exclaimed the King. "You must rest! Come, me give two huts for the night."

"We're very grateful," I said followed by a small yawn.

King Taiko waved the thanks away. "No. Pleasure is my."

Shaman Oring stood up. "Was honor talking with you. Hope can talk again tomorrow morning."

"Of course," said Josie. "But now we just need to sleep. It's been a long day."

CHAPTER 9

THEY GAVE US one hut for Josie and me and another one for Zach and Sage. I don't know where exactly Eket slept, but I knew he would be well taken care of. They also took Josie's backpack and promised to have it refilled with food supplies for the next morning.

Even as they did this, my eyelids drooped. I entered the hut and as soon as I found my bed, I collapsed on it. Then I heard Josie come in and climb into the bed on the other side of the room. We said good night to each other, but however tired I was and however much the warm duvet invited me into dreamland, I couldn't go to sleep.

The feeling was like homesickness. When you're busy the whole day, playing or doing whatever it is you do, you don't have time to miss home. But when you actually have the time to sit down and think about it, you feel homesick.

The second I had time to think, all of my old worries about Tom came flooding back. What if I had been wrong all along? What if my time had already run out? What if, what if, what if . . . ?

I lay in bed, tossing and turning, falling into a half-sleep then waking up again two minutes later. Finally I decided to go outside for some air.

I crept by Josie, who was sleeping soundly in her comfortable cot, and slipped out into the cool night. Stars winked above my head. Instead of walking deeper into the village, I walked out toward the lake, even though it scared me a little bit.

I gasped at the breathtaking view of the moonlight bouncing off the water and shivered in the night breeze. Out of the corner of my eye, I noticed a silhouette of a person, sitting in the sand not so far away. Not knowing who it was, and not wanting to startle him or her, I tip-toed up behind the shadow.

"Who is it?" said a voice, out of the blue, making me jump.

"It's just me. Isabel!"

"Oh. Isabel."

I crept closer to the outline of the person and realized it was Zach.

"What are you doing here?" I asked as I sat down next to him.

"I could ask you the same thing."

We sat there on the sand in silence, gazing at the lake's gentle lapping waves. After a while I said, "You know, Sage isn't all you think she is."

"What do you mean?"

"I mean that she's not stupid."

Zach only grunted.

"I'm serious! You saw how she knew about the tribe and the lake, and how she had the idea about the limo."

"Yeah," he said with a sigh. "I still miss that limo. I can't believe I didn't get to drive that thing!" He grinned.

"You aren't even old enough!" I laughed.

"That didn't stop you!" he shot back. After a few seconds, he broke the silence. "But seriously, why did you come out here?"

I hesitated, wondering whether I should tell him the truth. Finally I decided just to be honest. "I'm just scared, that's all."

There I had said it. Now I braced myself for him to start teasing me.

"That's okay," he said. "We all are." He paused. "Even me."

I looked at him, surprised he had been so sincere.

"But just a tiny bit," he added quickly.

I allowed myself a small chuckle before I became serious again. "I mean, we don't even really have a plan. We're just making it up as we go along. I keep on thinking I'm going to have this big breakthrough idea, but . . ."

"Don't worry, Isabel. We'll think of something."

"Still . . . ," I said and returned my gaze to the sparkling lake.

Suddenly I felt a sharp burning on my arm, as if

someone had just slapped me. "Ow!" I looked around to see who had just hurt me, but it was too dark to see anything clearly.

Then I felt another intense pain across my face. I glanced at Zach and seeing his face twisted with discomfort as well, I knew he had also felt the burning.

But what was it?

If only I had a flashlight or something. Wait, I did still have my Swiss Army knife in my pocket, and it had a small LED light on it.

I took it out, switched it on, and waved it around in front of us.

A weird kind of ball floated in front of us. At least, it looked like a hovering ball at first, but once I inspected it with more attention, I saw that it was actually hundreds of tiny creatures, their bodies forming a sphere.

One of them by itself was about as tall as the length of my hand. Their limbs were long and skinny, and no hair grew on their big, bulbous heads. Their green skin matched their huge green eyes, which made them really good at doing "puppy dog eyes."

"Aw," I said, "they're actually kind of cute! In a really weird way."

That was before I got another burning slap across the other cheek.

"Okay, maybe not so cute." I said, rubbing my face.

I then noticed that each one of them had a little whip they were using to slap us.

"Why are you angry with us?" demanded Zach. "What did we do?"

"Stay away from tree!" came their squeaky voices, speaking in unison.

"We're nowhere near a tree!" I said.

"Stay away from tree!" shrieked the voices again, along with another crack of a whip across my arm.

"Okay, that's enough!" I shouted. "We didn't go near any stupid tree, so quit whipping us!"

This time I felt three stings on my body. "That's it! I'm sick of you!" Before I could give it a second thought, I thrust my hand into the middle of the hovering ball of creatures. Then I waved it back and forth, destroying the compact sphere and sending the little creatures flying in all different directions.

Little squeals escaped their mouths as they dispersed. In a second, they had all disappeared into the night. I guess without the safeness of their fellow creatures, they didn't stand a chance.

"Quick thinking," Zach said as he rubbed one of the whip marks on his arm.

Usually when people praise me, I make a whole show about: I bow and blow kisses as if I had just won the greatest talent show in the world. I'm not boastful, but I'm not modest either, and I guess my little routine could make me look rather full of myself, but I couldn't help it.

However this time—and I don't know why— I just smiled. "Thanks, but I should probably get going."

I turned to leave when Zach said, "Wait!"

"What?"

He took a step closer to me, closed his eyes, and

kissed me on the cheek. My brain seemed to turn to mush, and I could only stand there, paralyzed. After what felt like a lifetime, he stepped away. I was so confused, I didn't know if I should smile or slug him in the stomach. I mean, we hardly knew each other; you can't go around kissing everyone you meet!

Then he gave me one last grin and rushed off into the night.

CHAPTER 10

JOSIE ROUGHLY SHOOK my shoulder, trying to wake me. "Isabel, we have to hurry, it's already eleven!"

When I heard that, I instantly sat up and got a head rush from doing it too quickly. I groaned and held my hand to my spinning head. "Eleven in the morning?"

Josie raised an eyebrow. "No, eleven at night," she said sarcastically.

"Sorry, I just feel like I've barely slept at all." I got up, slipped my shoes on, and followed Josie out of our hut to meet with the others.

The King and the Shaman crowded around Eket, wishing him safe travels. I overheard Sage speaking with Queen Prizma. She explained that we needed some sort of vehicle to use, but the Queen clearly did not understand. In the end, Sage gave up, deciding that, even though it would take forever, we had no choice but to walk.

I went up to Shaman Oring and asked him, "Have you ever seen smoke in the distance?"

He nodded.

"Which direction is it in?"

The Shaman shuddered. "No go. Is evil smoke." This sentence only confirmed my suspicions that the smoke was somehow connected to the Soul Sucker.

"But we have to go there," I said.

He shook his head and mumbled something under his breath, but he finally said, "That way," and pointed outward from the lake.

Josie and I thanked him and gathered up the others. We were about to leave when Shaman Oring jerked his head up, suddenly, as if he had just remembered something very important. "No go yet!" he cried. "Must read future!"

I immediately began to protest, "We really don't have time . . ."

Shaman Oring looked offended. "But is part of Good-Bye Ceremony!"

I glanced at my friends, who just shrugged their shoulders. Finally I gave an exasperated sigh. "I guess we could spare a few minutes."

The Shaman clapped his hands in delight. "Come."

We walked with him through the village and stopped in front of his house.

"Enter one at a time," he instructed us and went into his home, leaving us outside by ourselves.

We looked around at each other for a few seconds before Sage moved toward the door. As she walked into

Shaman Oring's house, she called over her shoulder, "I'll go first since I'm the oldest."

After a few minutes she emerged, her face pale. I opened my mouth to ask her what had happened, but she shook her head before I could say anything.

Zach went next, and when he came out again, he looked just as shaken up as his sister.

I was dying to know what the Shaman had told them. What did he say that had unnerved them this much?

Josie and I were the remaining ones. I had absolutely no desire to see my future, but I knew I had to be strong. After all, I had practically assumed the leader role of our team. I made for the door, but Josie stopped me. "I'll go," she said and entered the hut.

A few minutes later she came out, and it was finally my turn. I slowly opened the door and stepped in.

The inside smelled of tea leaves, and the only light came from a few candles.

Shaman Oring sat on a blood red pillow with his eyes closed. Without opening them, he motioned to the pale blue cushion that faced him. I nervously sat down.

"Hand," he ordered. I obediently held out my hand, palm facing up. He gently took hold of it and then drew out a small bejeweled needle and pricked my finger. A drop of blood oozed out and trickled down my skin. At the sight of the blood, my stomach churned. It was just a drop, but I always felt squeamish whenever I saw even a nosebleed.

The Shaman expertly caught the droplet in a tiny vial

of pinkish glass. He held the vial over one of the candles and murmured something in a strange language under his breath. Then he slowly tipped the blood onto a scrap of paper and gazed at it. I craned my neck to have a look at what he saw on the parchment, and when I did, I barely believed it. The blood formed symbols and unfamiliar letters on the paper as if it was red ink. I tried to understand what it wrote, but I couldn't make sense of it. I watched him in silence, the only sound being the tinkling of shells on his many magical necklaces and bracelets.

After scrutinizing the piece of stained parchment for a long moment he cleared his throat, then spoke in a voice that wasn't his own; it seemed like somebody else spoke through his body. "Worry is a misuse of the imagination, and it will get you nowhere. It will only weaken and corrupt your being. The strength is already inside you. Now you must take it out. Use it. Work with it. And beware: you are too responsible for the lives of others. On this journey there will be sacrifices. You must learn to live with them."

My heart beat hard and my breath came and went in short, quick gasps.

When Shaman Oring finished speaking, he took up the scrap of paper and held it over the candle. Smoke rose up from it, and when it had climbed high enough in the air, it took a form.

My eyes filled with tears as I stared into the smoky faces of my parents and brother. "Isabel, we love you!" they called out to me.

"I love you too!" I cried out.

"You will come back to us, won't you?" they called out in unison.

"I will. I will." I tasted the salt in my tears.

I tried to reach and grasp them, but the smoke dissolved into the air as soon as I touched it. The fragility of their forms made even more sadness fill my heart. Once the last wisp had faded away, I whispered, "I'll try."

I took a deep breath, stood up to leave, and wiped my eyes. "Good-bye, Shaman Oring."

Only when I reached the door did he respond, once again in his normal voice. "Farewell, Isabel," he said. "Safe travels."

*

Unfortunately the Erinav tribe didn't know what cars were, so we had to walk, which was a big setback. Eket carried our bags at least, so we didn't have to, and we started our journey.

At the beginning we walked in silence. I presumed each one of us was thinking about what Shaman Oring had said. I guiltily agreed with him about me being too responsible, but I didn't understand what he meant about having some sort of strength inside of me.

I wondered what the others had been told, especially Sage since it looked like the Shaman's words had affected her the most. But I knew it couldn't be shared with us—much too personal.

As we walked, my mind traveled back in time, going

over everything that had happened. I felt bad for how much my parents must be worried and how much the others' parents must be worried, too. Actually, I didn't know anything about Zach and Sage's parents. I had only met their grandmother and cousin. What was her name again? Maya. I wondered where their parents could be, and why they never talked about them.

Then I thought about the pixies, and how scared I had been, and how easily Zach had been put under their spell. The Soul Sucker was hundreds of times more powerful than the pixies. We were so vulnerable!

Thank goodness we had Eket, otherwise we would already be dead. I looked back at our pixie escape and thought how lucky we were that we had coincidentally bumped into Ian. Now that I thought about it, why had Ian been there, in the Pixie District, in the first place? Maybe he had been looking for us? But that didn't seem right. He had said he wasn't worried about us.

Before I could contemplate it any more, an earsplitting shriek pierced the air. I doubled over. The sound penetrated my very soul and woke all of my fears, old and new. I wanted to see if my friends were all right, but I couldn't. Pain wracked my mind, and I found myself sobbing involuntarily.

When the echo of that inhuman screech died down, I found I could straighten up.

"What w-was that?" asked Josie, in a trembling voice.

"That was a Psycho," said Zach, his voice shaking as well.

"A what?"

"Well, Psycho isn't its real name, but we call them Psychos because their scream can make people lose their minds. Make them go crazy," explained Zach. "But you have to hear it many times. You won't go crazy if you hear it only once . . ." He trailed off, but I heard him mutter, "I thought they were too dangerous to be let loose like this, though. That's why they were all closed in reserves. Unless there's a sanctuary near here?" He looked at Sage for her opinion, but she just shrugged.

"Where did the scream come from?" I asked.

"I don't know, but there must be a nest near by."

That didn't sound like such a good thing.

"So, um, what does a Psycho look like?" Josie asked.

"Like . . . like that!" Sage screamed.

Another blood-curdling shriek sliced through the air right behind me. Before I knew it, I felt strong jaws clamping around the back of my shirt, and something carried me away from my friends.

"Help!" I yelled, but everyone was still suffering from the effects of the Psycho's cry so no one heard me.

I opened my eyes to see ground rushing underneath me, making me scream again. The bottoms of my jeans were being shredded as my legs dragged on the rocky earth, forcing me to pull in my knees. I tried desperately to crane my neck around to see the Psycho that carried me, but I couldn't. I could only hear my shirt and hoodie tearing where the monster's teeth were holding me. And I could feel jarring shocks rattle through my body every time the Psycho's feet touched the ground.

It felt like an eternity had gone by when the Psycho finally stopped running.

He plopped me to the ground, but I was surprised when I landed on something soft. I lay in a bed of what looked like . . . cotton balls. This must be the Psycho's nest, I thought.

I rolled over to get a good look at this Psycho creature. But when I saw him, I wished I hadn't.

He was the same shape as a lion, only covered in shaggy, pale orange fur. Razor sharp teeth protruded out of his drooling mouth. His eyes were like dark pools of tar, swirling above two slits for a nose. The end of his furry tail was a huge, fluffy cotton ball.

I stared at that puff, confused. It really didn't match the rest of his body. All of a sudden, the Psycho jerked its head back, bit off the cotton ball from the end of its tail, and gently set it down on the other balls of fluff. Then he let out one final howl that made me almost lose consciousness and snuggled down in his nest of self-made cotton.

Before I knew it, the beast was letting out strange snoring noises, telling me he had fallen asleep. I thanked my luck, but I knew it wouldn't last. Probably when the Psycho woke up from his afternoon nap, he would have me as a tasty little snack.

I looked at my options: I could wait for my friends to find me or I could get out of this mess myself. I figured I should probably stay put until the others came, but they might never find me, and even if they did, it might be too late. So, moving to Option B, I decided to list what I knew about Psychos, which was not very much at all. They are supposed to be kept in reserves, although this one obviously wasn't. They create their nests from pieces of fluff that grows from their tails, and their screams make you insane.

Helpful.

The mountain of cotton that was its nest reached really high up off the ground, piled probably nine or ten feet high with white fuzz. I wondered why I wasn't sinking into the mound. Along the outside I could see that a transparent net held the whole thing together, which I imagined was what kept the Psycho and me from falling into the depths of the fluffy nest.

I turned my thoughts to escape. I could just start running while he slept, but I doubted I would get very far before he woke up, tracked me down, and ate me anyway. Then an idea formulated in my mind, and I swiftly tried to execute it before the Psycho woke up.

I pulled out my pocketknife and began sawing away at the net, making a hole big enough for me to wriggle through. It took me quite a while to do so, since the netting turned out to be stronger than it looked.

I was just finishing up when the Psycho started to toss in his sleep. I shoved the knife back into my pocket just as the beast opened his black eyes. He lazily stretched his cramped legs, and then began slinking across the net towards me. His snapping teeth glinted in the sunlight.

My heart caught in my throat, then he pounced.

I had been expecting it, so I was able to get out of the

way just in time. I launched myself sideways to where I had cut the hole. The Psycho cocked his head in confusion but quickly gained his bearings and leapt again. But he came too late. I had already begun to squirm my way through the hole.

I congratulated myself, but I had acted too quickly.

I made it halfway through the gash in the net but then got stuck. I hadn't had enough time to make the hole the right size! I thrashed and flailed, but I couldn't get past my hips. I felt the Psycho breathing on my legs from the other side of the hole. I kicked out and made perfect contact with something hard.

I hoped it was his face.

The Psycho quickly recovered from the strike I had given him and let out his ear-piercing screech. Even with my head stuffed inside a heap of cotton balls, the sound still got to me. My stomach lurched, and I felt like I was about to throw up.

Before the Psycho could scream again, I seized some of the cotton balls surrounding me, and thrust them in my ears, hoping that would block most of the sound.

Suddenly an intense agony shot up my leg. The Psycho's teeth tore into my flesh. A cry of anguish escaped from my mouth and tears sprung to my eyes. I wasn't used to this sort of torture, and I almost fainted from the pain.

Biting my lip, I struggled on. My hope that my plan would work was slipping away, but I kept wiggling my hips and pushing with my hands to get free. Finally, through gritted teeth, I managed to slide through the hole. I was shocked that I didn't sink to the floor, instead I "swam" in the snowy fluff quite easily. I could barely see a thing, however.

Sensing that the Psycho had followed me into the core of his nest, I tried to get back to the tear in the net as fast as possible.

Thankfully, I found it in a second, and this time, I managed to get back through the hole with ease. Climbing out was rather difficult, though, considering the raging pain in my leg. The Psycho was still in the depths of the nest, trying to find me. If he was shrieking, I couldn't hear it.

I seized the bits of ripped netting and pulled them together quickly, hoping to close up the hole and trap the Psycho inside his own nest. But I hadn't thought this part of the plan through. There was no way to close the hole.

The whole nest was shaking as the Psycho thrashed about inside of it. I felt around to see if there was anything, anything at all that I could tie the hole up with. My hand came to rest on my belt. In a flash, I had taken it off and woven it in the meshwork of the net, closing up the hole.

However great my handiwork was, though, I knew it wouldn't last forever. I slid down the side of the nest and staggered away from the Psycho, my leg throbbing. I didn't dare look down at it for fear of throwing up. The more blood I felt dripping down to my ankle, the weaker I became. But I continued to stumble on, yelling with all the strength I could muster, "Josie! Zach! Sage! Eket! I'm here!"

But only the wind could hear my frail voice.

When I could go no farther, I fell to my knees, all the time shouting for my friends.

The bleeding had stopped, and I finally got the courage to glance down at my leg. Seeing it swollen with dried blood caked to the wound, I cursed the Psycho under my breath. I was sliding into unconsciousness when I heard footsteps coming up behind me.

I whirled around, but my vision blurred and everything went fuzzy. The last thing I heard was, "It's all right. You're safe with me."

CHAPTER 11

"AAAAAH!" I howled in pain.

I sat up, my head spinning. Seeing that I found myself in a hut, I thought I was back in the Erinav village, but then all the memories of the Psycho came flooding back to me.

I looked around and saw a tall figure standing beside the fireplace. My fingers curled around my pocketknife and I said, "Who are you? And where am I?"

The figure turned around, and I saw that he was a well-built, middle-aged man with a stubbly beard.

"Oh, you've woken up. Drink this," he said and handed me a little clay cup brimming with a steaming liquid.

"How do I know I can trust you?" I asked.

"Well, I am healing your leg. When I saw you running around in the middle of the prairie and bleeding badly, the only think I could do was help you," he said. "Now drink this."

I warily took the cup and downed its contents. Instantly, I felt the effects. My whole body warmed and relaxed, and the pain in my leg eased.

"I'm Isabel," I said and handed him the empty cup.

"Luke, Luke Curador," he said as he took the cup from me with one hand and reached out the other to shake.

I stared at his hand for a couple seconds before accepting it. "Okay, Luke," I said as I offered as firm a handshake as I could manage. "So why are you helping me?"

He smiled. "I'm a healer. It's my job. And I also have what's called moral obligations."

"Well tell me," I said, wincing as I tried to bend my injured leg, "how does it look?"

"Well that medicine you just drank should help it a lot, especially with the pain, and I've bandaged it, so I'm pretty sure you will be able to walk in a few days."

I let out a stifled yelp. "A few days? I can't stay here that long! I have to get back to my team!"

"Well, you've already been here two days—"

"Two days? I have to go!" I jumped to my feet, and the next thing my face was squashed against the rug.

Luke helped me up and sat me back down on the bed. "You must rest, Isabel. What were you doing out there anyway? Why are you so far away from Malsama?"

I snorted. "I'm not even from Malsama. Or Eeba for that matter." The moment I said it, I wished I had kept my mouth shut. I am such a blabbermouth!

"Oh?" Luke said, very interested.

I hung my head. "Never mind."

"No, please tell me." In his voice, I heard the same honesty and fascination that Zach had in his the first time I met him at Grandma Martha's house—the qualities that had urged me to tell him the truth.

It was that, along with the fact that I had way too much on my shoulders to bear any longer, that made me break and tell him everything. I wanted to summarize it, but there was something about him that made me pour my whole heart out. He was such a good listener, I even almost told him some bits about Zach and I, but I caught myself at the last moment.

At the end of my ramblings, he didn't look as shocked as I thought he would.

"The smoke—the Soul Sucker's palace—isn't far from here."

"Really?" I asked, excitedly. "I knew it! I knew the two were connected! Oh, if only I knew where the others were!"

"Please, do me a favor, Isabel. Don't go anywhere near that wretched place. I know what goes on in there, and believe me, you don't want to know." His voice had dropped to a sinister whisper.

"Do you have any idea what I have been through?" I demanded, angrily. "I didn't come all this way to hear you discourage me! Now if you know anything that might be useful to me as I take on this Soul Sucker person, I would be very grateful." My voice softened at the end.

Luke stood up and walked to the fire. "It's getting late. I'll make some soup while you get some more rest."

"You do know something, don't you?" I asked in an accusatory tone and with a suspicious gleam in my eye. What had I just done? Even if he had helped me and fixed up my leg, he could be in league with the Soul Sucker for all I knew! I couldn't believe how stupid I had been. Too much stress and pressure wasn't a good enough excuse for pouring my heart out.

"Just rest," was all he said as he turned to leave the room.

I grunted but lay down on my back, mumbling, "Resting is the most boring thing."

Luke laughed, "You remind me so much of—" He abruptly stopped and frowned.

"Of who?"

He shook his head. "Just try to go back to sleep, Isabel."

*

This time, I woke up to the homey smell of warm soup. The pain in my leg had subsided to a dull throb, and I found that I could shuffle around the hut now.

Luke had made a vegetable stew, which I gulped down in no time.

"Luke? Do you think I could go outside for a second, just to see if my friends are anywhere near here?"

"I've already looked, but there is nobody," he said, shaking his head.

I looked down into my empty bowl. That was how

my heart felt: empty. Now what Shaman Oring had said about me being too loyal and responsible for my friends was really getting to me. Drips of anxiety leaked into my mind, but I wiped them up fast. I wouldn't let worry block out my good sense.

Another day passed without us saying much. Every hour Luke gave me another medicinal drink, and every hour I became stronger. With each gulp, I began to think that I had been a bit too hasty to judge him. It was only natural that he would know about the smoke if he lived right next to it. Plus, if he were actually teamed up with the enemy, I doubt he would have helped me this much.

When I finally managed to walk normally, I turned to Luke. "I'm so grateful. There is really no way for me to thank you enough, but now I have to go find my friends."

I made for the door. I had just wrapped my fingers around the doorknob when he yelled, "Wait! Come over here."

I went back to where he was and sat down opposite him.

"I should tell you something, Isabel."

"Yes?"

"You'll have to know how to defeat the Soul Sucker if you want to get out of there alive. And I haven't wasted all this time on healing you just to have you killed."

I leaned forward, eagerly waiting for what he had to say.

"You were along the right lines," he continued. "The

Soul Sucker does use the souls' power: to keep Earth and Eeba separated. All the souls are kept in a well at the center of the palace, so you'll have to release them, freeing your brother's, too, and then the two worlds will come together."

Freeing my brother's soul. Uniting Earth and Eeba. The two things I knew I had to do. The things I had guessed were connected, and in the end, my hunch had been right.

And now here was Luke telling me exactly what to do! Release the souls from the well, and everything would fall together perfectly. Now the only problem was getting to the center of the palace where the well was kept.

As if reading my mind, Luke continued. "But you'll have a hard time getting in there." Go figure. "The lair is surrounded by special kinds of guards."

What did he mean? But before I questioned him about that, there was something else I had to be aware of.

"How do you know all this?" I demanded.

Luke was silent for so long that I thought he hadn't heard the question. I was about to repeat it when he said, "I've . . ." He paused as he searched for the right word then continued, "studied that place for a long time, trying to get information."

My mouth gaped open. "Why? When? How?"

He scowled. "That's enough questions, and besides that would be my business. Just go find your friends. I've told you enough."

I knew that this conversation had ended, and however much I wanted to stay and find out more, I also knew that I had to find my friends before it was too late.

Before I closed the door, I whispered, "Luke, who do I remind you of?"

I could hear the buzzing in my ears at how silent the hut had become. Finally Luke choked out, "M-my sister." Then he turned away and said, "Good luck Isabel, and may our paths cross again some time in the future."

CHAPTER 12

ONCE OUTSIDE, I made my way across the flat, grassy terrain. Days had passed since I had last seen my friends, and the only thing I hoped for was that they hadn't gone too far.

Sometimes I would think I heard the flap of Eket's wings, but it was only the wind. Or I would think I heard someone calling my name, but it was only a bird cry.

Wait, a bird cry?

"Eket?" I shouted out.

"Isabeeel!" was the faint response.

"I'm over here!"

After a few minutes, there was a big THUMP behind me that shook the ground. I spun around toward the noise.

Standing tall and proud was Eket with Zach, Josie, and Sage sitting on his back.

"Isabel!" they cried and slid down Eket's spine to the ground. "Are you okay?"

Before I could respond, I was wrapped in Josie's hug. "You ever scare me like that again, you're dead. You understand me?" she whispered in my ear.

"Gotcha," I whispered back with a smile. "I'm glad to see you, too."

Once Josie let go of me, everyone else crowded around me as well. "Oh thank God you're all alright!" I sobbed in relief.

"Us?" asked Zach, raising his eyebrows. "Hello? You got carried off by a Psycho, and you were worried if we were okay?" He nodded and turned to Josie, "See? I told you she wasn't alright upstairs!" He tapped the side of his head with a grin in my direction.

I laughed. "Oh, like you are?"

Zach stared at me in mock insult. "Did you just call me crazy? How dare you offend me in such a manner?" He pretended to cry, which really made us crack up.

Then, becoming serious again, I told them how I had escaped from the Psycho and how I had hurt myself. When I started to talk about how I got better, Zach paled at the name "Luke Curador" and looked like he was going to be sick. But when I made eye contact with him, cocked my head to one side, and squinted my eyes, he just shook his head.

"This is great!" said Sage, once I had finished my story and assured everyone that my leg was feeling fine. "Release the souls, huh?"

"That's right," I said. "But I must admit I'm feeling a

bit uneasy about this. Between the guards, the Soul Sucker's henchmen, and the Soul Sucker himself . . ."

Josie waved my doubts aside. "We don't have time to worry now! We're so close! Did Luke tell you exactly where the palace is?"

I racked my brain, but even if he had pointed the way, I couldn't remember. So Eket quickly flew up and oriented us so we faced toward the smoke.

Once we knew which way we had to go, we began walking. I nervously played with my Swiss Army knife, flicking out the blade then pressing the dull side against my thigh to push it back in. My thoughts roamed on every bit of information that I knew. About Eeba, the Division, and the souls. Unfortunately, it wasn't much. At all. Nevertheless, I tried to memorize every word. Who knew what could turn out to be useful at the last minute?

I thought about what we would have to do once we got there. Get to the center of the palace and empty the Well of Souls. How exactly do you do that, anyway? Luke had said that some special kind of creature guarded the palace. What did he mean "special?" What were we in for?

I was starting to panic. There were too many things we still didn't know. We should turn back, I thought, and think everything through before traveling into the mouth of the enemy.

A memory of Tom, sweating and gasping for breath on his bed on Eeba, came to my mind, together with the picture of him sleeping in a hospital cot on Earth, a calm expression on his face.

Both images made me furious. What was I thinking? Turn back? I didn't even know if we would all get out of this alive. I didn't even know if we were in time to save Tom. But I did know that I would never forgive myself if I didn't even try.

Tearing my eyes off my moving feet, I saw a building emerging in the distance.

It seemed to be made of ivory or pearl and had the form of three enormous spikes; the one in the middle was higher than the other two. A dense cloud of black smoke billowed from the tip of the tall spike.

I scanned the grounds for the guards that Luke had talked about, but I didn't see anybody.

We cautiously crept up to the building but nothing tried to stop us. I began to wonder if Luke had been wrong all along. Then I felt something weave around my arm and yank me into the air.

"Aaaah!" I shrieked. I stared at my arm, but I couldn't see what was holding me.

One by one, my friends yelled in shock as they too were pulled into the air by invisible hands. A ray of sunlight bounced off something, blinding me for an instant. I scrutinized the air encircling me and caught a glimpse of a snakelike tentacle wrapped around my arm.

I looked with more intensity and the form of the thing holding me came into focus enough for me to see it clearly. It'll probably sound strange, and very hard to imagine, but it resembled a transparent lick of flame: thick, hard, and smooth, clutching my bicep without burning it.

The yelps of surprise from my friends told me they had seen these creatures, too. So these were the special guards that Luke had spoken of.

The transparent being shook me around and around as I desperately fumbled for my pocketknife. Before I could pull it out, I heard an ear-splitting squawk and Eket tore free from the grasp of the "flame" that had been curled around his claw.

As soon as he was free, Eket swooped around to me. Suddenly the grasp on my arm loosened and I was dropped from the air, landing painfully on my bad leg.

I watched with pride and amazement as Eket released Josie, then Sage, and finally Zach.

Now all five of the tentacle things were turned on Eket, who somehow managed to fight them all off at once.

"Go!" he yelled. "I'll deal with these, and then I'll catch up."

I limped after the others as we all raced to the entrance, which lay at the base of the central spike. Sage was the first to get there. She shoved open the heavy oak doors. "Go, go, go!" she screamed while holding open the door.

We all sprinted inside and stopped for a moment to catch our breath. Cautiously flicking open my knife, I looked around, expecting to have to a fight off an army, or something.

It was empty.

"What the—?" I said, confused, but a loud, booming laugh interrupted me.

A voice came from nowhere. "Hello Eebians, Zach and Sage, and greetings to you Earth people, Isabel and Josie. I've been expecting you for quite some time! I must say, you took longer than I thought you would, but no matter. Seize them!"

Before I could blink a dozen macho men in tuxedos encircled us. I waved my pocketknife pathetically at them, but I knew we didn't stand a chance. Powerful hands gripped my shoulders and those of my friends, and they dragged us down the hall.

CHAPTER 13

I COULDN'T SEE where I was going, but the fact that I couldn't see my friends frightened me even more. I couldn't get separated from them again.

"Where are you taking us?" I demanded the man nearest to me.

He just snickered and said, "You'll find out soon enough."

From the way he said it, a shiver trembled up and down my spine. At first I fought, kicking and biting, but after a while my struggle lost its force and then it drifted away all together.

I dreaded the moment when we would stop and we would have to face my worst nightmare.

And then that moment came.

The henchmen dispersed, but I knew they would still

be waiting in the shadows in case something got out of hand.

Now that I could see, I noticed we found ourselves in a room almost as big as the one we had first entered. In the center was a tall black chair that swiveled around to face us. I braced myself for the horror that sat on it.

Some sort of monster? A vampire man? Or another thug in a suit?

I looked up, and on the pitch black chair sat a tanned, dark-haired, and frankly quite beautiful woman.

"The Soul Sucker is a woman?" asked Zach.

The lady chuckled. "Ignorance can be quite amusing," she said, folding her hands together in her lap. "And yes, I am a woman. My name is Odette."

I could only gawk.

"Isabel, close that jaw, and please step forward," the woman ordered.

I felt a powerful push from behind, and I stumbled forward. "How do you know our names?"

She giggled again. "Oh I know a lot of things. I know about your visit to the Erinav tribe and your unpleasant encounter with the Galdur that you defeated with my limo. I know you were planning on being caught on purpose by my henchmen in that very limousine—but then the bird, Eket, got rid of them, and he is now outside fighting my guards."

I was paralyzed. How did she know all that?

"I also know," she continued, "that you have no chance of saving your brother." She leaned in closer to my face. "No. Hope."

Josie spoke up, voicing all our thoughts. "How do you know all these things? We never told anyone but ourselves about our plans!"

Odette smiled. "Are you sure about that? You did let something slip . . . to a certain someone. Don't you remember?"

For a moment, I thought that it had been Luke that betrayed us, but something told me he had nothing to do with this. But then who else? We had kept everything to ourselves, hadn't we?

After a minute of no one saying anything, Odette smirked and said, "You really don't remember, do you? I guess I'll have to give it away then." She sighed. "It's all thanks to him." She dramatically flicked her hand to the other side of the small room.

A tall man with black hair walked into the chamber. When he saw us he cringed.

Odette said, "Say hello to your old friend, Ian."

I felt like the world started spinning uncontrollably, and my heart almost stopped. "Ian?" Zach croaked. "As in . . . our Ian?"

Odette laughed at his distress. "The very same."

This was too much to bear. "That isn't possible!" I shouted. "He's a smudge! Ian, is that really you?" I forced the words out.

He nodded. "Odette promised she would give me back my soul if I helped her."

I seriously thought a meteorite had landed in my head. I didn't know what was going on anymore. I didn't know who was my friend or enemy.

Behind me I heard someone crying, then Zach began yelling, "We trusted you! How could you betray us like this? You piece of—!"

He tried to launch himself at Ian, but the men held him back.

I didn't want to believe it, but I knew it was true. That's what Ian had been doing in the Pixie District, that's why he had been so interested when we told him what we planned on doing.

"I didn't want to do it, but if you were just a hollow shell for as long as I was, you would do anything to get your soul back," said Ian. "Anything."

Odette beckoned for Ian to come to her side, and once he arrived, she lovingly weaved her hand in his black hair. "Now Isabel, what are you planning to do?"

I felt helpless.

In the distance, I could hear that Eket was fighting an endless fight outside while we were trapped in here, completely vulnerable, with all our plans known. I looked around the room in despair, trying to get an idea, but nothing came to me.

Then my eyes came to rest on a medium sized, circular structure made of stone, half-hidden by the Soul Sucker's chair.

"What's that?" I asked with a bravery I didn't even know I had and pointed at the stone thing.

Odette seemed almost pleased by my question. "You are quite observant! That's a well, and inside is something very special."

I hated the way she talked to me as if I were a two-year-old. But did she say "well?" The Well of Souls? It had to be.

Then I made a stupid mistake.

I wanted to show her that she didn't know everything. That we weren't just some show for her to watch. So instead of keeping my mouth closed, I had to go an open it. "Something special? As special as human souls?" I said. "So all I have to do is release the souls from the well, save my brother, and Earth and Eeba will come together, and you will be destroyed?"

The look of confidence that had been plastered on her face from the moment we had walked in vanished for a split second. But it returned so fast I couldn't be sure if it had actually happened.

"Bravo, Isabel! I may have underestimated you a little bit, but you have a problem. You don't know how to release the souls."

My shoulders sagged as I realized she was right. The last piece of the puzzle that we needed to complete the picture. Before she could say anything else, I said, "Oh really? And what if I do know how to release them?" It was obviously a lie, but I had to say something.

"Stop bluffing, Isabel. I can see straight through you."

Crap. That went well.

Then Odette laughed. "Well, that was actually quite entertaining for a minute or two, but I'm getting tired of this conversation, and you know too much." She snapped her fingers and commanded sharply, "Kill them."

Those words felt like a punch in the stomach.

Ian spoke next, which I hadn't expected at all. "Wait! That wasn't the deal! You promised you would imprison them, but not kill them!"

Odette snickered. "You should know by now that I hardly ever keep my promises completely."

A look of horror covered Ian's face. "No," he mumbled. "What have I done?"

I heard Josie and Zach yelling in protest and Sage quietly weeping.

Then Ian shouted, "Run children! Run!"

Odette snarled at him, "Hold your tongue. Or if that's too hard, I'll cut it off and make it simple for you." The men closed in on us. I tried to keep them at bay by waving my knife, but one of them snatched it up effortlessly and threw my beloved—and only—weapon over his shoulder.

I knew I would never see it again.

It took me a second to realize Ian was yelling, "Children, you must forgive me. I have been selfish and now I must make amends."

"Shut up, you weak, stupid man!" hissed Odette, but Ian was on a roll and no one could have stopped him.

He continued shouting, "To free the souls someone must sacrifice themselves. For the souls to be released there must be another soul but still in its owner's body!"

"I said SHUT UP!" screeched Odette as she leapt off her chair. In two strides she arrived next to Ian. She brought up her fist, and in one swift, powerful movement, struck him across the face.

He crumpled to the floor.

I had no time to fret over Ian. I was processing his words in my brain. To save Tom I had to sacrifice myself. I would do anything for my brother.

The Soul Sucker's henchmen had stopped closing in on us and were now just staring at what would happen next.

Odette was still looking down at Ian's crippled body.

For once in my life, I thought over the consequences before acting. If I sacrificed myself, Tom's soul would return to his body and he would continue to live. See our parents again. I wondered if the freed souls would go back to their owners' bodies or just roam the two worlds. Well, if it worked, Earth and Eeba would become one. I wished I could be around to see that. Something told me that even though the other souls would be going back to their initial bodies, I knew I wouldn't magically start living again.

But my mind was made up.

I straightened my back and began to make my way to the small stone structure.

But somebody had beaten me to it.

Sage stood there, next to the Well of Souls where their blue energy could be seen crackling and sparking and glinting off her glittery shirt.

She gave me a half smile. "Make sure Tom doesn't forget me," she said and then she leapt into the bottomless well.

A scream erupted from the mouth of every person in the room. Zach, Josie, and I howled for Sage. The men shouted in surprise. But the most horrible scream came from Odette. Her mouth stretched, and a shriek resembling that of a Psycho gushed from her mouth.

Then she stopped, cocked her head to one side, and an alarmed expression crossed her face.

She whispered five words, so quietly I didn't even know if she had said them: "You are making a mistake."

And then she was gone.

CHAPTER 14

DON'T ASK ME what happened next, or how exactly we got out of there. It was a blur.

I faintly recall being blinded by millions of little balls of blue light whizzing out from the well and flying around in the air before going their separate ways. Then Eket came in and, with Odette gone and her henchmen too confused and shocked to stop him, carried us away.

I remember the crushing weight of grief almost breaking my back. Even though I hadn't known Sage very long, we had been through so much together, it seemed like a lifetime. I remember the tears soaking my cheeks. I remember the expression of complete despair and misery on Zach's face. And I remember the overpowering feeling of loss that squeezed my heart, along with the sense of joy that we had succeeded.

After that it was all hazy. Then I found myself in a firm bed, wrapped in warm blankets. "What the—?" I sat up to see a familiar face. "Luke?"

He nodded. "I am so happy you made it out okay. I'm sorry about . . ."

I wanted to cry again, but all the tears inside me had dried up.

Josie sat next to me, clutching my hand tightly, as if afraid I would disappear any second and leave her too. I held her back with the same firmness.

Looking around, I noticed Zach sat at the opposite end of the room with his back to us. I wanted to go over to him, comfort him in some way, but I didn't know what I would say. I decided to just leave him alone for a while.

"Where's Eket?," I asked. "How did we get here?"

Josie replied, "He's outside, resting. He carried us all the way over here."

I stayed silent. I didn't know what to say, but I knew what we had to do. "We have to go find Tom. And my parents. They should be here, now that Earth and Eeba are one, right?"

"Isabel," said Luke, "worlds may not take years to come together, but it won't happen immediately either. My guess is a week or something, at least."

My shoulders sagged. This sucked. I thought it would be an instantaneous thing. Oh well, a week wouldn't take too long to go by, right?

"We should get some sleep; it's nighttime," advised Josie, sniffling. The last thing I wanted to do was sleep, but I knew I had to have as much strength as I could to start on our journey to get Tom in the morning.

I reluctantly lay down on my side and closed my eyes. Guilty happiness rippled in my heart. I could barely believe we had actually done it! We had saved Tom! I knew I shouldn't feel proud at a time like this—I should be mourning—but I couldn't help myself.

Also, along with my joy and sorrow, I noticed a little tug of emotion in my stomach.

It took me a second to realize it was jealousy.

At first I tried to deny it. Why would I feel envy of all things? But then I started to understand myself. I was jealous because Sage had gotten the glory. She was gone now, and that only made me even more ashamed of my feelings, but it was still she who had really saved my brother. Not me.

Loud snoring interrupted my thoughts, and I sat back up. I wanted to go out and see Eket, but I realized I was not the only one awake. Zach was standing by the small window, staring at the starry night sky.

I tiptoed over to him, making as little noise as possible. He was so absorbed in his own thoughts, he hadn't heard me get up.

I awkwardly placed my hand on his arm. He jumped a bit, but didn't say anything.

"Why? Why did she do that?" he whispered. "I would never have had the courage."

I didn't say anything at first. After a long, stretched out moment, I said, "She loved Tom. They met in their dreams, and they fell in love."

Neither of us said anything. "Why did I ever doubt her?" Zach said in a murmur, so quietly I hardly realized he had spoken.

I didn't answer. Instead I squeezed his arm gently. "We better go get Tom tomorrow. She would have wanted it."

"Then we'll go back to Malsama to tell my grandma, and we'll have a proper funeral."

I nodded, then I asked him something I had been wanting to know for ages. "Zach, what happened to your parents?"

I felt his arm stiffen under my hand. "We . . . I never really knew my parents."

"Oh. I'm sorry." I wanted to kick myself. Hard. Couldn't I see he was already miserable? Why did I have to bring up another delicate subject? I whispered "good night" in his ear and creeped back into my bed.

But before I fell back to sleep, I saw a movement next to me. I looked closer and saw that Josie was awake. She had seen, and heard, everything that had just happened. I blushed, threw the blankets over my head, and fell into my deep dreams.

The next morning I noticed Zach watching Luke's every move. At first I thought I was imagining things, but he had stared at the healer all throughout breakfast, and then I remembered how when I had first mentioned Luke's name, Zach had paled.

What was wrong? At the breakfast table I asked him why he was keeping such a close eye on Luke. But he only responded, "Huh? Oh, just thinking about something the Shaman had said." Then his brow furrowed, like he was deciding whether to say something or not. He made up his mind to speak, apparently, and awkwardly stood up.

We all looked up from our porridge to hear what he had to say.

"At the Erinav tribe, Shaman Oring told me something. He said that I would soon find my parents. He said that they had moved on, but the one could still be found, and not very far away. He said . . . he said . . . my father is called Luke Curador."

I dropped my spoon as I almost slid off my chair, and Luke began choking on his scrambled eggs.

"What?" I exclaimed once I had regained my balance. "Are you sure it's not a different Luke Curador?"

"Why, this is wonderful!" Josie gushed. "Father and son reunited at last!"

When Luke stopped coughing, he said, "This Shaman Oring person must be mistaken. I have no children."

"Hey, are we going to hit the road, or what?" Eket shouted from outside. He thrust his head through the open window. "What's going on? You all look kind of . . . whitish."

Nobody said anything for a moment or two, then I took a deep breath, gulped once, and said, "Luke might be Zach's father."

Eket pulled his head out of the window and fainted.

We all rushed outside, where the giant bird lay on his back, his claws in the air and his tongue lolling out of his beak.

"Oh my God," I muttered. I watched Josie climb, with some difficulty, up the side of Eket's face, taking care not to hurt him. When she got up there, she slapped the side of his cheek to wake him up. It woke him, all right.

He jerked up, sending her careening down into me so that we both landed in a heap at Luke's feet.

I quickly picked myself up, helped Josie to her feet as well, and dusted down my clothes. "Eket? Was that really necessary?"

He just looked at me and shrugged.

Luke cleared his throat. "No, no, you are mistaken, Isabel." He turned to Zach, "I can't be your father."

"I know, I know!" said Zach. "My parents died right after I was born, and Sage doesn't . . . didn't remember them either. But why would the Shaman say something like that?"

"I have no idea. I have nothing to do with you or your sister!" Even before Luke finished the sentence, he realized how mean he sounded. I think living by himself in the middle of nowhere for so long must have affected his social skills considerably. Instead of trying to apologize, or explain himself, he quickly turned around and walked into the house.

I rushed back in to see him putting out the fire. "What are you doing?" I asked.

He scowled and said gruffly to the smoldering ashes, "I thought you wanted to go get Tom. What are we waiting for?"

"You're coming, too?"

Luke looked at me. "Unless you don't want me to . . ."

"No, no, it's not that. I just wasn't expecting it."

"I've gotten too used to living alone. I need to reintroduce myself into the world."

"You should definitely come with us," I said, encouragingly.

He smiled. "I'm glad you're not too disappointed that I'm not Zach's father."

I shook my head. "Oh I am disappointed. Everyone is. Zach is probably going crazy right now. "

"But what do you want me to do?" Luke said. "I don't have any children. It's not like I can just decide he's my son! And besides, he knows it too. He said so himself that his parents are dead . . ."

"That's not what I mean."

"Then what do you mean?"

I sighed. "I don't know what anything means anymore."

CHAPTER 15

THE CASTLE WHERE Tom had been kept was further away than I would have liked, but the sooner you set out, the sooner you get there, so we got moving.

We were a pretty gloomy bunch, and we had every right to be. We trudged along with various packs on our backs without saying a word—except for Eket, who shouted out random jokes or sentences for no apparent reason. I guessed it was his way of trying to lighten the mood, but it wasn't working—and he wasn't doing a very good job of it anyway.

After walking for so long, I felt like my legs were going to fall off. We were all fed up with Eket's blabbing, too.

"Hey, guess what?" he squawked, for about the millionth time.

"Enough, Eket! Could you please just shut up!" Zach cried, finally losing his temper.

Eket shrank back. "I just wanted to say that I see a castle," he whispered.

Our hearts rose, and we tramped on with renewed energy. A tall, black spire emerged from the distance. We raced towards it, and with each step it grew larger.

When we finally reached the castle, Josie let out a long whistle of amazement. I was surprised too. It was much bigger than I remembered, and the glass walls shined as if recently polished.

I looked around for the entrance, but instead of the sliding doors, a centaur stood stiffly at the base of the castle: half-man, half-black stallion. He guarded a large set of wooden doors, holding a spear firmly at his side. When we stopped in front of him, he held it out at us, and declared, "State your business!"

I swallowed and said in a shaky voice, "I'm Isabel, Tom's sister, and these are my friends."

The centaur's expression softened. "Tom's sister! We must get you to him at once!"

He pushed open the double doors and beckoned us into the castle.

"I think I'll stay out here," said Eket.

"Are you sure? You know, you might be able to squeeze in. It looks pretty big in there," urged Josie.

Eket nodded vigorously. "I much prefer being outside. Plus, I don't do well with emotional reunions." He turned up his beak and sniffled.

So, leaving Eket behind, we made our way into the castle.

"I am Sir Fluffy, one of the castle guards," the centaur informed us. Zach snickered, but Sir Fluffy ignored him and continued excitedly. "You will be pleased to know that Tom is better. In fact, he's completely healed! He should be just up these stairs."

"Isabel!" Tom shouted as he turned the corner. When he saw me his face lit up like a million light bulbs.

"Tom!" I screamed and I threw myself in his arms. I wanted to say something more, but a lump had grown in my throat, preventing me from speaking. I found myself sobbing with relief and joy. When we finally pulled away from each other, I saw he was crying too.

"Zach!" shouted an elderly female voice. Grandma Martha came bustling out from behind Tom. She wrapped herself around Zach in a smothering embrace. "Young man, I am very angry with you! You could have been killed, you could have . . ." but Grandma Martha couldn't bear scolding Zach when she was so relieved he had made it out okay. Then she stopped. "Where's Sage?" she whispered.

Zach took a deep breath. "Sage . . . Sage didn't make it."

For a moment Grandma Martha didn't even react as though she didn't even believe us, but when she saw it was the truth, she let out a wail of distress. She trembled as a flood of tears poured down her cheeks. Then she covered her face with her hands and hurried away.

We watched her go. None of us tried to stop her. We knew she just had to have time to be by herself.

At the announcement of Sage's fate, Tom's expression lost all of its previous gladness, leaving his face a chalky white. He swayed on his feet, and I thought he was going to fall down, but he stayed strong and didn't let his knees give way. All the time he kept shaking his head. No. No.

"Guard, take them to the dinner hall," Tom ordered, his voice almost breaking. "I'm going to go find Grandma Martha." Then he, too, rushed away in the direction that she had gone. I felt anxious, seeing him go. I feared that if I couldn't see him, he would disappear, and I'd be alone again. But I told myself I was being silly and let him leave without complaint.

Sir Fluffy herded us down the corridor, the opposite way Tom had gone. "Come on," he said. "They have food prepared for you."

"Do you think she'll be okay?" whispered Josie.

Grandma Martha's breakdown had only worsened Zach's state. He didn't cry. He didn't shout. But I knew that under his stony expression a whirlwind of emotions spun around in his mind. Even so, Zach responded, "My grandma is a strong woman. She'll be fine." Unlike Grandma Martha, he had already gotten over the initial shock of grief. Not being a psychologist, I didn't know what the second phase would be.

And I didn't want to know.

We entered a large chamber that was occupied, for the most part, by a big table, surrounded by chairs of all sizes and colors. The end closest to us had a huge collection of plates and cups, sending out different aromas. After walking for so long, I was starving but I had almost forgotten my hunger with the excitement of seeing my brother. Almost forgotten.

We all jumped into different chairs and eagerly stuffed our faces. At one point, I saw a particularly muscular centaur dragging a giant dish covered with one of those old-fashioned bell thingies to the largest window.

I began to ask what it was for when Eket stuck his face through the window and stared keenly at the plate. When the centaur had finally brought it close enough to Eket's beak, the giant parrot knocked down the cover and gobbled up whatever he had been served.

We finished and sat back in our chairs, completely full. Just then, Tom walked in, his hand resting on Grandma Martha's shoulder. She had stopped crying and her lips now formed a straight, emotionless line. I admired how she and Tom had gotten themselves under control. I couldn't imagine how hard it must have been for them to remain calm on the outside while inside they were in misery. I knew that each and every one of us had to deal and somehow get over what had happened to Sage, and we would all do so in different ways. Some might think and cry over her every day, while others wouldn't want to face it at all.

A sobbing ten-year-old girl trailed behind them, not even trying to hide her sadness.

"Maya!" I exclaimed, as I recognized her. She looked up but didn't stop crying.

Once they all sat down Tom cleared his throat and said, "I'm sure I speak for Grandma Martha and Maya when I say I can't wait to hear about your adventure."

So I began to recount to them everything that had

happened. From going back to Earth and fetching Josie to being saved by Eket from the jellyfish monster. I told them how Sage had told me about her falling in love with Tom—here some color returned to Tom's cheeks—and about our meeting the Erinav tribe. Then about my escape from the Psycho, finding Luke, who had healed my leg (everyone congratulated him, so much, in fact, that I noticed his face turning red), meeting back up with the others again, and getting to the Soul Sucker's palace.

The whole time I talked, I kept glancing over at Tom, just to make sure he still sat there. A great joy bubbled up inside me each time I looked at him. He was okay! Along with my relief, I felt a confidence that warmed my body. I had done it! I felt like hugging him again and again, but I restrained myself and continued to describe our story.

When I got to the part about Ian's betrayal, Grandma Martha went pale. Her shoulders sagged, and she uttered something incomprehensible under her breath.

The last thing I said was what Odette had mumbled before she disappeared: "You are making a mistake."

When I finished, Grandma Martha uttered a small gasp of amazement. "So not only did you save your brother, but you also brought the two worlds together! This is brilliant, just brilliant!"

At that point, Zach interrupted her and told them what Shaman Oring had told him about Luke Curador being his father.

Silence.

"Now Zach," said Grandma Martha, gently placing her hand on his knee, "you know perfectly well that's not possible."

He stood up, forcing Grandma Martha to take her hand away.

"Then why did Shaman Oring tell me Luke was my father?"

"I don't want to call the Shaman a liar," said Luke, "but I'm not. Your father, I mean. I have no idea why he would say something like that."

We were silent for a while, and although I felt for Zach, I had to speak up. Hello? What the heck were we sitting around here for? It was time for Josie, my brother, and me to return home. "Tom! We have to go back home! Back to Earth!"

Even as I said it I knew it was easier said than done. I was going to miss all the fantastic things that happened in Eeba, and most of all I would miss the people. I guessed I could always open the portal and visit Eeba, but it wouldn't be the same. I would have to wait a couple of weeks, like Luke had said, until the two worlds joined together. I didn't know exactly what it would be like, but I imagined I would be able to see my Eeba friends on Earth. I silently congratulated myself on my instincts. I had known that I had to bring Earth and Eeba together to create one, balanced world. I had guessed it! Not anybody else!

Tom frowned as he thought about it. "I'm actually not so sure if, if I can . . ."

I leapt from my chair. "What the hell do you mean?"

My brother shrugged. "Well, you came through the portal, so you're fine. But only half of me is here, on Eeba. The other half of me is probably still in a coma on Earth. You and Josie can just walk through the portal again, but I don't know if it works the same for me."

I didn't know whether to cry or scream at the top of my lungs.

After everything we had been through to save my brother and bring him back to Earth, now he was telling me he might not be able to?

"Couldn't we try?" I whispered.

Grandma Martha cleared her throat. "In my opinion, I think he would be fine if he went through the portal. I believe he would just reunite with his other half, and that's it."

Josie looked confused. "How would that work? Would he find himself in the hospital?"

Grandma Martha shrugged. "Well, I would suppose that the weaker half of him would join with the stronger half, which is obviously the part that is here, on Eeba. So when he crosses onto Earth, the half that is in hospital would probably join this part of him. At least, that's what I think."

"Grandma Martha, how do you know all these things?" I said. So far this old lady had so many answers to our questions, and I started to wonder how.

She sighed. "Ian," she said with regret in her voice.

Grandma Martha brusquely wiped her shining eyes with the back of her hand and said, "I don't know what time it is, but I'm sure it's way past bedtime."

"You're right, it's late," Luke agreed.

Suddenly Grandma Martha jerked up, and she looked at Luke as if she had just noticed he was there. Her face covered with suspicion, she asked, "Luke, how did you know about Earth?"

Luke glanced around in every possible direction to avoid Grandma Martha's skeptical gaze, looking like a child squirming in front of a teacher's stern stare.

"Isabel told me," he said and pointed at me.

"Yes, but there were other things you knew, too. How come?" Grandma Martha said, quietly but fiercely.

"It's a long story . . ."

"Please tell," said Grandma Martha, rather menacingly, and making it sound more like an order or a threat instead of a suggestion. She sat back in her chair and added, "We can all stay up just a little longer for this."

I thought she was overreacting a bit, but then I realized she had every right to be distrustful. Even though I didn't want to, I couldn't help fearing that he could be one of the bad guys. Could he be a traitor, too? I had told him about Earth when he healed me, but he had known other things I hadn't told him. I also remember him never questioning my story. He hadn't even looked surprised.

Luke let out a loud exhale and said, "My sister, Lucy, would often visit me at my old house in the Forest of Foscor. One day she showed up on my doorstep, clutching some letters. She looked so distressed, but when I tried talking to her she would start spouting nonsense. And that wasn't the worst of it—she started talking about herself in the third person. She was acting so strangely, like she was a whole different person. Then one day she just . . . left without giving me any warning or explanation. I tried to follow her tracks, but I only came across the Soul Sucker's palace, and the moment I saw it, I became fascinated. I wanted to know who lived there and what happened inside. Little by little, I gained information. Not much, but enough to suspect about an alternate reality, and some bits about souls."

Luke looked around at us to see our reactions. At first no one said anything, and it was all quiet except for Maya's gentle snores .

He had already told me the last part, so I was obviously more interested in the beginning. "So what happened to your sister? She just went crazy and left? Did you ever read the letters?" I wondered how her story connected with the Soul Sucker, and if there was something behind this that we should know.

"I don't know what ever happened to Lucy, and I have never been back to my old house in the Forest of Foscor where she left her letters," Luke said, his face clouded with longing and sorrow.

I realized how much this meant to him, and after how much he had helped us, I felt like we owed him something. That, and also I was dying with curiosity and thirst for another adventure, so I said, "Luke, we've been through a lot together, so I want you to know that if you want to go back to the Forest of Foscor, or whatever it's called, I would be happy to go with you."

"Are you out of your mind?" Tom demanded. "I thought you were the one who couldn't wait to go home, and now you're going to run off on another stupid journey? I don't think so!"

I opened my mouth to defend myself, but Luke spoke first. "Isabel, I don't want to make you feel as if you owe me anything. I'm fine, really."

"But what if those letters contain valuable information?" I asked, hoping to make my case that we needed to retrieve them.

"About what?" Tom asked, skeptically.

"I don't know!" I spluttered. "Maybe the Soul Sucker or the two worlds?"

"No," said my brother. "Sure, it seems like they might be connected, that Lucy led him to the Odette's palace and whatever, but you can't prove it! And even if they were linked in some way, I wouldn't care. You've already risked way too much, Isabel. It's time to go home."

I scowled. "But what if I'm right? Besides, what would it change? Even if they aren't connected, at least we'd get to see more of Eeba, explore, and see awesome new things!"

All this time Zach, Josie, and Eket had remained silent, but now I looked at them and silently pleaded with them to take my side.

Zach spoke up first. "You know, Isabel may have a point. I mean, knowledge is power, and the more we have the better, right? Those letters could contain something interesting."

I looked into his eyes and sent him a silent thank you. Next to speak was Josie, who moved her hair out of her face and said, "I'm usually very cautious about things, but I agree, and besides that, another adventure would be exciting. I'm not really ready to go back to boring old Earth just yet. Even if soon enough it might not be as boring."

Then Eket piped up from the window. "I'm part of the team, so wherever you go, I go!"

I crossed my arms and looked at Tom and Luke, but they just frowned. Grandma Martha fidgeted with some fraying thread from her cardigan.

"Please let us go," I begged Luke.

"The house is too far away anyway," he said, but he was obviously hopeful at the thought of finding out more about his sister. "It would take days, even weeks, to get there on foot."

"But we don't have to go on foot!" I protested. "I say we go back to Malsama, get another hovercraft or something, and go to Luke's old house. Or maybe we could get jetpacks! Now that would be cool!"

"You're talking as if it's already been decided that we're going," Tom said with a sneer.

"Oh come on, Tom! Stop being such a wimp!" I said.

Tom furrowed his eyebrows and stayed silent for a moment. Then he said, "Fine. I guess we could make a short trip to the Forest of whatever, but then right after that we are going back to Earth!" I smiled, to which he quickly responded, "And don't think this means you can always have your way!"

But his last words were drowned out by Grandma Martha. "If you are going, then I'm coming with you!" she exclaimed. "I will not have you children traveling around unprotected!"

Zach, Josie, and I let out a slight groan, and we were about to protest when Eket said, "Beg your pardon, ma'am, but I don't think there's any need for that. Luke will be with them this time, and Tom. And also," he cleared his throat, "I can be very vicious and fierce when I want to be." He put on his "warrior" face, which just made him look constipated.

I coughed. "What Eket is trying to say is: we have lots of protection without your coming along, Grandma Martha. Besides, who would take care of Maya? Would you really want her to come with us?"

"You have a point there," Grandma Martha said.

Good going, Isabel, I said to myself.

Maya, who woke up just in time to hear the last part, crossed her arms and insisted, "I am coming, what do you take me for–"

"Hush, Maya," scolded Grandma Martha, as she thought for a minute or two, considering her options. Finally she made up her mind. "Fine, I won't come along, but you," she said, shoving her finger under Luke's chin and pulling his face towards hers. "If any of them come back to me with one bruise, so help me, I will . . ."

"I understand completely, ma'am," Luke said quickly.

Grandma Martha grunted and turned to Eket. "And if you lose another one of these children, I will tear out your feathers, one by one!"

Eket gulped loudly. "Yes, sir. I mean ma'am."

The elderly lady let out a loud humph and sat back down again.

Josie yawned. "Great, now that's decided, but I'm sorry. I can't keep my eyes open."

Tom jumped up. "Sir Fluffy!" he called out to the hall. The centaur immediately showed up beside him. "Take them to their bedrooms and show them the bathrooms. Grandma Martha, Luke, and I will be up there in a second."

Sir Fluffy obediently escorted us up the stairs.

Maya tagged along for part of the way, whining constantly. "It's not fair! Everybody thinks I can't do anything just because I'm little!"

I patted her on the shoulder, "It's okay. I'm sure your time for adventure will come."

She just grumbled in response.

With Zach and Maya already in their rooms, Sir Fluffy escorted Josie and me farther down the hall. On our way, I asked Josie, "Do you really agree with me about going to Luke's house?"

She grinned. "Completely. I actually really hoped you would offer to go and find the letters."

I smiled back. "I'm glad you think so."

Sir Fluffy stopped in front of Josie's room, and we said good night. Then the centaur and I continued to my bedroom. He quietly closed the door behind me as I walked in.

It looked like a room you would find at a fancy ho-

THE TWO WORLDS OF ISABEL

tel, with smooth marble floors that were cool to your bare feet and made you walk carefully, because you knew if you slipped, you would probably crack your head open. In the center sat a queen-sized bed with puffy pillows and a crisp duvet, all in white. One wall was just one huge window framed by a pair of white drapes. I walked over to it and could see Eket right outside, his head tucked under his wing, sleeping peacefully below me.

"Good night Eket," I whispered to the giant parrot. I pulled the curtains across the glass wall.

I dragged myself over to the adjacent bathroom, where I found all new toiletries and towels there for me.

I took a quick shower, just to refresh myself a bit, then brushed my teeth. Out in the main room, a beautiful wooden cabinet was filled with a bunch of different clothes and pajamas. Already my eyelids sagged. I threw on the first set of pajamas I could find and dove into the bed.

It didn't take me long to fall asleep.

CHAPTER 16

THUNK THUNK THUNK.

"What the—?" I sat up and rubbed my eyes. What was going on?

"Isabel!" came a muffled voice.

I popped out of bed and pulled back the curtains from the window. Outside stood Eket, loudly thumping his beak against the glass as he hovered above the ground. He had fear in his eyes as he tried to wake me up.

"What's the matter?" I asked, but I realized at least one problem immediately and my breath caught in my throat.

The sky was green.

At first I thought it might have been an effect of the sunrise or something, but it had nothing to do with dawn. I stood there, staring at the bizarre color of the sky, in awe and fear. I felt certain this was a sign of the worlds coming together.

"Eket!" I yelled to him, once I got over my shock a bit. "Do the others see this?"

He shrugged.

Still in my pajamas, I raced out the door. I had to get to the others. See what they thought of this.

Just as I walked out into the corridor, Tom turned the corner. "Did you see—?" I began to ask him.

Before I could even finish he said, "Yes, I did. Quick, we must get to the others!" He walked briskly down the hall with me trailing behind him. Rounding another corner, we met Grandma Martha and Maya. We didn't have to say anything to know we were all thinking the same thing. So without speaking a word, we continued down a long corridor and up a short flight of stairs, where we bumped into Sir Fluffy.

"Sir Fluffy, what are you doing here?" I asked.

"I found your friends roaming the castle. They were obviously lost so I brought them to you." From behind him emerged Josie, Zach, and Luke.

"Thank you, Sir," said Tom. "You may return to your post."

The centaur nodded gruffly and clip-clopped away.

"Did you see the sky? It's green!" said Maya excitedly, her eyes shining with wonder.

"What do you think it is?" asked Josie.

"A sign," I said with confidence. "A sign that the two worlds are coming together. It's got to be!"

The others responded with a round of excited whispering and nods of approval.

Luke spoke up. "I'm not sure exactly how long it will take for Earth and Eeba to completely unite. My guess is around a week, or maybe two. Anyway, I think it would be better if we left as soon as possible. As we talked about yesterday, let's go to Malsama first and find a hovercraft, and then we'll head on to the Forest of Foscor."

I could feel, just from the eagerness in his voice, how excited he was. He was going back to his old home, the site of one of his last memories of his sister. I wondered why he had not returned before. What had stopped him from going there until now? Whatever. I hardly cared. All that mattered to me was that we were going on another adventure. Clearly I had not yet learned my lesson about wishing for adventure.

Luke's enthusiasm was contagious and soon we were all impatient to leave on our journey.

Grandma Martha spoke up. "Last night I asked Sir Fluffy to prepare some food and supplies for you to take on your journey. Go get the bag, and then you may go."

She turned away so nobody would notice the tears filling her eyes, but I saw them. I couldn't imagine how hard it must be for her, to first lose a granddaughter, and then watch another grandchild go. Zach was right. Grandma Martha was a very strong woman.

CHAPTER 17

WE ALL STOOD outside the door of the castle. Eket held the bag of supplies in his claw, and Zach was saying good-bye to Grandma Martha. She had been fussing over him for at least a minute, and I started to think we would never leave.

"It's not fair!" complained Maya. "I want to go, too!" Her grandmother ignored her and continued telling Zach the dangers of not brushing his teeth.

Zach groaned. "Grandma, I know! I'll be fine, really!"

"Okay, okay," she muttered while smoothing his shirt with her hands.

Tom turned to go and we all followed him. "Don't worry Grandma Martha!" he yelled over his shoulder. "We'll all be fine! And we'll be back before you know it!"

"Bye, Maya!" Josie and I called to the little girl, feeling sorry for her.

Once we were out of sight of the castle, Luke reached into his coat pocket and pulled out a large piece of parchment paper. "Sir Fluffy gave me this map. It shows the part of Eeba where we are. My house is in the Forest of Foscor, right about . . . here," he said and pointed at the map where he estimated was his house.

"So what we do is go to Malsama, get some mode of transportation, then travel into the Forest to get to Luke's house," Tom said, trailing his finger to make an imaginary line across the paper.

We all nodded and began to walk, Luke at the front, holding the map, and everyone else in a huddle behind him.

"How long do you think it will take?" asked Eket.

"I don't know. Maybe a day?" Tom responded. Everyone groaned. We had walked so much in the past few days. Just the idea of the long journey ahead made me feel sick.

We hiked on and on, stopping every once in a while for a rest or to have a bite of food.

I thought about all I had been through. Compared to the past few days, my troubles with Ashley were laughable. I had battled monsters, I had made new friends, I had ridden a giant parrot, and I had driven a limo!

I wondered how the others were coping. Josie seemed fine, but I could never be sure with her. She could hide her emotions so easily and so well that sometimes it scared me. She was, of course, still the real Josie. My friend Josie: the one who always had my back, the one who was always there for me, the one who was careful and warned me if she knew I was going to do something I would later regret. I felt so lucky to have her by my side.

Then there was Zach. Ever since Sage had sacrificed herself it seemed like a veil had drawn across his face. He didn't joke or tease me like he had done before. Now he was more serious and always had a straight face. It made me uneasy. I wanted him to return back to normal, but I knew it was way too much to ask of him just yet. I was aware that everyone needs time to recover from a loss as great as the one that he had suffered.

I glanced over at Tom. Whenever I looked at him, a great happiness swelled in my heart, along with the feeling of self-confidence and pride. I was delighted to see my brother looking fine again, back to his old self. But I wondered if that was just his appearance. What if something had happened to him while Odette had been sucking his soul? Would he still be the "cool guy" at school, but with that slightly nerdy side to him? Would he still have his thirst for knowledge that made him stay up late at night working ahead in his schoolbooks? Would he still be the Tom that was hardly afraid of anything, except when it came to medicine? The Tom that could barely swallow a pill without taking an hour to just put it in his mouth?

I didn't want my brother to change. Well, I knew he already had, and that he would change even more as time went by, but I didn't want it to be anything abrupt. I wanted it all to come when we were both ready.

But I only had to look at him to see that Sage's sacrifice had hit him hard, too.

I gazed up at Eket, who towered over all of us. It felt strange, in a good way, to have a friend that wasn't human. Who would have thought that one day I would be walking beside a fifteen-foot parrot? Eket was one of a kind, even if he told really bad jokes. If it weren't for him, we would all be jellyfish poop by now.

Then I looked at Luke. I had known him for the least amount of time, but he still felt like an important member of the team. His face was screwed up with concentration as he tried to figure out our exact position on the map. I could tell he was happy to have something to do. I figured he was the kind of person who liked to keep busy so he didn't worry about something. He did have a lot to think about.

I felt reassured having Luke come along, though. Maybe it was because he was an adult (I guess technically Eket could be classified as an adult, too, but he didn't really count), or maybe it had to do with him being a healer, but either way, I felt safer with him at the front, leading us on.

I glanced up at the sky again, for about the millionth time. It had faded back to normal a while ago, but I still expected it to turn purple or something any second.

"Please! Must . . . stop . . . for. . . rest!" gasped Eket, collapsing to the ground, dramatically. He was obviously exaggerating, but I had been so wrapped up in thought that I had hardly realized how much time had passed and how far we had walked.

"Okay," said Luke. "We'll stop for a minute."

We all flopped to the ground.

I gulped down some water from my canteen. "Will we have to spend the night out here? Or will we get to Malsama in time?" I asked, suddenly imagining sleeping under a sky that could change colors, or worse, at any moment.

Luke shrugged. "I can't be sure. We'll just have to see."

After we got up and continued on for a bit more, it began to get dark, and there was still no sign of Malsama. The last thing I wanted to do was spend a night out in the middle of nowhere, but we had no choice.

We ambled on until the sun had set and we could walk no farther. Then we opened our bags and took out the blankets and travel pillows that Sir Fluffy had packed for us.

As soon as the sun had gone down, the temperature dropped as well. We would have made a fire, but we were in the middle of a grassy meadow and there were no trees in sight from which we could get wood. So instead, we had to huddle together and clutch our blankets tightly. I didn't want to sleep. I was scared of what might happen if I closed my eyes. We considered having somebody stand guard, but we knew it was pointless as that person would fall asleep anyway; we were all so exhausted.

I snuggled into my blanket, comfortable between Tom and Josie, and forced myself to stay awake, but I was too tired, and my eyelids drooped further and further until I finally drifted off into a deep sleep.

*

Something chased me. I didn't know what, but I ran like I had never run before, completely terrified of whatever creature was coming up behind me. My lungs burned, and my breathing came in quick, bursting gasps. I knew it was only a matter of time before I could go no farther. But that moment came sooner than I expected.

I slowed to a halt, bent over, and rested my hands on my knees, gulping air. I couldn't hear footsteps behind me or anything, but I could feel a presence. A great presence that loomed at my shoulders. And even though I couldn't really tell whether it was good or bad, I ran from it anyway.

But now I could feel it closing in on me and there was nothing I could do to slow it down. For the first time I looked around to see where I was and if my surroundings could help me in any way. Just as my eyes glanced around, the air encircling me shimmered and I found myself standing in the middle of a desert. A little wail escaped my lips, and I could feel the creature getting even closer to me. In one last desperate action, I tried to sprint forward, but I had no energy, and the sand that curled around my feet only made it worse.

Suddenly the wind that slapped my face howled louder and a voice pierced through the noise. It was neither male nor female, but it brimmed with ancient power: "You will never make it. You will save no one."

The voice sounded strangely familiar. For a moment I forgot my fear and glanced around in confusion. I tried to pinpoint exactly where the voice came from, trying to remember where I had heard it before.

I shouted out into the wind. "What do you mean? I have already made it! I have already saved my brother!"

A great thundering rumble met my ears, and I realized it was laughing! And it took me another moment to understand that it was laughing at me!

My stupidity won over my prudence and I yelled, "What's so amusing? I didn't do anything funny! So stop laughing at me!"

The rumbling stopped and suddenly I felt something pull at my hair. Tears welled up in my eyes, but I didn't cry out. Then I was pushed onto my knees to the ground. The wind grew even stronger and the sand flew up into my face, making tears stream down my cheeks in an attempt to wash my eyes.

Then the voice came again. "Stupid girl. You will see where your selfishness has brought you. Now everyone will suffer! You have saved no one!"

I finally realized why the voice sounded so familiar. It was the same voice that had come out of Shaman Oring's mouth when he had read my fortune. I realized I was talking with something more powerful than anything.

The future.

It seemed too strange and impossible to understand.

Talking with my very fate.

No wonder it was so cruel.

Hysteria began to rise in my throat and I cried, "What do you mean? Tom is alive and safe! Earth and Eeba are joining together. Everyone's fine!"

There was another deep rumbling. "That's what you think."

"I don't understand!" I cried out, but I felt that the presence had gone, and I knew that the voice wouldn't respond.

All at once, the wind died down, and I collapsed into the sand, lying on my back. The only sounds that remained were my labored breaths and the beating of my own heart.

*

"Look, here's another little girly!" said a nasty voice.

I jerked my head up, instantly awake. For a moment my mind flashed back to my dream, and I remembered the presence that had chased me. And that voice . . .

I tried to grasp the memory, but the more I tried, the hazier my dream became. And then I forgot it all together.

My mind finally came back to reality and I saw a man standing over me with a scraggly beard and a malicious, toothless smile. A fur cape was draped over his shoulders, and in his hand glinted a large, rusty knife.

I gulped. This could not be good news.

I tried to stand up, but the man had tied rope around my ankles and wrists. This was getting worse and worse by the second.

"Boss, found another one!" said a voice nearby, and another man came into view, dragging Luke behind him.

"Luke!" I cried out. By the looks of him, he probably tried to fight his captor, but it hadn't ended well. The healer had a long scratch running down his cheek and a bruised and swollen eye. He, too, had been tied up.

"Good job, Jasper," said the first man, who was obviously the boss. Jasper grinned and shoved Luke down next to me.

I looked around to see if the others had been captured as well. A little ways off sat Josie. She was roped and gagged, but even so, was yelling swear words at the men, muffled as they were by the piece of dirty cloth stuck in her mouth. Behind me Zach lay unconscious and bound up.

"What did you do to him?" I demanded, nodding towards Zach. The boss chuckled. "Put up a bit too much of a fight."

"Why you nasty little—" I began, struggling to get up, but Jasper pushed me down to the ground.

I looked around trying to see where Tom and Eket were, but I couldn't see them anywhere. At least they got away, I thought. I tried to think of an escape plan, but nothing came to mind. And these were dangerous men with knives that had managed to overpower Luke, the only adult. If Luke couldn't handle them, and neither Eket nor Tom were here, then we had no hope.

"Come on," said the boss, "we have to take you to the slave market."

I almost gagged. "The slave market?" I choked out. "You can't sell us as slaves! You just can't!"

The boss just laughed. "Come on Jasper, call the oth-

185

ers. Nobody else is here, so we better get these ones in the wagon."

Jasper put two fingers in his mouth and let out a long, high-pitched whistle. Almost immediately, two other men showed up. Jasper grabbed Luke by the arm and hauled him away. A second later, one of the other men yanked me by the arm and pulled me up off the ground. His grip was so tight, I almost cried out.

In the meantime, the other men had grabbed Josie and Zach, and they dragged us towards a big covered wagon that was parked a little ways off. Josie cursed louder. I began to struggle and cuss as well, but I instantly stopped when the boss began to pull out his knife.

At the sight of the dagger, Luke paled. I wished that Eket were here. He could have easily gotten rid of the slave traders. How could he have left us? How could Tom have left us? I felt a sharp pang in my heart as I thought of Tom leaving without me. He probably tried to wake me but couldn't. I tried to convince myself of this, but I became more and more desperate.

The man clutching me had arrived at the wagon. He threw me into the back. Pitching forward head first, I tried to put my arms out in front of me to break the fall, but I remembered they were tied behind my back. I landed painfully on my side. When I looked up, I saw that Josie, Zach, and Luke were already in the wagon.

"Josie," I whispered to her, "we have to think of a way to get out of here."

I heard a loud crack of a whip, and the wagon jerked

into motion. I couldn't continue talking to Josie because the men were sitting in the back with us. Only Jasper and the boss were out in the front, where I couldn't see them.

I tried to crane my neck to meet Josie's gaze, but I lay in an awkward position that didn't allow me to see anything but the floor.

"Pssst," I hissed to Luke, who was crouching beside me. "Psssst!"

I finally managed to get his attention, but at the same time, one of the slave traders bent down and whispered into my ear, "If I was you, I would cut that out. Got it?" I could feel his foul breath warming my cheek, and all I could do was nod helplessly and shut up.

The wagon bounced along the uneven ground, making me even more uncomfortable. I waited for us to get to our destination, but I wasn't quite sure I wanted us to arrive. Could they have been serious when they spoke about the slave market? Half of me just didn't want to believe it, but the realistic part knew that they had spoken the truth. So the longer it took us to get there, the better.

I could hear Josie weeping quietly, and I presumed Zach was still unconscious. My mind traveled to Tom and Eket, who had somehow managed to escape. Where did they go? When were they going to come back for us? I knew they wouldn't just abandon my friends and me, so where the hell were they? Why hadn't they saved us yet?

These thoughts rattled my brain right up until I felt the wagon stop moving.

We had arrived.

The door swung open and light suddenly burst into the back of the wagon. I squinted my eyes to try and see past the boss standing in the doorway, but his shoulders were so broad, they blocked almost everything out. His rough voice barked out orders. "Max, you get the man. Scuttle, you can get the boy, and Jasper, you grab the two girls."

A big burly man with long, oily hair grabbed Luke. I gulped. This guy was seriously built like a freaking mountain, and he had a nasty glint in his eyes that said he liked to hurt things for pleasure.

Zach suddenly came to, and a moment later, he was pulled out into the open by a tall, lean man with little, squinty eyes. His arms were ropes of sinewy muscle, and even if he didn't seem that imposing, I could tell that was the whole point.

Once we were all outside on our (roped) feet, our captors started pushing us along windy, narrow streets. We were probably entering a slum, somewhere in the periphery of Malsama. I stumbled along the filthy alleyways, looking anxiously around me, half-expecting Eket or Tom to burst out and save us. Or at least half-hoping.

No such luck.

They continued forcing us towards God knows where without interruption. Sometimes I saw hunched over figures, crouching in corners, and when we passed, they looked up at us with their dirty faces. Their expressions were hard to describe. No trace of happiness any-where, only sorrow and defeat. Their eyes bore into me, and I felt a sharp pang in my heart.

Suddenly the street opened up into a huge square with an unusually tall platform rising up in the middle. The expanse was empty, save for a few people who drifted around the edges for no apparent reason. The boss made straight for the platform, and Jasper, still clutching the arms of Josie and me, trailed behind him.

Once we reached the base of the stage, Max stepped forward and cut the rope around our ankles, allowing us to walk freely up the steps of the platform. Obedi-ently and in silence, we trudged up and arranged ourselves in a line along the front of the stage.

I looked out across the square, where all of a sudden, loads of people had started crowding around. And soon, the plaza was swarming and buzzing with chatter.

Would I soon be a possession of one of those people? What would happen to my friends? What had hap-pened to Eket and my brother?

My heart sank when I finally realized we were com-pletely trapped. This whole time, there had been a part of me, however small, that still believed we could make it out of there alive and free.

But now that I looked around me and at my friends with their heads bowed and hands tied, it hit me that this time, we would finally be defeated. So many times we had made it out of sticky situations, but now I really couldn't see any hope. Our luck had run out.

I was jerked back to reality by the sound of a gong

and then the voice of the boss yelling out to the crowd, "Now you all know why we are here, so let's just cut to the selling!"

A loud cheer rose from the public and the boss continued, "Here we have a nice strong man, ready to do any hard labor that you don't care to do yourself!"

Max pushed Luke forward so he was standing next to the boss. Out of the corner of my eye, I saw Zach open his mouth, but Scuttle nudged him in the back and Zach's mouth snapped shut.

Before anyone in the crowd could shout out a cost, Luke looked up, straight into the boss's eyes and said, "Please. You can sell me. You can sell me and I won't even put up a fight. But please, leave the children alone!"

I held my breath, waiting for a reaction.

The audience started to chuckle—not quite the reaction I was hoping for—and soon great roars of laughter escaped from their mouths. When they finally stopped, they started bidding on Luke as if nothing had happened.

I silently groaned, as I imagined the first loss of the day. I wondered how long it would take for Luke to get sold.

I didn't know anything about the currency in Malsama, but I could tell that the prices for Luke were rising fast. And then a man with a yellow hat shouted out, "Three-thousand pekkacs!"

A hush fell over the audience and the boss yelled, "Sold! For three-thousand pekkacs to the man with the yellow hat!"

Jasper gave a hard shove to Luke's back, sending him careening down the stairs. When he managed to regain his balance, he was already in the hands of his buyer. He desperately kicked out, but his feet never met anything but air. And soon he stopped struggling.

The boss then moved on to Josie. Anger boiled up inside me, replacing my despair. There was no way, I could let him sell my best friend. I had to do something quickly. But what could I possibly do?

The boss dragged Josie up next to him and yelled, "Now how much for this young lady? She can help you out with the domestic work and . . ." He let out a little chuckle and ran his rough fingers down Josie's cheek. "She's a right pretty little thing too, eh?"

I heard low, masculine snickers coming from the crowd and I just exploded. "Keep your dirty hands off of her, you sick-minded snake! You're nothing but a—"

Max clamped his hand over my mouth. At least I had managed to say the better part of my insult before he silenced me.

Silent tears trickled down Josie's cheeks as the bids started to fly. In the end, a sinister-looking man gave the highest price, and I watched my best friend being dragged down the stairs of the platform.

Without thinking, I clamped my teeth down on Max's hand (which was probably the most disgusting thing I have ever tasted) and as I felt his grip loosen, I shouted out, "Please! Leave her alone! You can't—"

Max backhanded me across the cheek so forcefully that I heard my neck joints crack. The blood rose in my face, and tears sprung to my eyes. I could feel the side of my face growing numb already. Out of the corner of my eye, I saw Josie being held tightly by the man who had bought her. He was slowly running his hand up her arm, and I glimpsed her shuddering at his touch.

That perverted sicko. I promised myself that if I ever got my hands on him, I would wring his sorry little throat. Threats kept going through my mind even as Jasper pushed me towards the boss, who grabbed me by the shoulders and held me so tightly I could barely move.

"Here we've got another little girl," he started. "A bit of a rebel, this one, but she'll be just fine if you know how to handle her."

At that moment, I remembered a very useful fact. My legs had been untied.

And so, without thinking about the consequences, I did the first thing that sprang into my mind. My leg swung up and then back again with all the force I could muster, kicking squarely into the boss's groin behind me.

I cannot begin to describe just how satisfying it was hearing him squeal.

With adrenaline pumping through my body, I reached down to where he was lying on the floor, gasping, and whipped out the knife from his belt so I could slit the rope binding my hands. Taking a second to examine the red lines cutting into my wrists, I dove to the ground, barely dodging Jasper's punch. I then swiped with the knife across his thigh, causing him to fall.

Pushing myself back up, I was just in time to see Scuttle and Max lunge for me. Moving on impulse, I managed to dodge bulky Max, but Scuttle was more agile, and he caught my hair in his fist and pulled me towards him.

I bent my arm back and struck out randomly and repeatedly with the blade. At first, I didn't connect with anything, but on the third strike, I heard a yelp and felt the grip on my hair ease up.

I immediately jumped towards Zach, who was just standing there, watching in awe. I quickly freed his hands.

By this time, the boss had recovered and was making his way towards us.

In a strange moment of calm, I looked out into the square, where the crowd had panicked and were running wildly about. I had a sudden urge to just jump off the platform and run away, but two things held me back. For one, the platform was way too high. I probably would have broken both ankles by leaping off with nothing to cushion my fall.

The other thing? Guilt. How could I even have thought that? Just abandon my friends and leave them to their own devices? I would never do that.

Finally, my mind tore back to reality, where a very angry boss was making his way menacingly towards me, his fellow slave traders close behind.

With Zach at my side, I started to back away, but soon we would be at the edge of the platform, and what then?

I held out my knife, but Max growled and hit my hand, knocking the blade away.

This was the exact moment when I needed a miracle.

And amazingly, a miracle came, like it had before, in the form of a giant bird.

Eket suddenly thumped down on the platform with such a force that it knocked me off balance and caused everyone to fall to their knees. But he didn't stop there. He continued jumping and pounding on the wooden planks of the platform until they started to cave in.

I felt the boards underneath me start to dip and slope downwards, almost making me slip. Zach and I managed to hold onto the edge of the platform to stop ourselves from sliding, but the slave traders weren't so lucky.

With all of Eket's thumping, the planks cracked, creating a hole in the stage, and the boss, Jasper, Max, and Scuttle were now falling down towards it.

I let out a sigh of relief, but I acted too soon.

At the last second, Jasper grabbed onto my ankle, and the next thing I knew, I was sliding down towards the gaping hole in the platform, dragged by Jasper's weight.

A hundred thoughts flashed through my mind. What would happen if I actually did fall through the hole? I remembered the platform being surprisingly high, but would it really be that dangerous to fall from that height? I decided I would rather not find out.

My nails scraped wood, trying desperately to slow me down. Splinters pierced the soft skin of my fingers, but

I didn't care. I had just almost lost my grip, when I felt arms around my chest, and I looked up to see Zach's face very close to mine.

I looked up into his eyes, seeing in his face the strain of holding Jasper's and my weight. His arms were looped under my armpits, and only the top of our chests were touching; the rest of my body was hanging over the edge of the hole.

I could feel his heartbeat almost in sync with mine. "Please," I whispered, "please don't let go."

He didn't say anything, but I could feel his arms tighten their grip. The pressure on my ankle was growing, and no blood was circulating in my foot. I tried to wriggle my leg and loosen Jasper's grip, but it was impossible.

I managed to look down into the hole, and I could see the broken bodies of the boss, Max, and Scuttle curled at the bottom, their limbs bent at awkward angles. I imagined they had probably banged into the interior beams holding up the platform and then landed hard on ground. Too hard. It was obvious they weren't breathing anymore. And I guess that answered my question about how dangerous a fall it would be.

Turning my head away from the disturbing sight, I met Zach's gaze again. With his face so close to mine, I noticed that glimmers of green streaked his brown eyes, which now darted from side to side in this desperate situation.

"Please," I said again, "you can't let go."

All of a sudden, Eket pounded the platform again. One last time, but just hard enough to make Jasper loosen his hold on my ankle. Zach somehow managed to keep hold of me, and once Jasper had fallen, he hoisted me up, out of the gap, where we both sat for a second, panting.

At that moment, I looked at him again, so full of admiration, and as I gazed at him, a grin flickered across his face.

God, I loved that smile.

Without knowing what came over me, I leaned forward, and in that perfect moment, I kissed him.

His lips were soft against mine, and his nose tickled my cheek. I felt my heart beat a little faster inside my chest, and happiness blossomed in my mind. The kiss lasted for only a few seconds, because at that moment, I heard someone coming up behind me.

I broke away from Zach to hear Josie's amused voice, "Oh, am I interrupting something? Please, continue as if I wasn't here." I could hear the laughter in her voice, and I turned to see a huge grin on her face.

"What are you laughing about?" I grumbled, embarrassed.

Out of the corner of my eye, I saw Zach giving Josie the thumbs-up sign. I laughed along with my friends, and in that moment, I almost forgot about the situation that we were in, and the fact that we were still sitting on a destroyed platform in some slum.

Then I saw Tom and Luke talking down in the square, and we all got up to join them.

"What the hell took you so long?" I shouted at my brother, hugging him at the same time.

"Well, don't bother saying 'thank you,'" said Eket, who had just landed beside me.

"We almost became slaves!" I continued, him. "Why did you take so long to show up?"

Tom began. "It's a long story, and one I don't really care to repeat just now. Why don't we just try and get to a nicer part of Malsama and then we can talk?"

Everyone agreed, so we made our way across the square and through the alleys, telling Tom and Eket about what had happened.

About fifteen minutes later, we emerged from a street and found ourselves in front of a large river. On the other side, I could hear and smell the strange yet kind of familiar senses of Malsama—the nice part of it.

"Hey, this is River Fluo! Once we're on the other side, we won't be far from the Plausible Quarter," Zach announced.

Only then did I look closely at River Fluo, and I gasped when I realized it was pink.

As the sun reflected on the water, the color changed to neon green, yellow, pink, electric blue. It was crazy! Every time the current twisted, even if just a tiny bit, the water changed color, and it moved from one shade of the rainbow to the next with amazing ease and grace, so I hardly realized I was then staring at a different colored river.

I had to tear my eyes away from Fluo because my friends had started walking towards the nearest bridge. Once we got to the crossing over the water, we slowly made our way across, cautiously avoiding the middle of the bridge where many weird vehicles whizzed by.

Halfway there, we were stopped by a man and a woman in matching silver jumpsuits, holding little black and white cubes. After checking our clothes and pockets, they finally moved on, leaving us free to continue.

"What were those little cubes they were holding?" Josie asked Zach once they were out of earshot.

"Those are Fluos, the weapons the police use," he explained.

"Whoa, wait. I thought Fluo was the river," I said.

"It is, and the Fluos are full of the water from the river. The water, once treated with a special chemical, creates this particular energy that when locked up in a closed space for long enough can have very serious effects when released," Zach explained. "If they shoot a Fluo at you, you don't die or anything. It's not like a gun, but you're still kind of screwed for a while anyway."

"Okay, okay, I get it," I said quickly.

We were nearing the end of the bridge, and when we finally crossed over, the effect on my senses was immediate. After being out in the middle of nowhere for so long, it came as an enormous shock to be in a city again. Especially the massive city of Malsama. All the noises and smells and things to see overwhelmed me. I felt like my brain would explode. It reminded me of going into a super crowded mall where everyone's talking and there's different music blaring from all the different stores, and I feel like crawling into a hole and never coming out again.

At least, that's what I felt like, and I could tell Luke

felt the same way. Josie just stared and gawked at every little thing, while Zach looked right at home.

"So?" Tom began to ask Luke, but Luke just shook his head.

"Don't look at me," he said. "I'm not a city person."

Zach spoke up. "Follow me. I know a place where we can rent a hovercraft and for a fair price, too."

At the word "price" I paled. "Oh, crap," I said. "We don't have any money."

Josie groaned and smacked the palm of her hand against her forehead.

"Oh no!" cried Zach, but then a smile crept across his face. "Nah, just messing with you. I have all the money we need in here." He patted his pocket. "Grandma gave it to me before we left."

We all sighed in relief, then began following Zach down the big crowded streets of Malsama.

"Oh my God, did you see that?" Josie kept exclaiming, her hand shooting to her mouth. I grinned at her excitement. I had been on Eeba for enough time to be prepared for anything out of the ordinary.

Zach weaved in and out of streets and we all trailed behind him.

Suddenly we heard a group of voices. "Zach? Dude, is that you?"

A small gang of boys emerged out of nowhere and stood in our way.

"Guys? What are you doing here?" exclaimed Zach, surprised, but in a happy way. Must be his friends, I thought.

They exchanged friendly shoves and pats on the shoulder, and then the boys seemed to finally notice the rest of us. A black boy with curly hair raised an eyebrow at us. "Who are these people?"

"Friends of mine, Dylan. I'm showing them around town," replied Zach.

"Oh, where are they . . . whoa." The boy's jaw dropped as Josie came into view. The others saw this and playfully nudged his shoulder.

Dylan cleared his throat. "Um, won't you introduce me to your . . . friends?" he said, still staring at Josie.

Zach smirked while stifling a laugh and said, "Isabel, Josie, Luke, Tom and Eket. this is Dylan."

"Nice to meet you, Josie," said Dylan.

Josie laughed. "Hi."

The other boys cracked up and pulled Dylan back towards the group.

"So where have you been?" asked another one of the boys. "We haven't seen you for quite a while."

"Oh, I've been, er, sick," responded Zach. He put his hands in his pockets and looked around nervously. "Look, guys, I gotta run. See you around!"

I was afraid the boys would start pushing us to stay or not allow us to leave, but thankfully, Zach's friends were really understanding and let us go with no problems. Wait. Cancel that. Girls are understanding; boys just didn't care.

"See ya!" they said.

"Bye, Josie," Dylan called. Josie gave him a playful closed-mouth smile that made the other guys chuckle even more. Then we rounded the corner, and the gang went out of sight.

"Your friends seem nice," I told Zach.

He grinned. "Yeah, they're a blast. I've known them forever." The way he said it made me wonder if he would prefer hanging out with them than being with us.

We walked on until we came into a little alley. "The store is just over— "

"Well, if it isn't Zach Fowler."

I whirled around to see a group of three or four teenage boys, a little older than me. For a second I thought they were Zach's friends that we had just met, but these boys had a cruel glint in their eye, telling me they definitely were not associated with Zach. The boy that had spoken stood a little taller than the others, and his spiky hair just added to his height. He was obviously the leader.

"Zeb, we don't want any trouble," said Zach.

"Oh, we ain't gonna give you no trouble," growled Zeb. "I'm just gonna show you what happens when you mess with us. I don't suppose you remember what happened the last time one of you set foot on our turf. Well let me tell you this. It wasn't pretty."

The other boys laughed nastily, and one spoke up. "It's been a while since the two Zs stood in one place."

I couldn't believe I was hearing this. We only had to do one simple thing, and we had to be stopped by a rival gang? We didn't have time for this. So I did something without thinking, something I would greatly regret. I guess after all we had been through I had gotten cocky and overconfident. I gently pushed Zach aside and sauntered over to Zeb.

"You look here, mister. I have been through a hell of a lot. Stuff that you and your little gang only have nightmares about. So I highly suggest you move aside before my giant parrot here rips you to shreds."

"Oh no," I heard Eket mutter behind me. "I couldn't do that. It's against the law!"

Zeb heard what the parrot had said and he laughed. "You see? I guess your plan won't work so well after all."

That was my cue to back off, but I refused to be so easily defeated. "Do you really think I'm scared of a few scrawny teenage boys? Move out of the way and let us pass."

Up until then, Zeb had been entertained by my little burst of sass, but now he was starting to get sick of it. A scowl crossed his face, and he began to bounce back and forth on his heels.

I took a deep breath as my anger rose. "If you don't step aside right now," I said while putting my hands on my hips, "we will have to move you by force, and there's nothing you guys have that could stop us."

Zeb brought out a little black and white cube that I immediately recognized as a Fluo.

I gulped. "Except maybe that."

Zach's jaw dropped open. "Where the hell did you get a Fluo?" he cried out, more amazed than scared.

Zeb stepped forward.

At that moment Luke stepped forward as well. "Now you kids run along, or I will be forced to do something drastic." I almost snorted at Luke's effort, like he thought he could intimidate a bunch on teenagers with a dangerous weapon by playing the part of the "grown-up."

Zeb and his gang sneered and started to close in on us.

"Cut it out, Zeb," came a voice to my right.

Dylan stood to the side, arms crossed over his chest, with the rest of Zach's friends at his shoulders. They did not look happy.

"Zeb, we made a truce," said Dylan, glaring at the leader of the other gang. "Now scat, before I make you."

Zeb sneered. "Wow, I'm really scared now." He casually spun the Fluo across the palm of his hand and said, "But if I were you, I'd be even more scared. I'm sure you know what this is, right?"

Dylan just laughed. "Yeah, right. Who would be dumb enough to leave a Fluo just laying around? I don't buy your crap. It's probably not even charged."

Zeb paled visibly as Dylan called out his bluff, and he took a slow step back.

Dylan smirked, then he glanced at Josie to make sure she was looking at him. He stuck two fingers in his mouth and whistled. Two seconds later five other boys arrived on the scene. Along with the original group and now the other five that had joined them, Zach's gang had more than double the number of people that Zeb's had.

Dylan grinned. "Okay, now you're scared."

Zeb's eyes almost popped out of his head. He began nervously twitching and moving his fingers. Then he rolled his eyes and stuck the Fluo back in his pocket. "Whatever," he said as he turned and jogged away down the street, followed by the rest of his band. "But don't think this is the end!" he yelled over his shoulder, and then he was gone.

Zach beamed at his friends. "That was awesome! You guys rock!"

"Yeah," said Josie, "thank God you came just at that moment."

Dylan grinned and straightened his back. "Oh, it was nothing."

"Well, thank you so much," said Tom, "but we really have to get going."

Zach nodded. "Yeah, we do. Bye, guys, and thanks again!"

Dylan nodded, and he, with the rest of the gang, turned to go. "See ya, dude!" he yelled to Zach, then more quietly he said, "Bye again, sweet Josie."

"Bye, Dylan," Josie said with a laugh. Then she turned and followed the rest of us down the street towards the hovercraft shop.

CHAPTER 18

"LOUIS'S HOVERCRAFT RENTAL" said the sign hanging above the door to a large garage. We walked in, and a tall man with a mustache greeted us.

"Hey Louis," said Zach. "We need to rent a hover-craft."

Louis twirled his mustache nervously. "I don't know, Zachy boy. You see, something's happened."

"What do you mean?" Zach asked, concerned.

"Well, almost all of the hovercrafts have just disappeared overnight! And it hasn't happened only to my shop. Pegasus saddles have vanished; jetpacks have melted away into thin air. I don't know what's going on!"

A strange thought struck me. What if this was another side effect of Eeba and Earth coming together? What if Eeba was losing some of its magic because it was joining with Earth? That would explain why these magical things were vanishing!

"I'm sorry to hear that," said Josie, "but are you sure there are no more left?"

Louis shrugged. "Come with me."

We followed him deeper into the garage. It was much more empty than I expected it to be, even after what Louis had told us. Finally we came upon a little group of roofless hovercrafts. Looking more closely at them, I noticed they weren't in the best condition—rusty with worn leather seats.

Luke sighed. "Oh well," he said, checking out the pathetic machines. "We'll take that one." He pointed to the best one.

"Okay," said Louis. "I'll have to see your driver's license."

Luke paled. "My driver's license. Um . . . sure." Living in the middle of nowhere for so long, he obviously had no need for a car or a driver's license. He frantically searched his pockets, hoping he would find something in one of them.

Suddenly Tom's face lit up, and he pulled a little plastic card out of his pocket and placed it in Louis's open palm.

Louis raised an eyebrow and turned the driver's license over in his hand. We all held our breath, and he finally said, "This is a driver's license, but a right strange one!" He inspected more closely, "Wait . . . Pennsylvania? Now where in heck is that?" He looked at Tom suspiciously, "And where exactly are you from anyway?" Tom hesitated, not knowing what to say. But thankfully Luke spoke up at that point, saying, "He's from up north."

"I see . . ." said Louis.

"You know, the Difal regions." Luke continued.

Louis fell for it. "Oh yeah of course, I've heard some right strange things about those countries. Oh well, how long will you be needing it?"

Tom shrugged. "I'd say about a week."

"Okay, that'll be twenty big ones," Louis said.

Zach's jaw dropped. "Twenty? That's crazy!"

Louis shrugged, looking upset about having to charge his friend so much. "Sorry, but the prices have gone up with all the merchandise disappearing."

Zach scowled as he began counting out his money. Finally he placed a small stack of strange silver bills in Louis's outstretched hand.

Louis took a key out of his pocket and handed it to Tom. "Here. Gas tank's full. Safe driving!"

We all climbed into the hovercraft with Tom sitting at the driver's seat. He looked surprisingly chill, considering he had never driven a hovercraft before. Holding the wheel loosely, he slowly turned the key in the ignition. The hovercraft drifted up a few feet. Then Tom lightly pressed the gas. We shot forward and out of the garage with Eket flapping in the air above, easily keeping up with us.

Luckily, Louis's shop wasn't located too far inside Malsama. To leave the busy city we only had to cross River Fluo again and then weave our way through Malsama until the buildings started to thin out.

Once we found ourselves in the big open country-side, Tom drove faster, getting more confident the farther we went. I watched land rush away from under us and felt the wind whip my face and hair. We were moving quite fast, and the hovercraft had no roof, so the wind roared loudly in our ears, forcing us to yell if we wanted to be heard.

Nobody really wanted to shout, but I had gone so long without talking that it was getting on my nerves. "Have you thought of what our parents must be doing, and how worried they must be?" I asked my brother.

He nodded. "I'm homesick, and I'm sure mom and dad must be out of their minds. But I don't really want to think about it. It just makes me depressed. I'll worry about it when the time comes."

"What about you, Josie?" I asked my friend.

She frowned and took a second before responding. "I love Eeba, and I think it's awesome. But I wouldn't want to stay here. I mean, my place is on Earth, where I understand things, and with my family. I really miss them."

Then an uneasy thought popped into my head.

What if Earth and Eeba coming together wasn't the best thing after all?

I had acted so quickly, and to tell the truth, joining the two worlds was just incidental to releasing the souls and saving Tom, so I hadn't really thought too much about it.

Maybe Odette had been doing the right thing by keeping the two worlds separated. A being as powerful as the Soul Sucker must have had a reason for separating the worlds, not just a simple whim.

This thought disquieted me, and it made me as scared as ever. I kept this theory to myself, though, since I didn't want to worry the others.

"How about a lunch break?" Zach suggested, interrupting my thoughts.

Tom slowed the hovercraft to a stop. Then we all climbed out to stretch out legs and began to eat the food in our packs.

I sat cross-legged on the grass, eating a sandwich, when a chilling feeling came over me. It unnerved me and made me shiver. I glanced at the others to see if they had felt it. By the looks on their faces, I could tell they had.

It felt like millions of people were watching me but not giving me their full attention. It felt like being in an overly crowded bus, squished between throngs of strangers.

Then, as quickly as it had come, the sensation subsided.

"What . . . was that?" asked Eket, his eyes wide with discomfort. Everyone wondered the same thing, but none of us knew the answer.

We quickly finished eating and continued driving.

*

It was at times like this that I really wished I had brought my iPod or something. We had been cruising towards the Forest of Foscor for what felt like years, and I was so bored. For a little while I had played tic-tac-toe with Josie, drawing the grid on my arm with a pen, but then she felt sick. So I played with Zach for a while. But then I ran out of space on my arm, so I returned to doing nothing.

I was getting tired of seeing the same landscape for hours and wished we would get to the Forest soon.

"Eket, you okay up there?" I yelled.

"Sure," he shouted back. I wanted him to say he was tired so we could stop and stretch our legs for a bit, but he didn't. I thought of asking to stop myself, but I didn't want to seem like I couldn't even go a few cramped hours in a hovercraft, so I kept my mouth shut and didn't complain.

I decided to try and start a conversation. "So Luke, what was it like living in the Forest all by yourself?"

Luke smiled. "Great, actually. I don't do so well with lots of people and big cities. But in the Forest it was peaceful and quiet. Just me. Obviously a few problems sprouted up here and there—wild beasts and stuff like that—but I got rid of them easily. Every day I would go search for different medicinal herbs and explore."

"But didn't you get lonely?" asked Josie.

"Well, another healer lived by herself in a house not very far from mine. Her name was Agatha. She became a great friend of mine, but she was old, and she passed away many years ago."

"Oh, I'm sorry," I whispered.

Luke nodded. "Her time had come. Besides, I hardly

remember her. I lived in the Forest such a long time ago," said Luke.

A moment of silence passed before Tom took his focus off of the road for a second and asked, "What about you Eket? Where's your family?"

Eket called down, "Well, I moved out of the nest not very long ago. And since I have a great singing voice, I decided to try and get somewhere with music. Listen." He began singing loudly and off-key.

Zach covered up his ears. "Good luck with that."

Eket didn't hear the sarcasm in his voice. "Why, thank you."

"Geez, that was . . . nice," Josie added politely.

"Well, that's the reason I was on my way to the concert the day we first met," Eket continued, "and now I'm here. And I've got to say, this is the most fun I have had in ages!" He paused. "Except for us almost dying a few times . . . and having to attack men with knives . . . and fighting an oversized jellyfish . . . and—"

"Okay, we get the picture," I interrupted him.

"Hey, is that the Forest of Foscor?" asked Josie, sitting up and staring out into the distance. Sure enough, an expanse of densely packed trees stretched along the horizon.

It was hard to see, though, since the sun had set and darkness had already fallen. "We'll stop here, then we'll arrive at the Forest, fresh, tomorrow," said Tom.

I practically dove out of the hovercraft. We had been driving for a day and a half already and now that the Forest of Foscor stretched out just ahead of us, I could hardly hold back my excitement. I shivered. The clean clothes that I had grabbed at the castle weren't really warm enough for cold nights. Of course, I still had my hoodie, but it didn't make me that much warmer.

I wrapped my blanket around me and took some food out of our bags. I scarfed it down and lay down on my back, staring up at the stars.

I tried to go to sleep, but that horrible thought kept returning to my mind. The thought that joining together Earth and Eeba was wrong. I tried to push it away. I told myself I was crazy. Even Grandma Martha had thought it brilliant when I told her we had destroyed the barrier between the two worlds! But then why did I feel this way? And why did this idea keep coming to haunt me every time I shut my eyes?

The sound of everyone snoring made it even harder for me to fall asleep, but at long last, I did.

CHAPTER 19

I WAS THE first one up the following morning. Awful nightmares had filled my mind and all night I had tossed and turned in my blanket, trying to clear my head and just waiting for the relief that morning would bring. I opened my eyes and sunlight flooded my vision. I lay there for a moment or two before sitting up.

Rubbing the sleep out of my eyes, I got to my feet. When I looked around I almost fell back down again.

I found myself back on Earth.

At least that's what I thought for a second. All the brightness of the grass and the sky had left, leaving the landscape almost colorless.

I remembered that when I had first arrived on Eeba, I had almost been blinded by the intense shades of green and blue. By now, I had gotten used to it, but that morning, it seemed like all the vividness had been sapped from this world.

It must be another effect that Earth and Eeba are coming together, I thought, with a sick feeling in my stomach.

One by one, the others woke up and stared in shock at the dull colors of Eeba. I explained to them I figured it was another sign that the two worlds were joining, like when the sky had turned green. With this idea, they became less nervous, but they still remained fidgety.

We each grabbed an apple and jumped into the hovercraft. We all practically buzzed with excitement of being so close to the Forest.

Tom drove with extra speed, and in no time we hovered in front of a thick wall of trees. Tom tried to drive the hovercraft into the Forest, but it was too hard to navigate it through the line of trees. We had to leave the hovercraft at the border and travel into the Forest of Foscor on foot.

We took our supply packs and headed into the woods. Behind us, Eket forced his way through the small spaces between every tree.

Soon, the trees became more spread apart, allowing us to move more freely. Deeper into the Forest, the trees grew tall, but not very thick, and their branches spread out in the air above us, blocking out most of the sunlight. Strangely, I wasn't scared. After all the other monsters we had encountered, I expected myself to be trembling with fear when we entered a dark forest that could be crawling with beasts. But I wasn't. There was something about the Forest of Foscor that made me think only of the beauty of the trees instead of all the dangers that could be hiding in their shadows.

Crunchy red leaves and small bunches of shrubs covered the forest floor. Once in a while, a thick tree root protruded out of the ground, causing one of us to trip (and you should know that by "one of us" I mainly mean Eket).

Luke walked in the lead, looking around for anything that might help him get his bearings.

"You know where we're going, right?" Josie asked warily.

"Of course," Luke answered. "I just have to get on the right track."

He peered around a tree, and I was pretty sure we were lost. "Luke, admit it. You have no idea where we are," I said.

Luke ignored me and kept going forward.

A rustling in the leaves behind me stopped me in my tracks. I slowly turned around, nudging my friends and mouthing, "I heard something."

They turned around, and we all stared out into the Forest, but there was nothing to see. We nervously continued walking again, but I kept looking over my shoulder to see if something was following us.

After a few minutes I again heard something moving behind me. I whirled around and yelled, "Who's there?"

No response.

My friends looked at me like I was crazy. They hadn't

heard anything. But I knew there was something behind us, and I wanted to know what it was.

"Come on!" I shouted. "Show yourself!"

All of a sudden, there was another movement on the ground, this time much closer to me. I let out a little yelp and grabbed onto Tom's shoulder.

Right at my feet stood a little furry creature. It had big puppy dog eyes and was no bigger than my hand.

I bent down towards it.

"I wouldn't do that," Luke warned.

I ignored him, never one to resist an adorable animal. "Aww, he's so cute!" I crooned. Suddenly his mouth stretched to show a row of little pointy teeth.

"Or maybe not so cute," I managed to say, just before he jumped up and nipped my leg.

"Get away, you little pest," said Zach, kicking at the creature that had just bitten me.

"Zach. Don't," said Luke, grabbing Zach's hand and mine at the same time.

He dragged us away from the tiny thing, with Tom, Josie, and Eket right behind him.

"Those are dangerous creatures," he said. "We've got to get away from him as soon as possible. Thank God he didn't bite you!"

I gulped. "Um, he kind of did," I said, lifting up my pant leg to reveal a small wound. "Is that going to be a problem?"

Luke's eyes widened. "Quick, get behind that tree. We'll deal with this little monster."

I rushed to sit behind the tree, but with each step, I

became dizzy. Even though the tree was only a few feet away, I barely made it. My surroundings started to look fuzzy and out of focus, and with every breath I took, the weaker my legs became. I slumped down at the base of its trunk and willed my head to stop spinning.

I glanced over my shoulder to see how the others were doing. Eket was closing in on the creature, flapping his wings forcefully.

But suddenly the little thing shot towards Eket and bit him on the ankle. The creature moved so fast, I could barely see him. Eket blinked in surprise, then he began to sway, until he fell in a heap on the forest floor.

I groaned for two reasons. One, the little beast had knocked out our best fighter, and two, my head was spinning faster and faster.

My eyelids drooped, and my head felt as light as air, but I knew that fainting would be the worst thing to do right now. I slapped the side of my face to keep myself awake. I looked back over my shoulder to see how the others were faring. It didn't look good.

Luke shouted instructions, and Zach and Josie were trying, frantically, to do as he said. Wait, where was Tom? I anxiously looked around and saw my brother slumped over a tree root, passed out. He had been bitten, too.

I wanted to cry with despair. I couldn't believe we were so close and were going to get defeated by some stupid little creature with bad social skills, cute as he was.

Pain rose to my head. I was afraid I was going to

puke. I gave one last glance behind me, expecting to see the rest of my friends unconscious on the ground. Instead, Luke stood in front of the creature, taunting and provoking him. The little monster had all of his attention on Luke, and didn't see Josie and Zach creeping up behind. In their hands was a burlap sack. Where had they gotten that? I remained conscious long enough only to see Zach and Josie drop the bag over the creature's head.

CHAPTER 20

"YEP, SHE'S COMING round."

I blinked, slow and sluggish. My head pounded so hard I felt like my skull would break from the pressure. Groaning as I sat up, I remembered about getting bitten by the little monster. Then I recalled that Tom and Eket had been bitten as well.

"Is Tom okay?" I asked. "And how's Eket?"

Josie handed me a bottle of water. "Oh they're fine," she said. "They woke up a while before you. You had its poison in you the longest."

"Am I going to be okay?" I asked and then took a sip of water. It tasted so good, I wondered how long I had been out.

"Of course. Luke fixed you up just fine," Josie assured me.

"Thank God. Oh, and by the way, you rocked when you captured that critter," I told her.

She blushed. "You saw that? Well, I guess it was pretty cool . . ."

I unsteadily got to my feet. We were standing in a small clearing next to a stream. I walked away from the bed of leaves I had been lying on, and, leaning on Josie for support, I reached the chirping creek.

I bent down and dipped my hands in the freezing water. I cupped my hands and splashed my face and hair. "Where are the others?" I asked, noticing with some concern that we were alone in the clearing.

"Tom and Zach went to get some firewood, Eket's standing guard, and Luke just went off to get some herbs or whatever."

"Isabel! You're okay!" I heard a shout behind me. I turned around to see my brother with Zach trailing behind him. Their arms were full of sticks and chips of wood.

"Of course I'm okay. You didn't think you could get rid of me that easily!" I replied.

The two boys set their little piles of wood down on the ground and walked up to us. "Luke finally knows where we are," Zach told me. "Now all we have to do is follow the stream north, and we'll be at his house."

"That's right," said Luke as he entered the clearing. "We leave as soon as you feel good enough to walk."

Luke sat down on the forest floor and took out a bulging sack of berries he had been collecting. We called Eket over and tucked into the fruit.

Once we had all eaten our fill and wiped our mouths clean of berry juice, we set off up the stream.

A different mood had settled over us. Maybe it was from the joy of being so close to Luke's house, or maybe we were just happy, but whatever the reason, the walk up the stream was filled with chatter and laughter.

We didn't talk about anything particularly significant, or things would get too serious. Instead we chatted about silly unimportant things that were fun to speak about anyway.

We all laughed when I told them about my encounter with Ashley and Colin that one night at Charlie's. And Zach told us all about his school, his friends (he went into a lot of detail about Dylan), and about the rival gangs he always had trouble with.

Luke even began to tell us about his childhood and when he was our age, recounting a bunch of funny, embarrassing things that had happened to him. Then Josie described a hilarious story about one of her sailing trips with her friend, and this guy that she hardly knew, and how they ran into a party boat and managed to do the craziest things. And then Tom started to tell us about when he went to the school prom—not expecting to dance at all—and how he ended up having to bust some moves by himself in front of the whole school!

Throughout all of our journeys and adventures, we hadn't really talked much to one another on a personal level. But after a few hours of cheerful conversation, I felt like we had all known each other for our whole lives.

"Should your house be somewhere around here, then?" Tom asked.

Luke nodded. "We should come across it at any minute now—" He froze. His brow furrowed as if he felt something strange. I felt it too.

That cramped, sickening we had all felt a while ago had returned. I could feel the presence of millions of people, pressing against me and moving around, brushing past me, but I saw nothing.

We were silent as we waited for it to go away. At long last, it did. We all exchanged fretful looks. The feeling had remained a lot longer than the first time we had felt it.

"Isabel?" Josie whispered. "What is that?"

"I have no idea," I responded with a shiver. The others were exchanging uneasy glances, and I knew it would only be a couple of seconds before Eket had a nervous breakdown.

"Come on!" I said, trying to sound like there was no trouble. "We're so close to Luke's house! Don't spook yourselves out. I'm sure it was nothing."

What a big, fat lie.

The others bought it, though. Or at least they pretended to. We ambled on up the course of water until we came to a little clearing. I trembled when I looked with more attention at the opening. The ground was covered in ash, and the trees' trunks were burnt all along their sides. I heard Luke swiftly draw in his breath as we observed what was in the glade, or what had been.

Once upon a time a house had stood there, but now, all that remained were two crumbling walls surrounded by scorched bricks.

I sidled up to the remains of Luke's house, feeling tears of defeat prick my eyes, and lightly touched the bricks. They were cold.

"There must have been a fire," choked out Josie.

"And a pretty long time ago judging by the temperature of the ash," I added.

Luke stared straight ahead and said nothing.

Eket spoke next. "We better get some rest. We have to have all our strength for the journey back to Malsama." I could tell he was trying his best to be mature and controlled, but he, too, was as sad as the rest of us.

In gloomy silence, we took out our blankets and camped out right there. Nobody had an appetite after we had just seen all that remained of Luke's house, so we all just went to sleep.

The moment I laid down, I began forming new ideas and plans in my head. Even though I wasn't the oldest, I still felt like the captain of our team. I began to ponder those strange sensations we had been having, then I was again tormented about my new fear: that I was wrong and had messed up by bringing Earth and Eeba together. The more I thought about it, the more I was convinced that this theory was right, even though I didn't really know why.

I went over all that had happened since Sage had jumped into the Well of Souls, and after comparing recent events to everything before that, I hit upon the strangest awareness.

I only realized it then, but ever since Sage had sacrificed herself, Eeba had begun to feel more and more forced and labored. It was like I was trying to violate some unbreakable law of nature.

This whole time I had relied on feelings and suspicions—no solid facts. And now my trust in my instincts had become a lot stronger.

I knew I had done the wrong thing.

Once I became conscious of this, I only grew more troubled. So what was I supposed to do now? Try and divide the two worlds again? Had Sage died for nothing?

I tried to ignore my breakthrough. I tried to convince myself that Earth and Eeba were supposed to come together, but I couldn't.

I thrashed around under my blanket, but it was impossible to sleep knowing what I had just realized.

The sun was already starting to rise by the time I had managed to close my eyes.

"You guys! Wake up!" shouted a voice.

I was instantly up. "What? What's the matter? Is everybody okay?"

Zach was running into the clearing, grinning from ear to ear and shouting, "Quickly! Wake up!"

At first, I thought he was being chased by some horrible monster, but then I reminded myself he was smiling. What was wrong with him?

In the meantime, the others had woken up and were obviously wondering what was the matter with Zach as well.

When he got to us, he bent over and put his hands on his knees, trying to catch his breath.

"What's the matter?" demanded Tom. "Tell us!"

Zach straightened up and said, "There's another house! Just that way, a few hundred yards from here!"

Luke's eyes widened and he sprinted in the direction where Zach was pointing. Tom rushed to follow him, and the rest of us ran to catch up with them, dragging our blankets behind us.

In front of me, I could see Tom and Luke had stopped and were both staring at something. Once I arrived to where they were standing, I gasped. Zach had been right. Just ahead stood another house, perfectly intact, ringed by a garden filled with weeds.

"M—my house," whispered Luke. "There's still hope!"

"Wait, if this is your house, then whose was that burnt one?" Eket asked, between pants.

Luke thought for a moment, then said, "Remember my friend Agatha I told you about? That must have been hers!"

"Well, come on then!" Josie exclaimed, making towards the house. We all followed her.

CHAPTER 21

AFTER PICKING OUR way through the overgrown garden, we finally made it to the door. With some difficulty, Luke forced it open and we walked inside.

Unfortunately, Eket couldn't fit through the door, so he had to wait outside, much to his annoyance. "It's not fair," he grumbled. "Why do I have to be so big?"

"You can keep watch," said Josie, trying to make him feel better.

It was obvious that nobody had been in that house for a long time. Cobwebs covered the walls, the smell of mold hung in the air, and each time I inhaled, I coughed from all the dust that had accumulated during the years. The sound of little paws scuttling across wooden floor boards made us all cautious of where we stepped.

A disgusted look crossed Josie's face as she looked

around. "So what exactly are we looking for again?" she asked.

Luke responded, "Well, right before Lucy left, she got these letters. She never let me read them, but I could tell they spooked her out. We should try and find them."

Tom shook his head. "I seriously doubt they would still be around." Then he continued in his scientific voice, "Over the course of the years the paper on which the letters were written would have biodegraded by now. Or at least be very, very moldy."

We all glared at him, furious that he was destroying our excitement. He shrugged sheepishly. "Well, it also depends where they were kept. I could be wrong."

I began peering into different corners of the house, searching for where the letters might be and soon everyone else was doing the same thing.

"Where exactly is Lucy's room?" Eket called from the window, peeking in on us to see how we were doing.

"Oh, it was just over here," said Luke, walking over to the door on the other side of the room. The rusty hinges squeaked as he opened the door, making me cringe.

We all filed into what had been Lucy's bedroom and continued our search in there. After about five minutes, I still hadn't found anything, and I was starting to lose hope. The others hadn't spotted anything either.

I was about to propose a breakfast break when Tom yelled, "I found something! I found something!" as he pulled his hand out from underneath the moldy mattress on the bed.

We all bolted up and crowded around him. "What did you find? What does it say?" we all demanded.

"Hey! I want to know, too!" shouted Eket, who had heard Tom's yelling. We all raced out of the house to where Eket stood waiting for us.

We huddled around Tom, who slowly unfurled his hand to show three thick envelopes. They had already been opened, so Tom just unfolded the top. As soon as he had done so, a great cloud of dust erupted from the envelope. But the letter inside was still mostly intact.

We all started chattering excitedly, but we shut up when Tom cleared his throat, and began to read.

Dear Lucy Curador,

I bring you information that will transform you forever. Literally.

You have been chosen to be the next Anima Magna, an all-powerful being, capable of things you've only dreamed of. Soon, you will start to lose all memory of this life, and you will be reincarnated as the Anima Magna.

Don't be alarmed. Once you have finished the transformation, the life you are currently living will seem like a dream.

Let me explain a little bit to you. The world you are on is actually just half of the world that used to be. At the beginning of time, there was one planet, but then it was Divided into separate alternate realities: Earth and Eeba.

What I did—and what all the Anima Magna before me did and now what you will have to do—is keep the two worlds separated by using the power of all the souls and spirits of people passed on.

People may call you evil, and you may think it as well at first, but you aren't. If we weren't there, all the souls would roam the two worlds, making it unbearable to live.

Tom paused and gulped. "Are you guys thinking what I'm thinking?"

"I don't know. What are you thinking?" Zach asked.

"You know that feeling we've all been having? That squished, crowded feeling? What if it's the presence of all the dead souls that we've released?"

I felt like someone had just slapped me.

"Guys, I think I should tell you something," I said. I needed to get it off my chest, and my friends had a right to know. "Ever since we destroyed the barrier between Earth and Eeba, this weird feeling has been growing inside of me . . . the feeling that we've been trying to break some important law of nature by bringing the two worlds together. I'm beginning to think that we did the wrong thing by releasing the souls."

Everyone was silent for a long, long time.

"You mean my sister died for nothing?" Zach growled with so much ferocity and hurt, it made me turn white.

"No, she didn't," I stammered, but Zach ignored me. He looked like he was going to hit someone—probably me. I tried to calm him down by saying how brave and courageous Sage had been, but that didn't do it.

Finally Eket said, "She didn't die in vain, Zach! She

died saving the boy she loved." He pointed a wing at Tom. "If she hadn't done what she did, Tom wouldn't be alive."

It surprised me to hear Eket speak with such wisdom and composure. He had always seemed rather childish to me.

Tom hung his head and whispered, "Zach, I miss her as much as you do."

For a second I thought Zach was going to burst into tears, but he shook his head, getting his emotions under control, and choked out, "Read on, Tom."

And so he did.

However, if people were to know there is another world just next to their own, they would get scared and try to bring them together, which would be a grave mistake.

That is why sometimes we must take drastic measures.

Every once in a while, somebody from Earth can see Eeba, and when that happens, you must suck their soul and add the power of their spirit to the others. None of us like doing this, but it is our duty.

"So this Anima Magna is obviously the same thing as the Soul Sucker, right?" Eket asked.

Josie nodded. "And if Odette is the Soul Sucker, then that means she's the Anima Magna, and that means Odette was . . ."

"Lucy," I finished, looking at Luke. "Your sister."

At first Luke didn't say anything, and we all felt that if somebody had to break this awkward silence, it should be him, so we all waited for him to speak. Finally he said, "That's not—that's not possible! My sister is not an ... evil being. She doesn't kill people, she doesn't . . ."

"You heard what it said in the letter," said Josie. "It was her duty."

Tom whipped his head around to look at her. "Are you saying that Odette was right, Josie? That she was right to suck my soul?"

I had never heard my brother speak so menacingly to anyone, and certainly never to my best friend! Josie just gulped and looked down at her lap, but she didn't nod or shake her head.

I could feel the tension rising quickly to its breaking point, so I said, "So what if that sensation we've been feeling actually is all the dead souls gathering around us? What do you say about that?"

"I don't want to decide anything right now," Josie said cautiously, not wanting to upset anyone again.

Zach nodded. "I agree."

Tom placed the letter back in its envelope, since the rest was too rotted away to read any further, and took the second. But it looked like that letter had gotten wet, because the ink was so smudged it had become totally illegible, so he went for the third.

Lucy Curador,

Your time to become the Anima Magna is nearing.

I will remind you: do not tell anyone about these letters or about anything you have learned. It would lead to Ultimate Disaster.

After reading my previous communications, you may have asked yourself why it's so important that Earth and

Eeba remain separate. Well this I will tell you: It is all a matter of a science.

The Second Law of Thermodynamics, also known as entropy, states that everything, all particles, must go from "complex" to "simple," from "order" to "disorder." That is why every building crumbles. That is why things break and fall apart.

Ever since the Big Bang, entropy has been increasing, that is, all the particles have been becoming more and more disorderly. This is why the world separated in the first place: to make the universe more chaotic.

If you were to try to bring Earth and Eeba together again, that would be, essentially, trying to break the law of entropy, and this would cause pure pandemonium.

You must guard the barrier of souls with your life. The state of the Universe depends on it.

I don't have to tell you any more. All the remaining information that the previous Anima Magna have gained will pass directly to you once you have completed your transformation.

Only after a minute did I manage to get my head around all those scientific laws and principles. But one thing was clear, with or without the science: I had made a terrible mistake. Just like Odette/Lucy/the Soul Sucker/Anima Magna had said.

We were all devastated. No one spoke as we went over in our heads what we had just heard.

"What have I done?" I breathed.

"What have we all done?" Josie corrected, but I wasn't listening to her.

"This is all my fault!" I shrieked, beside myself with frustration, hopelessness, and shame. "I have just done the most horrible thing that could be done! And I forced all of you into it!"

"Isabel, you didn't know," said Tom, moving to my side and putting his arm around me. "What if these letters are lies?" he added, trying to make me feel better and at the same time trying to convince himself that what he had just said was possible. But every single one of us knew the letters were right, and we were wrong. We felt it in our bones.

I slumped over on the ground, sobbing. "You read it yourself, Tom! Earth and Eeba are going to go into chaos, and it's all because of me!"

"Isabel, it's not your fault," began Josie, but I was hysterical.

"No, no, no. You're wrong! I've destroyed everything, and there's nothing we can do about it!"

Josie looked me directly in the eye. "Isabel, snap out of it. This was necessary to save Tom! You didn't know what you were doing. You just wanted your brother back, and you succeeded! We'll figure out a way to sort this out."

I sniffled and looked up, embarrassed at my breakdown. I shyly held out my arms to Josie. She smiled and hugged me.

Meanwhile, Eket turned to Luke. "Does this mean Odette was the good guy?"

But Luke didn't respond. He was gazing up at the sky, his face expressionless, and said, "Lucy became

Odette. Lucy is the Soul Sucker, the Anima Magna. Before I would have thought this was a bad thing, but after reading these letters . . . I don't know what to think anymore. It seems like she was the good guy."

"I'm glad you finally figured that out," said a female voice behind us.

We all jumped up, ready for another monster attack, but all we saw was a shadow between the trees.

"Come out where we can see you!" ordered Luke.

Obediently, the shadow made its way towards us, where it took the form of a woman.

"Odette?" I exclaimed.

"Lucy?" Luke shouted out at the same time.

The woman gave Luke a strange look. "Who's? I'm Odette. I'm already acquainted with the children, but who are you? You do look strangely familiar though . . ."

Luke grimaced as he remembered that this woman was not the same one she used to be. She wasn't his sister anymore, and the amount of pain that crossed his face as he reminded himself this almost made me cry.

"I'm Luke. Luke Curador," he said with a wince.

"Didn't you? Weren't you? Oh, never mind," she said, giving up as she tried to grasp a memory of her past life, but couldn't.

"What do you want with us?" Tom demanded. We were all wary of her, but we didn't feel the same way as we did before. After we had read those letters, we saw her in a different light.

"I listened to what you were saying," she said. "Now I hope you understand that what I did was for a reason."

We all silently nodded. At least I thought we had all nodded, but then Tom burst out, "I don't care why you did it! You tried to steal my soul! Don't come near me!"

I realized how much harder it must have been for Tom. I mean, he was the one who had nearly become a smudge, and all because of Odette. It was only reasonable that it would take more time for him to forgive her.

Suddenly, Odette seemed very tired and old. She sat down on the ground, exhausted, and put her hands over her face. "I remember . . . I remember I wasn't always like this. I remember I was someone else before Odette, but I can't . . . remember. As soon as I had enough energy, I followed you. And now this house . . . I don't know . . . there's just something about it."

I knew I had to say something. I knew we needed her help if we were going to set things right again. I swallowed my pride and forced my voice out. "Odette, I understand why you did what you did, and I know that what we did was wrong—well, partly wrong. I did what I did to save my brother, but that was it. We want to Divide the two worlds again."

Odette stared up at me. "Do you mean that?"

I nodded, and so did everyone else.

Odette gave a weak smile. "I hoped you would say that. There is only one thing that we can do. We must capture all the dead souls again and re-channel their power to recreate the barrier."

My eyes lit up. I felt like I would melt with relief and joy.

"You mean there's a way to fix things? This is great!" I shouted.

Odette's eyes shone for a second at seeing us so happy, but then she began coughing furiously.

"Ma'am, are you all right?" Eket inquired.

Finally Odette's coughing fit ended, and she got wobbly to her feet. "We need an ancient spell that the first Anima Magna left behind if something like this ever happened. It's a sort of calling to all the dead spirits to put them back in the Well of Souls."

"Well, where is it?" demanded Tom.

"Back at my palace, in a secret vault that only I can open," Odette told us between coughs.

"Then we've got to get back to your castle as soon as possible!" cried Zach. "Before Earth and Eeba join together and everything becomes a mess."

And so began another long journey to set things right again.

CHAPTER 22

AFTER STOMPING THROUGH the Forest for almost a day, we still hadn't found the hovercraft that we had left on the border.

We all stayed silent for the most part, all of us having a lot to think about. Luke trudged on in front of us, doing everything he could to not look at his sister—or what his sister had become.

I walked between Josie and Zach, trying to keep as much distance from Odette as possible. I know she was kind of the good guy now, but it was still terribly awkward, knowing that she had tried to destroy my brother, and then I had been the one to destroy everything. And in the end, I had screwed up. Sure, if I hadn't done it my brother would be a smudge by now, but I still felt awful.

I also didn't really understand how we were going to

fix it. Quite a lot of time had already passed since we had emptied the Well of Souls, and Earth and Eeba were dangerously close to merging together for good. Also, the cramped feelings of all the dead spirits were becoming more frequent and lasting longer. More of the color was being sapped out of Eeba, and it was just feeling more and more of a mess.

I glanced over at Odette. The first time I had seen her, she had looked like a gorgeous, healthy, young woman, full of self-confidence. But now she was paler and weaker and when she coughed, she had trouble stopping. Obviously there was something wrong even though she tried her best not to show it. She walked on, head held high, looking straight ahead of her.

Behind me, Eket banged into another tree again, but everyone ignored his loud ouch! We were all completely concentrated on getting to the hovercraft as soon as possible.

"This is hopeless!" complained Tom, after another half hour of walking.

Luke kept on going forward. "We'll be at the border any minute now."

"Yeah right. We're lost, admit it," Tom said.

"We are not lost," Luke said, glaring at Tom. "Just be patient."

Even though I wanted to believe Luke, I had to agree with my brother. It hadn't taken us this long on our way to the house.

"Can we take a break now?" Eket whined. "My feet hurt!"

Tom rolled his eyes. "Sure."

At the same time, Luke said. "No."

They glowered at each other, and I knew I should do something before they did. But to tell the truth, I was never good at breaking up fights. I'm usually the one in it.

Thankfully, Odette spoke up. "I think I see something behind a tree up ahead."

Luke instantly rushed forward to see what was there. When he turned around again, a smug look crossed his face. "It's the hovercraft."

We all cheered, except for Tom, who crossed his arms over his chest and looked at his toes.

We all raced to climb into the vehicle and rest our tired feet, even Tom. Even though it was a rather tight squeeze, we still all managed to fit comfortably enough. I felt sorry for Eket that he couldn't get in too, but he seemed happy enough to fly over our heads.

Feeling the sun on my face and the wind in my hair reminded me how good it felt to be out in the open, out of the dark, restricting Forest.

Hours flew by as quickly as the landscape did, until, before we knew it, the sun had set and the air that was blowing into my face grew cold.

We wanted to find a place to shelter under, but only plains stretched on either side of us. Luke slowed down, and he was about to give up and stop the hovercraft when I saw something in the distance.

"Look!" I exclaimed and pointed to a little bump in the ground not so far off. Immediately, Luke picked up speed, and in no time we had stopped in front of the weird bump.

I quickly climbed out of the vehicle to inspect it. As I neared, I realized it was a kind of hut, partially underground with only half a door and a window protruding from the floor, just enough for me to be able to see and identify them.

I moved to open it when Tom called from behind me, "Be careful, Isabel! Who knows what could live in there?"

"Don't worry!" I shouted back. "It looks pretty safe." I gently knocked on the door as the others came closer. When nobody answered, I knocked again, this time harder. I was almost at the conclusion that it was empty, when I heard a great commotion from inside.

The sound of footsteps neared the door, and we all held our breath as the door creaked open.

A veiled face appeared and grumbled in a female voice, "Who is it?"

I was instantly suspicious. The black cloth covering the woman's face didn't allow me to see anything. I was about to suggest that we leave when Odette spoke up. "Excuse me, we have traveled long and far, and we were wondering if you could let us stay for the night."

I nudged her in the stomach, "Odette!" I hissed. "This person is kinda creepy. I don't think this is such a good idea."

"We?" said the woman at the door.

"Yes," Tom replied, trying to show that he was one of the important leaders of our group as well.

"I guess you can come in," the woman said and pushed the door open wide. We all shuffled into a dark, cramped house, except for Eket, who assumed his typical position just outside the hut with his head peeking through the window.

We descended down a few stairs to get to the main part of the house.

I tried to take a better look at the interior, but there wasn't enough light. "Aren't there any lamps in here?" I asked.

"Yeah," Josie agreed. "I can hardly see a thing."

A sharp giggle emerged from under the veil. "Lamps? Light? Why would I need those?"

I glanced at the others to see if they were thinking the same thing I was—that this lady was a fruitcake.

Then Zach spoke up. "Why are you wearing a veil?"

I silently groaned. It's obvious that someone wears a veil to hide something, and when someone wants to hide something, they normally don't want to talk about it.

Of course, I was dying with curiosity too, but still . . .

Thankfully, the woman didn't seem offended by Zach's blunt question. She just chuckled again and said, "See for yourself."

Her hand grasped the edge of the black silk and with one dramatic flourish, she pulled it away from her face. Everyone except Odette gasped as we saw that where a pair of eyes should have been, there was only white. Not a milky white, not a creamy white, but an intense dazzling ivory that seemed to look deep into me and light up the darkness around us. And then I understood why it didn't matter to her if there were lights or not.

She was blind.

CHAPTER 23

IT TOOK US a few minutes to get used to her eyes, but it seemed rude to ask her to put the veil back on, so we learned to handle her white stare.

"I'm Rosie, by the way," she said, breaking the uncomfortable silence. On cue, we all introduced ourselves as she gestured for us to sit down. "Actually, I think there might be a few candles in that drawer over there," she muttered quietly to herself as she went to get them. Even though she was blind, she knew her way around her house perfectly well.

Once the wick had been lit, I felt much more at ease. We all sat down on a bit of a shabby sofa, and Rosie took out some sheets from another drawer. When she finally turned around, it was the first time I managed to see her face clearly.

She was much younger than I thought she would be,

and she was actually quite pretty, although I doubt she even knew it. She wore a plain, black dress made of the same material as the veil, and her black hair was held up with a big leather clip.

The contrast between her white eyes and her dark clothes and hair was quite striking.

Rosie said, "Over the years, I've gotten many visitors looking for lodging, but never quite so many at the same time!"

"We are very grateful to you for letting us stay," said Josie.

"Oh, it's nothing," she replied. "Here, I'll show you where you will be sleeping." She gave us two rooms: one for the girls and one for the boys. I could tell Luke and Tom weren't excited about sharing a room. They were both acting so stupid, each of them fighting to be the leader.

Even with so many thoughts and worries swirling around my head, I fell asleep just as my head touched the pillow.

*

A cold hand lightly touched my shoulder, and I instantly jerked awake to find myself staring into Rosie's sightless eyes. It took all my self-control not to scream at the top of my lungs. I half-expected her to take out a knife from behind her back and stab me like some sort of maniacal killer. But she only held a finger to her lips and motioned for me to follow her.

"What's the matter?" I whispered as I got out of bed. I noticed that the whole house was silent except for a few snores, so I knew my friends must have still been sleeping. Rosie just handed me a candle and continued walking down the hall.

Why would she wake me up in the middle of the night? Where was she taking me? All of sudden I realized that maybe this wasn't such a good idea. After encountering so many horrible and vicious monsters, I had become skeptical of everything, and I couldn't help pondering if this blind lady was leading me into some sort of trap.

Abruptly, Rosie stopped in front of a small cellar door. Even though she was sightless, she moved with surprising smoothness and grace. She quickly pushed open the door and shuffled in and I had no choice but to follow her.

The sound of the door creaking as it closed behind me made me feel sick. Here I was, trapped in a cellar with a creepy blind lady in the dead of night. This didn't really seem like such a great situation to be in.

"Don't be scared." Rosie said, which didn't make me feel much better. I slowly edged away from her, but she only came closer, as if she could sense me. She whispered, "Isabel, I may not see, but I can tell you're not from around here. Not from this . . . world."

I gulped. "I-I think I should go b-b-back to bed," I said and reached for the doorknob behind me. In a flash, her hand shot out and grabbed my wrist in an unexpectedly strong grip. I whimpered, "Please don't hurt me."

"I wasn't planning on it." And she let go of me. "Isabel, listen to me. No matter how much you try and convince yourself, and no matter how much Luke and Tom bicker, you are the leader. You're the one who brought all these people together."

"How do you know . . . ?"

"I may not see what is happening in the present, but I can catch glimpses of the past and the future, that is why I have brought you—and only you—here tonight. As a Diviner, I am permitted to give you something to help you on your journey into the future. I won't tell you exactly what will happen. That would be no fun at all! But I can give you this." Rosie reached into the darkness behind her and brought back her fist clenched around something that I couldn't quite see just yet.

I held my breath as Rosie unfurled her hand and brought the object to the light of my candle.

I admit I had been expecting a sword or a magical cape, something heroic and enchanting, so when a saw a plain, orange marble sitting in the palm of her hand, I couldn't help feeling disappointed.

"Um, are you sure this is it?" I asked.

"Of course! But don't think to thank me," Rosie said, slightly offended.

"Oh, thank you. Er, I guess I should go back to bed."

"Oh yes, naturally. But Isabel, if you tell another soul about the gift I just gave you, it won't work when you'll most need it," Rosie warned me.

I nodded and made for the door, but then I hesitated. A question had just sprung into my head. "Rosie?

You said you were a Diviner. Are there others like you who can tell the future?"

"Of course there are, and most of them much better than me," Rosie responded.

"You wouldn't happen to know Shaman Oring of the Erinav tribe?"

"Oring? Why of course I know him! He thought he was so much better than the rest of us."

"Well, he's changed now. He's very nice," I assured her. "But is it possible that he could have made a mistake? That he messed up telling the future?"

Rosie scoffed. "Oh no. If Oring said something about the future, then it's true. That old goat, always was something special. Why do you ask?"

I frowned. "He told us something. He said that Luke is Zach's father, but it's not possible, right?"

At this, Rosie's expression softened. "My child, Diviners have no real sense of time. Maybe it's not something that is or was, but something that will be."

"What's that supposed to—?" I tried to ask, but Rosie interrupted me, placing her hand on my shoulder. "I think it's time you go back to sleep."

In bed I couldn't stop thinking about what she had said and the gift she had given me. What was waiting for me in my future? And what was this thing that could be defeated with a marble?

CHAPTER 24

KEEPING MY MOUTH shut about Rosie's gift was proving to be quite difficult. I so wanted to tell Josie and ask her what she thought about it. But if I did, it wouldn't work. Or maybe Rosie had just said that to scare me. No, that wasn't very likely. I had to keep quiet, period.

All throughout breakfast I kept glancing over at the blind lady, in case she would give me some sort of sign that would help me know the marble's power. But then I realized how stupid I was being. She couldn't even see my brief looks in her direction. How could I expect her to respond to them?

As soon as we finished eating, Rosie showed us to the door, saying, "Go on. You'd best be on your way."

We all said good-bye to her and squeezed into the hovercraft, Eket standing alongside it. Luke started the engine and we zoomed forward, leaving Rosie waving behind us.

"Oh my God, she was creepy," muttered Tom, once we were far away from Rosie's little hut.

"Tom!" I snapped, "She was really nice to let us all stay the night. You shouldn't say that about her."

"Oh come on, Isabel. She was totally freaky, with those white eyes and black veil. It was a wonder she didn't kill us all in our beds!" Tom continued.

Why was my brother acting like such an idiot? First he was fighting with Luke, now he was saying mean things about a woman who had helped us. What was wrong with him?

"Tom, just shut up," I said sternly. He rolled his eyes, and everyone else stared out at the landscape, not wanting to get between our brother-sister argument.

A rough jerk of the hovercraft broke the tension.

"Luke!" Zach complained.

Luke's eyes widened. "It wasn't me!"

"What's the matter?" demanded Odette, "What's going on?"

All of a sudden, the hovercraft started halting, then zooming forward, then abruptly stopping again. "The hovercraft! It's gone crazy, I can't control it!" shouted Luke.

Then the vehicle began to spin, all the while shooting forward at a speed that increased every second.

Eket squawked as he flew to catch up with the hovercraft, and everyone in it screamed and hung onto the sides so we wouldn't fall out.

It was going so fast that the wind stung my eyes, but I forced them open and saw in the distance a giant hole in the ground. I instantly realized that the hovercraft would probably go down that hole and we would, too, if we didn't get out as soon as possible.

"Eket!" I yelled, "Get us out of here!"

Miraculously, he understood me and wrapped his two claws around Odette and Luke's waists, pulled them out of the moving hovercraft, and tossed them onto the ground.

I let out another shriek as I saw that we were nearing the hole. Eket managed to grab onto Tom but as he reached for Josie, the hovercraft gave another jerk, and the giant parrot was sent flying with just Tom in his grip.

I only succeeded in glancing quickly over my shoulder at Tom, Luke, Odette, and Eket sprawled across the landscape behind me, before Josie, Zach and I were sucked into the big gap in the ground.

*

As I opened my eyes, I felt a sharp pain in my wrist. I tried to move it, but I couldn't. I looked around and realized we were in a long tunnel, but I couldn't see the big hole that we had come in through. I inspected my wrist and saw that it was stuck to what looked like a large slab of metal. I called out, "Josie! Zach! Where are you?"

I heard a groan and a muffled "Over here!" to my right. I tried to get up to walk over to the sound, but I couldn't. My wrist was stuck fast to the hunk of metal, and it wouldn't allow me to budge.

I scanned my left side and saw the hovercraft, crumpled against the hunk of metal. Then I heard Josie screaming, "I can't move!"

"I can!" came Zach's voice from further off in front of me. "I'll come to you."

There was a loud crash of tumbling rocks, and then the top of his blond head came into view.

I strained my head to the side to get a glimpse of Josie to see if she was all right. Finally her blue eyes met mine, and I asked, "You okay?"

She gasped. "I guess, but my neck is attached to this big block of whatever this is."

"It's okay," I reassured her. "Zach's coming to help us."

Zach trudged up to me and stared at the chunk of metal that Josie and I were attached to. Suddenly, his jeans' pocket bulged and pointed towards us. "What the—?" he said. It was as if something in his pocket was pulling him towards the metal. He reached into his pocket and pulled out a coin. He abruptly let go, and it shot forward and stuck to the chunk Josie and I were attached to.

His eyes lit up and he said, "I think I understand what happened. Here's my theory . . ."

"Hurry up, Einstein," Josie managed to choke out.

"I think this block of metal is a really strong magnet. That's why the hovercraft was drawn to it!" Zach continued.

"But why are we stuck to it?" I demanded.

"Are you wearing anything metallic?" he asked.

I thought for a second and examined my wrist. "Oh

yeah!" I exclaimed. "The buckle on my watch!" With my other hand, I managed to unbuckle the watch from my wrist, and I was free.

I ran over to Josie with Zach right behind me. The back of her neck was stuck fast to the magnet and her face was turning purple.

"Your necklace!" I shouted, as I noticed a thin chain with a flower charm dangling at the end. With the intent of trying to unclasp the necklace and release her, I moved toward Josie, but Zach beat me to it. His hands were already around her neck, and I felt my cheeks turning scarlet with jealousy and anger when I saw how close their faces were.

I spun around on my heel and stalked off to the crushed up hovercraft. It had been attracted by the magnet with so much force that when the vehicle slammed into it, it was destroyed. There was no way we would ever drive in it again.

I peered inside to see if there were any bags or supplies we could salvage. I pulled out one of the backpacks and opened it. There was still some food intact in there, but I couldn't reach any of the other bags.

At that point, Josie and Zach came over and stood at my side. "So, what are we going to do now?" Josie whispered.

Only then did our situation really sink in. We were separated from the rest of the group, trapped underground, with hardly any food, and we were in a rush to get to Odette's castle, but now we had no idea where we were!

"We're doomed," I muttered, plunking myself on the ground. We found ourselves in a long tunnel with a high ceiling. We were obviously underground based on the earthy smell and a dampness in the air. But I still couldn't see the hole that we had been pulled through.

"Come on, Isabel. Pull yourself together," said Zach, sitting down next to me. I edged away from him. After seeing him and Josie, I wasn't really in the mood to have him cheer me up.

Josie said, "It'll be easy. All we have to do is find our way back to the surface."

I looked at her. "Yeah, easier said than done." I put my head in my hands and stared at the ceiling. Then I noticed something that I hadn't noticed before. A squiggly line carved into the dirt all along the ceiling traveled down a hall. A strange sensation came over me, and I knew that there was something very important about that line. I pointed it out to Josie and Zach, but they didn't say anything.

I grabbed the only surviving bag and began to follow the line. "Come on," I instructed them.

"What are you doing?" demanded Josie. "You have no idea where you're going."

"Yes I do," I responded. "I'm following the line."

"That sounds like a completely foolproof plan," said Zach, sarcastically.

I glared at him. "You have any better ideas?"

When he didn't respond, I whirled around and continued walking with Josie at my side.

In a few minutes we arrived at a fork in the underground passage. "Well?" asked Zach. "What do we do now?"

I looked up and saw that the line went down the tunnel on my left. "This way," I replied and kept going.

"Do you think the others are okay?" Josie asked me, after another few minutes of walking.

I remembered what Rosie had told me, that I was the leader everyone depended on. I wasn't so sure myself, but I knew I couldn't let the others get scared. But on the other hand, I didn't want to lie to my best friend and give her high expectations, so I answered in full truth. "I don't know. But I hope so."

She nodded as if that was the reply she knew I would give.

Zach trudged along behind us in complete silence, and I started to feel bad that I had been so hard on him. I realized he must have felt pretty lonely and left out. I mean, with Josie and I being best friends, there wasn't really any space for Zach. I mean, he was literally from another planet. I decided to try and include him a bit more.

I slowed down to his pace and tried to start a conversation. Josie followed suit.

"So," I said. "What do you plan on doing when we've re-Divided Earth and Eeba again?"

He shrugged. "Go back to school I guess. Although it'll be really weird after all these adventures."

"Yeah," Josie agreed. "I—"

She was interrupted by the strong, cramped feeling of all the dead souls around us, and this time it was more forceful and fierce than ever. It made my eyes water and my knees wobble as my skin brushed the essence of so many lifeless spirits.

Once it stopped, I straightened myself up and looked at Zach and Josie. "We really have to hurry," I said, telling them what they already knew.

We walked on, nearly jogging, all the while glancing up at the ceiling to check our track. We had gone on for maybe a couple hours, and I was getting tired, when I stopped. In front of us the path we were going down had split into four other tunnels, but the one that the line continued down was glowing a strange green light. I didn't know if this was good or bad.

I pointed it out to Zach and Josie and asked, "Shall we keep going anyway?"

"Well, we've followed it this far," Josie pointed out.

"I say we go for it," agreed Zach. Then in a lower voice: "Even though it creeps the hell out of me."

Cautiously, we made our way towards the emerald glow. The tunnel led into a great cavern where large lanterns hung from the ceiling, emanating the green light. My nose wrinkled as I smelled something. It wasn't exactly a bad smell, but it was just strange. And really sweet.

"Can you smell that—?" I started to say but was interrupted by Zach's elbow in my ribs.

"Look," he whispered and pointed to the far end of the room. I didn't see anything, except shadows. Wait. Shadows of what?

Without warning, a monstrous figure emerged from

the darkness, and with it came an unbearable heat. In fact, it seemed as if a fire was surrounding this creature because with every step it took, the hotter the air became. Then it stopped in front of one of the lanterns and green light flooded over it, letting us finally see it clearly.

"A d-dragon?" Josie stammered.

She was right. Standing before us was a dragon the size of Eket. Scales the same color as the green light covered his skin and coal black spikes ran down his spine, coming to a stop at the end of his long tail. He opened his mouth revealing rows of razor sharp teeth.

Seeing this terrifying monster before me, I did the only sensible and noble thing I could do.

I threw myself to my knees and whimpered, "P-please don't e-eat us!"

Then I felt a great wave of heat washing over me, and I knew he must have been breathing fire on us. At the same time I heard Josie and Zach screaming and diving for cover next to me.

Only a few seconds went by, but they felt like hours, and still the dragon hadn't give us any mercy. The heat was insufferable, and my hair was plastered to my face as sweat streamed out of my pores.

Finally, I got the guts to look up, and when I did, I could scarcely believe my eyes.

The dragon was laughing.

"What's so funny?" I demanded, trying to sound fierce and confident. Which is hard to do when you're lying on the floor in front of a dragon.

"Silly girl," it said in a deep, gravelly voice. "Why would I eat you?"

I slowly got up, followed by Zach, and then Josie. I cleared my throat and said, "You're a dragon, right? Isn't that what you do? Eat people?"

The dragon looked taken aback and replied, "I wouldn't do that. I don't eat meat."

Seriously? Was this a trick? Or was he vegetarian dragon?

I turned to the other two and whispered, "Do you think he's telling the truth?"

Zach observed the dragon, thoughtfully. Finally, he said, "I'm pretty sure he is. At school, I studied dragons—there's a particular kind of species that are herbivores—and they all have that sort of pearl thing on their forehead. Trust me, dragons are the only thing worth studying about."

I craned my neck to try and see what he was talking about. Sure enough, stuck on the dragon's brow, was a scale that had become spherical and white. And pearly.

I couldn't believe our luck! Of all the dragons on Eeba, we had come across a vegetarian one. Thank you, God!

Josie spoke up,. "Excuse me Mr., um, Dragon, but do you happen to know how we can get back to the surface?"

The dragon smiled his toothy grin and said, "Why, you just follow that wavy line," and pointed to the ceiling. "In about a day you will reach a giant hole that will lead you up to the outside."

I smiled. Finally I had done something right! We

were going the correct way, and I had figured it out all by myself. But then I started, "Wait," I said, "did you say 'a day?'"

The dragon nodded vigorously. "Precisely. But you'll probably want to start your walk tomorrow morning. It's not very wise to head out at this hour."

"Why?" Josie asked. "How long until night time?"

"Not very long," he replied, "and that's when all the under-crabs come out. Horrible creatures. Always messing around with my experiments."

"Under-crabs?" Josie asked.

"Experiments?" said Zach at the same time.

The dragon chuckled. "Why don't you come with me? You could stay the night, and I could answer your questions."

I hesitated. "I don't know . . ."

Zach interrupted me. "Don't worry, it's fine. We can go with him."

I raised an eyebrow at him.

"Trust me," he said.

"Fine," I said, giving in, "but if we die, I will so kill you."

He grinned. "Whatever you say."

The dragon led us to the back of the cavern, where we followed him down another smaller tunnel (but still big enough to fit him), but this one didn't have the wiggly line carved into the ceiling. We ended up in a bigger cavern than the first. In the middle of the room was a big slab of rock that was carved into what looked like an enormous couch.

The dragon sat himself down on it and said, "I am Rasoqi. Now what are three kids like you doing underground? And why isn't there an adult with you?"

After we had all introduced ourselves, I told him about how we had gotten separated from the rest of the group because the hovercraft lost control on account of the giant magnet.

The dragon nodded. "You wanted to know what my experiments were about? Well, that's it. I have spent forever trying to find out the properties of that metal. Sometimes its magnetic tug is stronger, sometimes it's weaker. I want to find out how it got here, and how exactly it was created."

"So you're a scientist?" Zach asked, interested.

"Yes. But enough talk about me. You wanted to know what under-crabs were?" Rasoqi asked Josie.

Before Josie could respond, Zach butted in, saying, "Under-crabs live underground, and they look like giant crabs . . ."

"Wow, genius," I muttered sarcastically. "I had figured that much out from the name." The words were out before I could stop them.

Zach scowled. "Fine. If you're so smart, why don't you tell us all about under-crabs?"

I guess I was too proud to let him think I would back off just because he snapped at me. So I continued, "Well, using my brain, I can understand that under-crabs are dangerous crab-like creatures or something that come out at night and live underground."

Zach rolled his eyes, "What an expert."

"Thank you," I retorted.

Out of the corner of my eye I saw Rasoqi standing up and saying, "Um, Josie, could you help me get some water from the well over here?"

Josie got the hint and said, "Oh, yeah, sure."

Once they left, Zach and I glared at each other. He opened his mouth to say something when I snapped, "Good grief Zach! Can't you just let me have the last word for once?"

I expected him to shout something back, but instead he grinned and said, "Isabel, you are such a donkey."

"Where the hell do you—!" I began, but Zach just laughed. I crossed my arms and frowned at him. "What's so funny?"

"Do you even have to ask for the last word? You technically already had it. My God, you are just so stubborn, you don't even realize it!"

"Hmmph," I said, trying to sound like I didn't care, but actually I was doing my best not to laugh myself. Just looking at that ridiculous grin stretched across Zach's face made me want to crack up.

I went a few seconds with a straight face, but then he grabbed my hand and said, "Come on, Isabel! Lighten up!"

Just the feel of my hand in his sent shivers up my spine, and my frown instantly dissolved into a smile.

But then his words went to my heart. Lighten up? Was he crazy? How was I supposed to do that if I had the responsibility of the fate of two worlds on my shoulders?

Before I could say anything else, Rasoqi and Josie came back, and seeing the smiles on our faces, understood that we had made up.

As soon as Josie sat down, she yawned, making Zach and I do the same thing. Only then did I realize how heavy my eyelids felt.

The dragon said, "You better go to sleep if you want to make it to the surface by tomorrow evening."

"Do you have any blankets?" asked Josie. "Or maybe pillows?"

Rasoqi looked confused. "What are pillows?"

"Oh, God," Zach groaned under his breath.

"They're fluffy things that you can lay down on when you sleep," Josie explained, patiently.

Rasoqi shrugged. "I sleep on the rock. If you like, I'll give you some space . . ."

Josie and I looked at each other. I shook my head and said, "Thanks, but I think I'll pass."

Once we had all gotten as comfortable as we could on the dirt floor, I tried to go to sleep. Listening to everyone's breathing calmed me down, and soon I heard the breaths slowing down and becoming deeper and more steady. However I couldn't fall asleep so easily. There was something nagging me at the back of my mind.

I reached into my pocket and gently took Rosie's gift out. Rolling the marble between my thumb and index finger, I gazed at it, trying to figure out its secret.

As I stared more intensely, I noticed a little spark of blue that gleamed in the center of the marble. I gasped and turned it over to try and see it more clearly. But as soon as I did so, the glint vanished, and the marble returned to an orange and white swirl. I sighed with disappointment and rolled over onto my side. Rasoqi was curled up just a few feet away. For a second, I cursed my madness. What the hell was I doing here with a colossal dragon at my side? But if he really planned on eating us, he could have done it a lot sooner.

With that reassuring thought fresh in my mind, I shut my eyes.

Chapter 25

Here's a piece of information you probably already know: sleeping on a dirt and rock floor without a blanket or a pillow is not comfortable.

At all.

I woke up and my bones ached all over. I glanced at my wrist to check the time, but upon seeing bare skin I remembered I didn't have it anymore. It was still stuck to the giant magnet.

I checked to see if anyone else was already awake, but they were all fast asleep except . . .

Suddenly the ground began to shake as Rasoqi walked in. Zach and Josie were instantly awake.

"Where did you go?" I asked.

Rasoqi replied, "Just fixing up one of my experiments. I see you are all awake."

"We are now," Zach muttered.

Josie stretched and yawned. "OK, I'm up. Now could you please show us the way to the tunnel that will lead us to the surface?" Josie asked.

"Right this way."

Sure enough, in a few seconds we were standing underneath a ceiling with a wriggly line etched into it.

After thanking Rasoqi again and again, we began to make our way down the tunnel.

Almost an hour had passed when I started to feel hungry. We hadn't had any dinner or breakfast, and we had been walking non-stop since we had woken up. We only had a small amount of food, and we had already eaten most of it for lunch the day before. We had to save it. So I just let my stomach keep talking.

The mood was oddly cheerful, considering we were a day closer to complete chaos than we were yesterday and we still hadn't found the others. Another hour passed, and we chatted about nothing of great importance.

So far, the journey had been unexpectedly smooth, but I knew that on Eeba, it was only a matter of time before something dangerous would happen.

Touch wood. The problem was that there wasn't any wood underground.

As Josie and I talked about what we were probably missing at school, out of the corner of my eye I saw Zach's brow furrow. I wondered what was wrong, but I didn't think much of it. We had just come to a turn in the road when I heard a strange crackling noise in the tunnel up ahead.

We all snapped to attention. Creeping cautiously forward, we made our way towards the sound.

A blinding light came out of nowhere, and we were smothered in a barrage of heat.

"What's happening?" I screamed. But nobody answered.

After a great effort, I managed to open my eyes, and I saw that we were surrounded by a hurricane of flames.

"Josie! Zach! Can you hear me?" I yelled, trying to find them. But the fire was impossibly thick, and I couldn't see anything except for giant, compressing walls of orange and red.

The heat pressed on my lungs, and I began to feel dizzy. But something didn't make sense. If there had been a fire this big, we would have smelled the smoke first and from farther away.

"Zach!" I shouted. "What's happening?"

After a painstakingly long moment I heard his response. "This is a magic fire! It starts without a cause and can only be extinguished with a huge amount of water, which we don't have!"

I tried to think straight, but my head was feeling light, and I could hardly breathe. The fire was getting closer and closer to me, and the sound of its hissing and snapping roared in my ears.

I gasped and tried to think of something to do, but the heat was too unbearable. I opened my mouth to yell something to my friends, but no sound came out. I tried to take a deep breath, but only a minute amount of air entered my lungs. And even if it was a pathetic breath, I knew it could very well be my last.

My knees crumpled, and I finally collapsed to the ground, choking. As I did so, I heard a small smash, but I didn't even have enough strength to look up.

I braced myself, preparing to be overcome by a final wave of heat . . . but it never came.

On every side, I heard fizzing and hissing, but I didn't open my eyes. Then I felt a bit of wetness curl around my body. Only when I felt myself being lifted up off the ground by something did I open my eyes.

I was floating on a great swell of water! The fire was out and the huge waves of flames had been replaced with enormous waves of water. I had no idea how it had happened, or how it had happened so fast. All I knew was that I had to find my friends.

I dove under to spot them more quickly. Josie was treading water just to my left, and I saw Zach a bit farther away. I swam to where Josie was spluttering and coughing. When I reached her, and I had surfaced, she gazed at me, wide-eyed.

"What happened?" she choked out. "One moment we're surrounded by fire, now water? This is a nightmare!"

I opened my mouth to tell her I didn't know but we had to get to Zach, but a giant wave broke over our heads and I got a mouth full of water.

It made no sense! How was it possible to have waves underground? Well, no time to question it. We had to find Zach and get to somewhere dry as soon as possible.

I waited for the surge of water to pass over me and

then I came back up again. Thankfully, Zach had already found his way to us, and I saw him treading water next to me. The moment I noticed him, I seized his arm and with my other hand grabbed hold of Josie.

"Come on! We've got to stick together!" I yelled.

I looked around, searching for a place to go, but the tunnel had become completely flooded and still the water was rising, bringing us closer to the rough, jagged ceiling.

Suddenly, I felt a sharp digging in my arm, and I turned to see Josie, white with terror as she stared at something behind me while pinching my skin with her nails.

I slowly turned around. Gulp. Towering over us was a ten-foot tall wave that I could feel sucking me backwards before it broke on top of our heads.

Now generally, I hate water. I mean, pools and lakes are fine, but when it comes to the ocean, I don't do well. I hated the idea of being degraded so easily by this force of nature, and the only thing I could do was let the immense waves toss me around like I was nothing but a rag doll. I wanted to be the one who changes things, and I like having things under control, but in the middle of the ocean, that's not really possible.

And now, seeing this enormous wave hanging over us made me feel sick. I was so wrapped in dread that at first I didn't hear Zach yelling, "Come on! Let's swim!"

"What the hell are you talking about?" Josie hollered.

"Let's swim ahead so we can catch the wave and ride it!" he yelled back.

Only then did I understand his words. "Are you freaking insane?" I screamed. "We can't ride that wave! It would kill us!"

"We have to try!" Zach shouted. "It's the only chance we've got!"

Before I could protest, he and Josie were already pulling me through the water, trying to get ahead of the wave before it broke on us.

I didn't dare look behind me. Panic was already consuming me, and if I glanced back, I wouldn't be able to go on. I kicked my legs and pushed myself forward with all my strength, at the same time holding onto Josie and Zach.

The moment the wave crashed down, I thought I was going to die right then and there. I had never seen a wave that big, and when I felt all of its watery power behind me, propelling us forward at such a breakneck speed, I knew I never wanted to see one that big again.

So many times I thought I would break from my friends' grasp, but I clung on and didn't let go. I screamed and screamed, consequently choking and gasping, but I couldn't tear myself away from the notion of all that water—and power—behind me. I didn't know exactly how much time had passed, but at some point, I felt the water calming, and the push behind us begin to slow down.

I looked up and noticed that the ceiling was much farther away than it had been before, and I realized that the water we were floating in was magically going down.

In only a few seconds, all that was left were a few puddles on the ground. Immediately, I began spitting and coughing up water while wiping the wetness out of my eyes. Only then did I become aware that I was practically on Zach's lap. I jerked up and began wringing out my shirt, trying to ignore Zach's smug smile.

"Oh, wipe that stupid grin off your face!" I laughed. But his smile only grew even bigger.

"You can't admit even for once that I was right?" he asked, amused.

I jokingly narrowed my eyes at him and continued shivering in my soaked clothes.

"Ahem!" Josie cleared her throat loudly to get our attention. "Excuse me? Would someone like to explain to me what the heck just happened?"

"Well, that was a kind of magic fire we ran into, also known as bioflames," explained Zach. "Bioflames are a kind of fire that's almost alive. Nobody can start it, and it just appears without warning and surrounds you. Then over time, it consumes its victims, as if it were eating them."

"Isn't it really dangerous to have a fire like that, just, on the loose that is practically impossible to control?" asked Josie, in a tone higher than her usual voice.

"Bioflames are actually really rare. We were pretty unlucky to run into them. Anyway, it's not the bioflames that I'm confused about. It's all that water! Where the heck did it come from?"

I shrugged. "I know! It makes no sense! Unless . . ." I trailed off as my hand found its way into my pocket. I felt around for the smooth surface of the marble, but it wasn't there. The only thing that I found was a small orange and white husk of glass.

Suddenly, I understood. That little blue spark I saw must have been a water sign. Then when I fell and I heard something smash—that must have been the marble cracking and releasing that power, creating all that water!

"Isabel? What is it?" Josie inquired, when she saw me gasping with amazement.

"Oh, nothing." I said quickly. "Just got some water . . . in my throat . . ." and I faked a bit of coughing. I don't know why I didn't tell her. Maybe it was because Rosie had told me not to say anything, and even though I had already used it I didn't want to take any chances. Or maybe because it was such an absurd idea, and I didn't want Zach to laugh at me. Whatever the case, I kept my mouth shut.

CHAPTER 26

ABOUT TWO-THIRDS of all the time I had spent on Eeba, I had been walking. And I was sick of it. Always moving. Always on the go. I just wanted to sit down and stay there without having a care in the world. Obviously my wish wasn't granted.

Hours trailed into the next, and hunger clawed at my empty stomach. I figured that our journey wouldn't take as long since the wave had swept us a long way ahead but it was still dragging on.

I didn't know how long we had walked, but at one point I looked up to check our course but the line had stopped! It just ended right there!

Panic rose up in my throat as I pointed it out to Josie and Zach. "Shouldn't there be a hole that will lead us up to the surface then?" asked Josie. She jogged ahead and then shouted back, "Guys! It's up here!"

We caught up with her and saw that the ceiling of the tunnel opened up, allowing us to see the outside world.

I felt the breeze coming from up there and I smiled. It felt like we had been stuck underground forever! I couldn't wait to stop breathing stale air and feel the sun!

But then a thought struck me. "Wait, how are we supposed to get up there?" The hole was quite a stretch above us, and there was no way we could reach it.

Zach smacked his palm on his forehead. "Oh my God."

I crouched down to see the hole at a better angle, but it was no use. We could never get to it by ourselves. "Well that's just brilliant," I muttered, sarcasm dripping from every word.

Josie sat down on the ground next to me. "So how will we—?"

I screamed as I saw a giant face shove its way down into the hole. I instantly regretted it when I noticed that it was a parrot's face.

Zach and Josie had jumped up in alarm but started laughing when they saw the cause of my shock.

I caught my breath but couldn't help chuckling too. "Holy crap, Eket! You scared the hell out of me!"

The bird grinned as much as his beak would allow and yelled, "Luke! Tom! Odette! Look who I found!" Then he turned back to us. "I just knew you guys would pop up somewhere unexpected. You're really quite good at that."

As Eket helped us all out from underground, I

couldn't believe how lucky we had been to meet up with the rest of the group at the perfect place at that precise moment.

We were all hugging each other when Odette said sharply, "Come! We don't have much time left." She pointed behind us.

I turned around and followed her finger up to the sky where I saw a vast cloud that crackled purple and black. It came from the direction of Malsama, and everything it passed over turned grey and collapsed to the ground. As I studied it with more attention I realized it was growing, albeit slowly, and it was gradually making its way closer and closer to where we were.

"Holy shit," Tom murmured.

We stared speechless as we watched the cloud advance like a great, looming deadline.

"Come on!" Odette insisted. "We're so close! We can't slow down now!"

In an anxious silence we trudged along, glancing fearfully over our shoulders. The only person who didn't look back was Odette. She walked ahead with her gaze fixed on the horizon. I admired how strong and powerful she was, and how beautiful and calm she could look even if we could all die at any moment. I wished I could be a leader like her.

But suddenly she started coughing. Her whole face paled and her body shook, and in a moment she changed to looking like a weak, lost little girl.

I guess I must have had a concerned expression on my face, because Tom leaned over and whispered, "She's been having coughing fits, and she hardly sleeps at night. I don't know what's wrong with her."

I shrugged. "Have you asked her?"

"Of course," Tom replied, still speaking under his breath, "but she never tells us anything. She's too proud."

"Where did you go after you lost us?" I asked, changing the subject.

"We went straight. Odette just kept leading us to her palace, and we found you!"

I nodded. "How long do you think it will be until we get there?"

Tom shook his head. "You should ask Odette. I have no idea."

I gulped. I knew Odette was surely on our side now, but her presence still made me nervous. Just thinking that her body was possessed with the Anima Magna made me tremble.

Ignoring the butterflies in my stomach, I caught up with Odette and asked, "How long until we get there?"

When she didn't acknowledge me, I thought she hadn't heard me. But then she responded without even turning her head, "Not long now. You can see it. Look."

I stared ahead over the flat, grassy plains and saw she was right. I could see the familiar pearl tower that rose like a needle towards the clouds.

Hope burst into my chest. "We're almost there, everybody!" I yelled and continued walking with renewed energy.

But it didn't last long. My knees began to feel weak

and shaky from lack of food, and when I looked at the others, I could tell they felt the same.

"Luke?" I asked. "You don't happen to have anything to eat?"

But I already knew the answer before he opened his mouth. If he did have food, he probably would have given some to us ages ago.

Just as I thought things couldn't get any worse, it started to rain.

Go figure.

And it wasn't one of those little showers either. Big drops fell from the sky and splattered my body.

Unfortunately the rain came from in front of us, and the wind blew all the water straight into our faces, making it hard to see ahead.

I wanted to talk to the others. Maybe by making conversation it would lighten the mood and make time go by faster. But I knew that if I opened my mouth, only complaining would come out: about the hunger, about the rain, about the long journey ahead of us. So instead I just continued going onward in silence.

*

I didn't know how long we walked, I just remember looking up right when I thought I couldn't go any farther and seeing the palace a few hundred yards away. Even though the sheets of rain obscured it a bit, I could still tell that we had almost arrived.

I gasped with joy and raced ahead of the others.

When they looked up too, they all ran to catch up, laughing and exclaiming with glee and triumph.

We had made it! We had gotten back to Odette's castle!

But our delight quickly vanished when we heard a booming crackle in the sky behind us. We all slowly turned around to see the evil cloud closing in on Odette's palace.

"Quick!" Eket shrieked. "Everybody into the castle!"

None of us needed to be told twice. We all sprinted toward the wide double doors. Luke and Tom shoved them open with their shoulders, and we all filed inside and caught our breaths.

This time the palace was completely empty, other than us, of course. Odette's henchmen were nowhere to be seen, and I've got to say, I didn't miss them.

Luckily for Eket, the ceilings were very tall, and he managed to fit inside without even having to hunch over.

I shook my head full of wet hair, dispersing some extra water, and I squeezed some rain out of my clothes, creating a small puddle at my feet.

"So?" I demanded. "You said there was some sort of spell?"

She nodded. "Yes. It calls the dead souls to recreate the barrier. It's down here, quick!" She coughed and dashed down the hall with everybody else at her heels.

At the end of the stone corridor we found ourselves in front of a small steel door. It looked like some sort of safe, but there wasn't any handle or combination lock.

"Um, Odette?" Zach began but was silenced by a

stern look from Luke. Odette had closed her eyes and placed her hand on the metal.

I leaned in closer to see what she was doing but Tom held me back. "Isabel . . ." he warned under his breath.

I saw Odette's lips move, but I couldn't make out the words she said. Then suddenly, the steel of the vault began to melt away, pulling back from her hand and making a little hole.

We all leaned in to get a better look of what was inside, but the little vault was too dark.

Odette gingerly reached in and we all held our breath.

This was the moment we had all been waiting for! My mind flashed back to when I had first left to save Tom. It felt like years ago; it was like I had been a whole different person. I had learned and gone through so much since then.

Also, my point of view at looking at things had changed more than once. First I thought the Soul Sucker was evil and that I had to destroy her. Then I was desperate and furious at myself when I found out I had had it all wrong. And now I was hopeful. I had finally figured out what I had to do, and I was so close! All we had to do was read a little spell . . .

"Here it is," Odette murmured. At that point, even she had anticipation in her voice, and there was no way she could have hidden it.

Her hand withdrew from the darkness of the inside of the safe, and when she held her fist up into the light we could all see an old crumpled piece of parchment that was covered with strange symbols.

"What does it say?" Josie said, her voice breathy and quiet with excitement.

Odette shook her head. "It is impossible to translate." She turned it over to examine it better. I noticed her eyes skimming over the little images on the page.

"Hmmm," she said to herself. Then she looked up and saw all of our excited looks and said, "The spell must be spoken at the Well of Souls."

We were all practically falling over our feet as she led us to the main gallery where we had first seen her.

She stood on the stones of the Well and closed her eyes. She began to chant and sway like she was dancing to a silent song. Then she fingered down the front of her dress and pulled out a thin, gold necklace with a glowing ball dangling at the end of it. The sphere gleamed an enchanting turquoise and the gem was encircled with small strips of gold.

Just the sight of it made me sigh with awe. It was the most stunning thing I had ever laid eyes on.

With the necklace in her grasp, Odette opened her eyes and began reciting the spell.

I didn't understand the incantation, but the way she read it was almost like she was singing it. The words made me more alert, and they seemed to reach inside me and make me want to go toward them.

I had to use all my willpower to keep myself from wandering forward and jumping into the Well. I glanced around to see if the words had the same effect on the others, and they clearly did.

Everyone was staring at the Well as if they couldn't

decide whether to leap into it or get as far away from it as possible. Eket even took a few steps towards it, but Luke placed his hand gently on the giant parrot's side and Eket stopped moving forward.

As Odette read on, little globes of sparkling blue light appeared and began to whizz around the room. I immediately recognized them as souls. They flew around for a minute before finally coming to rest and disappearing into the Well. When the first few vanished, more globes took the first ones' place until the whole chamber was almost filled with little orbs of light.

Odette was just reaching the climax of the spell when she suddenly cried out and crumpled to the floor. I jerked my head around to see what had happened. Standing above her was a wild-eyed, black-haired man. My mouth dropped open.

"Ian? What the hell are you doing?"

CHAPTER 27

I COULDN'T BELIEVE my eyes. The expression on Ian's face was that of a complete madman. Eyes bulging, nostrils flaring. His only goal was revenge.

"Ian! What have you done?" Josie shrieked.

"I have taken my vengeance on that filthy traitor!" he announced. "Come children, you don't have to thank me."

"But Ian, "Zach protested. "We made a mistake! She was actually kind of the good guy."

Ian whirled around, his face filled with spite and bitterness. "What did you say? You mean now you're with her?" He spat the words out like they tasted awful in his mouth.

"Ian, she's not that bad—" I tried to say, but Ian wasn't having any of it.

"No!" he shouted. "I can't believe you've betrayed me as well!"

"Ian, if you would just listen—" I pleaded.

"No!" he yelled and slapped me forcefully across the face. My cheek stung, and I fell to my knees.

Zach and Josie rushed to my side. Tom's face grew red with rage as he saw what Ian had done. "How dare you treat my sister like that?"

Ian turned around, shocked. "You, too? After all Odette has done to you, you're on her side?"

"It's not that simple," Tom tried to explain, but Ian turned his back on him.

Meanwhile, as all this was happening, Luke had rushed to his sister's side. "Lucy? Odette? Speak to me!" he begged.

At the growing violence, Eket backed away, whispering, "Please stop, please don't fight . . ." but no one heard him, and even if they did, nobody listened.

Once my eyes stopped watering, I stood up, shaking off Josie's warnings to sit back down. I looked around and saw that the bright blue spheres were growing restless. I knew if the spell wasn't finished soon we might lose our only chance of Dividing Earth and Eeba.

Ignoring the stinging pain in my cheek, I hurried to where Luke was kneeling over Odette, who was just gaining consciousness.

"Odette!" I cried out. "You have to finish the spell!"

Just as she turned to me, her face lost color and she began to cough. "No!" I groaned. "Not now!"

"I, I can't . . . d-don't have enough s-strength. You d-do it," she choked out. With labored breathing, she handed me the parchment and her necklace.

"Whoa, what?" I exclaimed, panic rising in my throat. "I can't even read this! I really don't think I can—"

"Isabel, the power is already inside you! All you have to do is bring it out," Odette told me between gasps.

As she said this, I had a strange sense of déjà vu. After a moment I remembered: they were the words Shaman Oring had said when he had read my future.

I took a deep breath.

With revived confidence in my heart, I grasped the necklace and the paper and slowly walked towards the Well.

Suddenly a loud scream met my ears. Looking behind me, I saw Tom and Ian wrestling on the ground. Josie shrieked again as Ian delivered a hard punch to Tom's stomach. My brother crumpled to the ground.

"No!" I yelled, and was about to go help him but I heard a voice in my head:

Isabel, for once in your life, think about the big picture. You must do the right thing for the well-being of everyone. Put your emotions aside. As a leader you have to think in everybody's best interest. If you go to help Tom, you'll lose the chance of saving the two worlds! Isabel, think before you act.

I looked around and met Odette's gaze. She nodded. I realized that it was her voice in my head. I gulped. The Soul Sucker's power never failed to amaze me.

Her words traveled to my heart, and I knew she was right, however much it pained me.

I winced and turned back to the parchment.

The page was covered with symbols and weird letters that swam before my eyes.

The power is already inside you. All you have to do is bring it out.

These words echoed inside my head as I focused on the spell.

Deep in concentration, I stared at the page, but it still made no sense to me. In fact, it seemed the more I looked at it, the less I understood.

The power is already inside you.

I closed my eyes and turned my gaze inward. I reached inside of me to pinpoint that spark of magic—however small it was—and use it.

Finally I found it. There, close to my heart sat a small ounce of magic that sparkled and leapt, just waiting to be wielded. As soon as I discovered it, I seized it.

When I opened my eyes again and looked at the parchment, the words made sense to me. I cleared my throat and began to read:

Souls! You have departed from your bodies, but still you continue forward. You were once contained, but now you have been released. With your departure, chaos reigns and havoc roams the two worlds. We call you, we plead to you, to come back. Return to your rightful home.

The spell continued, but I hardly acknowledged the meaning of the words. I just let them swirl from my mouth and hang in the air.

As I read, everyone looked up from what they were doing and gazed at me in wonder, even Ian.

I was almost at the end of the spell. The only thing I had to do was toss the necklace into the Well.

Just when I was about to throw the golden chain, Ian seized his opportunity. Seeing everyone distracted, he crept his way towards me. I saw him out of the corner of my eye, but I couldn't stop now. All I had to do was fling the necklace . . .

"Hah!" Ian yelled and grabbed it from my hand.

"No!" we all yelled at once.

I wanted to go for him, but there was still a part of the spell that I had to recite. Luke was busy with Odette. Tom lay on the floor, and Zach and Josie knelt beside him. The only one who remained free was . . . Eket.

I groaned. Eket may look like a big fierce parrot with large talons, but in real life, he was just a nervous bird with a phobia of, well, practically everything.

I mean, he could be really vicious when he wanted to. For instance when he beat up that big jellyfish thing in Korral Lake, or when he got rid of those nasty slave traders. But those were times when our lives were at stake, and I didn't think Eket understood the urgency of this situation.

It turned out I was mistaken, and I have never been so happy to be wrong in my life.

Eket straightened his back so that he brushed the tall ceiling. "Hey Ian!" he shouted. "You know what?" He took a deep breath and thought of the meanest thing he could say: "You're not very nice!" And with that, he charged.

I had just finished uttering the last word of the incantation when my brain registered what was going on around me. Without thinking I yelled, "Stop!"

Everybody froze.

I don't know why I did it. I guess I felt sorry for Ian. He was just so hurt and angry, and it wasn't really his fault he felt so betrayed. Now he looked around and saw only people who were once on his side.

I jumped off the edge of the Well and made my way cautiously towards him. "Ian. Will you just listen to me?" I implored. "I know you must be feeling terrible, but I can explain . . ." I looked in his eyes for any sanity left, but I searched in vain. I couldn't do anything else to help him. No one could. The only person who had any chance of saving Ian was himself.

"No!" he shrieked and pushed me away. Then he slowly walked towards Odette with his eyes full of suffering and wrath, and I could tell that all of these emotions were directed towards her.

I had no idea what he was planning on doing, but I didn't want to find out.

"Eket," I said, sadly. "Stop him."

This time the giant bird walked more gently towards Ian and put his claw lightly on his shoulder. Now all of our anger towards Ian was replaced with sympathy, and we felt sorry for him. But Ian didn't want our compassion. Instead he just became even madder.

"Keep your filthy claws off of me!" he shrieked and quickly backed away. "I don't need you!"

When I saw where he was heading I tried to stop him. "Ian!" I shouted. "Look out!"

"I don't need your help!" he continued, still walking backwards, his eyes lit with a deranged fire. "You all betrayed me! I always knew I was alone in this world! In both worlds!"

"Ian! Snap out of it!" I cried. "Look behind you!" But it was too late. He didn't watch where he was going and tripped, falling backwards into the Well of Souls.

There was silence for a really long time.

Then suddenly a gleam caught my eye. Laying at the base of the well was the necklace. It must have slipped from Ian's grasp and it hadn't fallen with him. Glancing up I saw the souls were even more agitated than before.

"Quick!" I shouted. "The necklace!"

Thank God Josie understood immediately and snapped into action. She raced over to the Well of Souls and scooped up the gold chain, then with one swift movement, launched it into the Well.

The effect was instantaneous. There was a sudden, blinding light that was so powerful it flung me back against the wall.

When I could finally open my eyes again, the blue orbs were gone. Instead, a turquoise light shimmered and glinted from the opening of the well.

I stood up. "We did it," I said, quietly at first. Then louder, "We did it!" Filled with a burst of joy, I did a little happy dance and raced to where the others were sprawled across the floor at different corners of the room.

I laughed with glee, first grabbing Zach's hand, then linking arms with Josie, then skipping over to Tom and giving him a great big bear hug.

Zach and Josie laughed with me, their eyes twinkling with merriment. Tom only managed a weak smile since he was still recovering from Ian's slug in the stomach.

Then I turned to Eket, whose grin stretched from one side of his beak to the other. He stamped his feet and gave me a great feathery whoop on the back that almost made me fall on my nose.

Finally I looked around for Luke and Odette, expecting to see them as happy as the rest of us were, but instead they were still huddled up on the ground. My happiness instantly vanished.

I rushed to them, the others hot on my heels. "What's the matter?" I asked, nearly in a whisper. "We did it!"

Luke looked up, sadly, "It's Lucy, I mean, Odette. I don't know what's wrong with her."

I kneeled next to Odette. "Odette? Can you hear me?"

Her eyelids fluttered open, and I sighed with relief to realize that she was still alive.

"Isabel," she gasped. "I'm almost at the end."

"End?" I said, alarmed. "What do you mean? We did it!"

She coughed and said, "The Anima Magna's essence is leaving me. My time is almost over."

"What will happen to you?" asked Eket, his brow furrowed.

"I will melt away. Once the Anima Magna has no need of this body, that is my fate," she replied.

"No, no don't say that!" Said Luke, "I can help you, I can heal you . . ."

"Please," Odette whispered. And Luke just closed his eyes.

There was a question nagging my mind that had to be answered, "But Odette, how did you know? How did you know that I would be able to recite the spell?"

Odette propped herself up on her elbows and managed a weak smile, leading me to think that she might be feeling better. "How else would you be able to open the portal?"

"So you mean I could have done it as well?" asked Zach.

"I'm not sure," Odette answered. "Isabel has more power than you."

"Go figure," Zach muttered.

"That's why I went to get you in the first place," Odette continued. "I could have just done the spell without getting you, but even then I didn't have enough strength, so I needed your help."

Suddenly Odette began to cough again, this time even harder. Finally she uttered, "This is the end. It has been an honor knowing such fine beings."

Then she looked up at Luke, who was cradling her head in his hands, as if she was seeing him for the first time. "Brother," she whispered, "my brother . . . I remember now . . ."

And then she dissolved into the air. The last thing we saw was a small blue sphere of light fly up from where her body last was and soar into the Well of Souls.

Chapter 28

LUKE WAS DOING a really bad job of trying not to cry. I could see his shoulders shaking, but still he refused to actually let his tears flow.

Tom laid his hand on Luke's shoulder, trying to comfort him, but Luke hardly noticed. Then Zach stood up and made his way towards the older man. He looked straight into Luke's eyes and said, "I understand. I lost my sister, too."

As soon as Zach had uttered that last word, they both cracked and he and Luke both dissolved into tears. I shifted around on my feet and glanced at Josie; we wanted to help them in some way, but . . . better to just leave them be.

Then I watched Tom and realized I was one of the lucky ones. I had managed to save my brother, but in doing so, two of my friends had lost their siblings. A confused feeling washed over me. Why me? Why was it that my brother had been saved?

Eket sat in the corner and sobbed just because of all the emotion building up inside the room. Then suddenly there was a voice, a weak female voice that said, "Zach? Is that you?"

Zach jerked his head up in surprise and stared into the shadows, trying to find out who had spoken.

Then there was a shimmer, and I saw a glittery shirt emerge from the darkness.

"Sage!" Zach yelled and threw himself into his sister's arms. There was so much emotion in his voice as he saw Sage that it made me weep.

When Zach finally got a hold on himself, he untangled himself from his sister and wiped his face. "But how—?"

He didn't get to finish his question, for at that moment, Sage's gaze fell on Tom. She gasped. "T-Tom? Is that you?" she managed to stammer.

Tom grinned, "It's me."

They slowly walked towards each other. Sage self-consciously wiped her eyes, trying to clean up her trickling eyeliner.

"It worked," she whispered. "You're here."

"I am," said Tom, "and so are you."

Then they threw their arms around each other and kissed.

Josie and I laughed and hugged each other, crying at the same time. Eket stomped the floor with glee. Only Luke's expression remained a bit downcast.

There was so much happy confusion, I hardly realized what exactly was going on. When it died down and all of us had calmed down considerably, we tried to make sense of what had just happened.

"Sage," Tom said, "how come you're still, I mean . . ."

"Alive?" Sage finished.

We all nodded. Sage shrugged. "I have no idea. I remember jumping into the Well, and then all of sudden, I was here again. I don't know what happened. But I'm glad it did."

"So am I," Zach said, and everyone nodded in agreement.

Taking our time, we made our way out of the castle. Not rushing, just enjoying the feeling of victory and each other's company.

We exited the double doors and I looked up. The great cloud had vanished, and Eeba possessed its amazing colors again. The grass wasn't a dull green anymore, and the sky had regained its bright blue color.

I smiled. It felt so good.

"Hey guys!" Eket shouted, interrupting my thoughts. "Look what I found!"

We all turned to where he was pointing. It was another hovercraft but nothing like the other ones that I had seen. This one was slimmer and pointed, made of sleek shining metal.

Zach and Sage gasped. "Oh my God! Do you realize what this is?"

I shook my head.

"This is like the Ferrari of hovercrafts! It's the fastest

there is!" exclaimed Zach. "And look! It has exactly five seats! One for each of us! Well, except Eket I guess."

"Whoa, whoa, slow down," said Luke. "Are you suggesting we steal it?"

"Well, who else is going to use it?" Zach argued.

"I'm with Zach," I said and moved toward the vehicle. "I am not walking another step."

In the end we decided we would drive it to the Fading Castle where Grandma Martha and Maya were waiting for us.

On the way, we explained to Sage most of what had happened, once in a while stopping for a small break.

The second we got to the castle doors we were greeted by a loud cry from a familiar centaur. "Sir Fluffy!" Tom cried out happily.

When Sir Fluffy saw us he, too, smiled. "You have returned! Grandma Martha will be so happy!" He led us through the door and up to Grandma Martha's quarters. Eket stayed outside and was given a nice place to rest. At first I felt sorry for him that he would be missing everything, but then I thought better of it. Eket didn't do so well when he was emotional.

We all made our way excitedly up the stairs. Even Luke had to crack a grin at seeing all of our happy faces.

We stopped in front of a dark wooden door. Sir Fluffy stepped forward and knocked loudly. Instantly the door opened.

As soon as she laid her gaze on us, her eyes began to twinkle.

"You made it," she whispered. "You made it!" she said, more loudly. Then her face paled. "S-Sage?" she choked out. "Is that you?"

"Grandma!" Sage cried out and wrapped her grandmother in a warm embrace. Grandma Martha shed many happy tears as she hugged her granddaughter.

"Sage!" Maya raced into the room and practically dove on top of her cousin.

Grandma Martha looked at us questioningly, "But how . . . ?

Luke shook his head. "It's complicated, and it will take a while to tell you the whole story, but we really need some food and a good rest."

At the word "food" my stomach growled. I had been distracted from my hunger for a little bit, but now I was beginning to feel it again, digging at my belly.

"Why, yes, of course!" Grandma Martha exclaimed. "If it is more comfortable for you, I will have it delivered to your rooms."

Her idea made me sigh with anticipation. The thought of food, a bed, and a warm shower was the perfect combo.

We were all shown to the rooms we had stayed in the previous time we were here.

"Go on," said Grandma Martha. "We shall talk tomorrow."

In my suite I dove into the bath and sat there, soaking in the warm water. When I felt as good as new, I put on some pajamas that I found in one of the drawers.

With the feeling of clean clothes on my skin, I made my way back into the bedroom where I saw a tray filled with food was waiting for me.

I dug in with relish, and when my stomach was full, I jumped into bed. The feeling of contentment washed over me, and for that moment, I was perfectly happy.

My eyelids were just dropping when I heard some urgent muttering coming from the other side of the wall. I snapped awake and silently cursed whomever was talking in that moment. I had just been falling asleep!

Who was that anyway? What were they talking about? I had to know.

I leapt back out of bed and tiptoed to the wall on my left. I pressed my ear against it to hear the voices better, and even though they were still pretty muffled, it would have to do.

"Why would you offer such a thing?" came Grandma Martha's voice.

"He has felt the same thing I feel right now." That was Luke. "Plus, I like the boy. He's intelligent and full of spunk."

What the heck were they talking about?

"I don't know, Luke. I'll have to think about it, and I have to have their consent as well," said Grandma Martha.

Before I could hear any more, there was a knock on my door. "Who is it?" I called out, jumping away from the wall.

"It's me," came Josie's voice.

The door creaked open, and I heard the padding of Josie's bare feet on the cold floor. "Isabel?" she whispered.

"What's the matter? I thought you would be asleep already," I said.

"I couldn't," she said. "I can't stop thinking about everything that had happened. It's almost too much for me to take!"

I sat on the big double bed, and she took a seat next to me. "I know," I said, trying to sound reassuring. "But all we have to understand is that everything is better now."

"Not everything," she corrected me. "We still have to go back to Earth and explain to our parents where we were! I can't even begin to imagine how worried they must be."

"I'm going to miss Eeba," I said with a sigh.

Josie nodded. "Me too. But hey, we can visit it whenever we want! You and Zach can open the portal, and we can just pop in and out as we please!"

"I guess," I said, "but I don't think it would be a great idea to come here all the time. I mean, it's good to have one foot in a real world and one in a more magical one, but we can't forget that we're from Earth, and we have to pay more attention to it than Eeba."

"Whoa!" said Josie, raising her hands. "You're sounding like 'the wise old man' or something!"

We both laughed for a moment, and I said, "Yeah, but don't get used to it," which made her giggle even more.

"Hey," I said, when an idea had sprung into my head, "why don't you sleep here in my room, in the double bed like when we have sleepovers?"

Josie grinned, "Yeah!"

We quickly got under the covers and snuggled down, giggling with the satisfaction of having our best friend close to us.

We whispered to each other under the covers, telling each other our secrets, and what we were feeling, just like we did on Earth.

And it felt great.

CHAPTER 29

I'M USUALLY AN early riser, and it always drove me crazy on a sleepover when I had to wait for Josie to get up so we could have breakfast (usually an hour later). But today she woke up before me, so when I opened my eyes, I saw her already dressed and ready to go find the others.

I wasn't awake right away. To tell the truth, once I opened my eyes I wanted to go straight back to sleep again. But anticipation for the exciting day ahead dragged me out of bed.

I got myself ready and, with Josie at my side, we walked out and tried to find the others.

We roamed the long halls for a while until we came across Sir Fluffy. When he saw us he said, "Good morning, Isabel; good morning Josie. The others are already awake, and they're out in the garden with Eket having breakfast. I will show you to them if that is what you wish."

"Yes, please," Josie replied, and we followed the centaur outside into the chilly morning air.

As I breathed in the sunshine, it occurred to me that it was because of us that the sun was shining so brightly and that the crisp breeze smelled like wild flowers. Imagine if we hadn't triumphed? If we hadn't succeeded in our mission? Both Earth and Eeba would have been destroyed.

The more I thought about it, the more I scolded myself. Why was I even thinking those negative thoughts? We had done it! That was all that mattered. My chest swelled with pride.

Then I saw my friends sitting on fold-out chairs, deep in conversation. At seeing them, I smiled. These people had gone through everything with me, and without them, I wouldn't be here right now.

Josie and I neared the group, and I noticed we were the last ones to have woken up. I opened the two remaining chairs that I figured were for Josie and me, and we sat down with the rest, greeted by a round of joyful good mornings.

They told us they had already recounted most of our story to Grandma Martha. Josie and I ate while they finished.

At the end, there was a moment of silence that was finally interrupted by Grandma Martha inquiring, "But I don't understand, how did Sage—?"

Before she could finish asking the question Tom said, "I was brainstorming about it last night, and I think I found the answer: Ian's soul was in his body, right? Just like Sage's was. What if, when he fell in, he involuntarily replaced her soul with his?"

"Like a trade?" said Zach.

"Exactly," Tom concluded.

Grandma Martha shook her head miserably and murmured, "Oh, Ian. What happened to you?"

The mood had gone from victorious to sorrowful in the time it had taken me to eat a piece of toast. I didn't want this morning to be a mournful one, so I swallowed the food in my mouth and said, "Come on guys, let's not be sad, at least we're still here, safe and sound. And just think of how many people we saved!"

Everybody instinctively smiled.

All of a sudden Luke stood up. With all our eyes on him, he took a deep breath, then said in a loud clear voice, "This must seem like an extremely unexpected and, frankly strange, announcement. But these past few days I've been seriously considering adopting you two." He turned to Zach and Sage, "Yes, you two."

My jaw fell open. I couldn't believe it! So that was what he and Grandma Martha had been discussing the night before. Personally, I thought it was a great idea. I wasn't so sure about Sage, but I was certain Zach would be happy.

I looked around to see the others' reactions; Grandma Martha just smiled, along with Tom. Josie was clapping her hands and skipping around, trying to get Eket to dance with her. The giant bird was merrily squawking but refusing to dance, and Zach and Sage just stared at each other and at Luke, not believing their ears.

When neither Zach nor Sage still hadn't said anything, we all stopped our gleeful gestures. I wasn't sure whether they were happy about it or not. I couldn't tell by the expressions on their faces. We waited for a sign in an awkward hush.

Then a grin broke across Zach's face and he said, "Yeah, that would be cool." At the end his voice cracked with emotion, and we all burst into joyful confusion.

We gave them hugs and shook their hands. Finally Tom backed off a little to give them space and gave the signal for the rest of us to do the same.

So Luke was now Zach's father. Rosie and Shaman Oring had been right. Luke wasn't Zach's flesh and blood, but Diviners don't always know how to tell the difference between the future, the present, and the past.

We all sat down again, with Luke taking a seat next to his soon-to-be-adopted children. I gazed around at this circle of people. Oh how I was going to miss them! But I couldn't wait a moment longer. I wanted to go home.

I glanced at Tom, then at Josie, and I knew they were thinking the same thing. We didn't need words to express so great a longing. You could see it in our eyes.

Tom was the one that said, "I think it's time we go back home."

There was silence, then we all stood and went around giving each other hugs and farewells. There was a calmness in our movements that was strangely reassuring. Nobody got muddled up or stammered their good-byes, even if everyone was very emotional. It was like a wedding: everyone knew what they had to do and what they had to say, but it wasn't like a show. Our feelings were real. I already had tears in my eyes, and when I got to Zach it was all I could do to not cry. "Hey," He said. I stared down at my hands, but he nudged my chin up so we were looking into each other's eyes.

"I'll miss you." I said.

"No you won't," he said with that grin. "I'm going to visit you so often that you'll be sick of me in a couple of weeks."

I laughed, "You do that."

He kissed my cheek, and I wrapped my arms around him. Behind him, I could see Sage and Tom talking a bit away from the others.

I finally stepped away, and Tom and Josie were at my side.

Then I closed my eyes, and I found that bit of magic inside of me.

"Open," I said, in a confident voice.

In front of me the ground started to spin as the portal appeared. I glanced inside to check if it had opened exactly where I wanted it to open.

It had.

Josie, Tom, and I waved one last good-bye to our friends and to Eeba. We weren't too sad; we knew we would see them again. And with that, we all jumped through the portal, back to Earth.

EPILOGUE

I still visit Eeba. Sometimes with Josie, sometimes with Tom, and sometimes by myself. Every time, I go with love in my heart, and I leave with serenity in my mind. Even though I love the magic and fascination of that other world, I still love Earth, and I don't feel attached to one more than the other. They are both part of me, they are both my home, and I love them both.

At the beginning of this story I told you that adventure was something to be careful of. Well, I'm sorry if I hung on to the bad things too much. I was wrong because in everything there is a little bad, and a little good, but you can't be too attached to one or the other.

Before, I was too fixed on the sadness and fear that my adventure had brought me, but now I look back, and I see all the thrilling, wonderful, and amazing things that happened to me as well.

So you know what? In the end, it was totally worth it, and I wish for you as much adventure as you can handle.

ABOUT THE AUTHOR

Giulia's love of books began at an early age when she read her first chapter book at age 6, "The Lion, the Witch and the Wardrobe". At 12, she was motivated and encouraged to write this - her first book about Isabel and her brother. Giulia was born in Rome, Italy and at 9 years old moved to Bali, Indonesia with her family for 2 years. Returning to Italy, her family moved to Orvieto, a small medieval hill town in Italy and she began a new journey - Liceo di Scienze Umane - a high school with a focus on philosophy, psychology, sociology, subjects she plans to incorporate into future characters and plots. Travel has always been a big part of her life as well as her interest in gender and social justice issues. She hopes to inspire others, especially young girls, to tell their stories.